# REPO

## A Henchmen MC Novel

--

Jessica Gadziala

Cover image credit: Shuterstock.com/Dewald Kirsten

## DEDICATION:

To Shelbi Adams, for agreeing to beta read for me when I needed feedback. Without that, I'm not sure I could have written past the insecurity. Also for finding all the "easter eggs" in my books.

Avocados, blech. Just sayin'.

—

# PROLOGUE

*Maze*

I've been a magnet for trouble my entire life.

It has never been by my own doing, mind you. I've always been on the up and up, the straight and narrow, the right side of the law. But as for the people around me, yeah, therein was the problem.

It all started with my mother who somehow managed to illegally obtain social security benefits she wasn't entitled to for ten years before they found her. By that time, they had attempted all the nice ways of contacting her and trying to get her to settle her debt. My mother, being the selfish, stubborn woman she was, never responded. So then one day, they stopped by and dragged her to jail and me into the system.

It only lasted for two weeks before my grandmother from Vermont made the trip down to the City and picked me up.

For the next eight years, there was no trouble, no fear of the police, no pit in my stomach. I had a good, albeit rather boring, childhood and adolescence.

About two months after I turned eighteen, my grandmother died. She left me the house and her car and what little money was in her bank account as well as completely and utterly alone in the world.

Then, well, what is a story about trouble without involving a boy, right?

I was nineteen, attending the local community college, taking classes in accounting, going home to an empty house filled with the ghosts of the woman who had lived there for sixty some-odd years, studying and eating dinner alone.

Then one day, behind me at the line at the coffee shop, I met him.

His name was Thato and he was tall and blond and beautiful with the most hypnotic gray eyes I had ever seen in my life. He asked for my number, his voice with a slight accent I couldn't place at first that sounded almost British, but wasn't. I learned when he took me out on our first date that it was South African, that his parents had moved to the states when he was thirteen and he never shook the slight inflection in his tone. Which was fine by me because it was one of the things I liked best about him.

Thato lived in an apartment above his mechanic shop and it wasn't long before I sold off my grandmother's house, stacked her belongings in storage, socked away the money, and moved in with him.

What could I say? I was young and in love.

And, as it often followed with a woman being young and in love, things didn't exactly go to plan.

Meaning, one night eight months into our relationship, I was shocked awake by the front door of our apartment being busted open with a battering ram and half a dozen of Burlington's finest burst into the bedroom before I could even pull up the blankets to cover my naked body.

See, as I learned later that night after being allowed to dress before being dragged down to the police station for questioning, Thato *did* own a mechanic shop. Sort-of. It was a mechanic shop in the way that it was a building with lifts and oil-stained floors and tire irons and torque wrenches and all that kinda stuff.

But it was not the place anyone went to have their cars fixed.

No, see. It was a place that Thato and his employees (or as the cops called them: accomplices)brought cars that they stole to dismantle and sell off as parts.

It was a chop shop.

The biggest one in Vermont.

So... yeah.

My little fairytale turned into Thato being hauled off to jail, me being scared out of my skin, and the decision for me to leave Vermont and start over again in New York City.

Then things went well for the next four years.

Or so I thought.

Then on one fateful January morning, I found out something.

And that's when everything went to hell.

# ONE

*Maze*

"You can do this."

I paced the small space of my cheap motel room from door to window wearing nothing but the scratchy towel that came with the room, stiff from way too much bleaching. The room was dominated by a queen bed in a room not meant to hold anything bigger than a full, covered in a God-awful brown and red paisley comforter that in no way matched the faded blue window dressings and carpet. It wasn't much, but it was home.

Temporarily.

I hoped.

If I couldn't calm my nerves and focus, it might end up being my home-home. And, well, that wouldn't stand. I may not have had much left in the world, but I had my pride. And my pride told me that no matter what shitstorm I had lived through the past six months, I was way above living in a sleep-and-fuck motel on the highway full of truckers and whores.

"Focus," I said, turning back to the bed where I had my clothes laid out. Really, they weren't my clothes; they were my uniform. They fit the part I was playing, the part I would be playing for weeks, months, hell... maybe even years. That was the thing. That was why I was so stressed out. It wasn't like this was some no big deal interview for some job I could walk away from at anytime.

This was my life.

For, well, however long it was necessary for it to be my life.

I sighed hard, grabbing the thong and bra and heading into the bathroom. The porcelain of the sink was still slightly tinted purple from where I had dyed my hair the night before. I pulled the black t-shirt off my head and let my damp hair fall in a straight, heavy, deep purple mass down almost to my waist. I raked a brush through it then dried it with the hair dryer the bathroom boasted that smelled like burning rubber.

It was alright.

I could get used to it.

K told me to go for a drastic change.

He told me to cut off most, or even all, of my long blonde hair. And, well, I was willing to do a lot of things, but I wasn't willing to cut off my hair.

But, still, he would approve.

I didn't even look like me anymore.

Sure, I had the same face with a slightly square jaw, generous lips, and hazel eyes. My eyebrows had been dyed as well, but not purple, dark brown. I was covering all traces of my former image. I needed to not look like that trouble-magnet accountant from New York City, then Vermont, then New York City again.

I wasn't her anymore.

Chances were, I would never get to be her again.

That morning, with purple hair, mascara-darkened lashes, black-lined eyes, and a slightly pear-shaped body that was wide of hip, generous of thigh and ass, but with a small waist and acceptable-sized boobs, I wasn't me.

I wasn't even me playing at someone else.

I was Maze.

Case closed.

I took a deep breath, shaking out the tension in my shoulders, and made my way back out to the bedroom. I grabbed the red snake-skin leather pants and the black wifebeater I had picked out as my first outfit. I slipped into my clothes, sitting off the side of the bed to roll on socks and slip into a pair of clunky black combat boots. The ritual of dressing calmed me, grounded me, as I did what K taught me to do when I was stressed: go over the plan. Go over the plan until you knew it inside and out, into all the nooks and crannies, until the running monologue of it threatened to drive you insane.

"I'm going to finish getting dressed. I'm going to grab my wallet with my fake IDs. I'm going to get onto that God-awful motorcycle and pretend I love it, that I was practically born on two wheels. I am going to drive to the compound and demand to see Reign."

If Reign wasn't available, I could demand Cash. If Cash wasn't available, Wolf would do in a pinch. Then, well, I had to use whatever I had in my toolbox to get the outcome I needed.

With Reign, that meant being a badass, challenging him, not shrinking away from his dark and dangerous persona.

With Cash, that meant I needed to be both strong and feminine. I needed to flirt if he flirted, but brush it away if he actually tried to follow through. He wouldn't respect me as a prospect if I gave in too easily.

With Wolf, well, I would have to do all the talking and pray that he had some kind of soft spot, some Achilles heel I could exploit.

I wrapped the strap of my wallet around my wrist and grabbed my keys as I went to the door. My heart was a slamming bass beat in my chest and the summer heat blasted me and did nothing to help the nervous sweat I felt all over my skin.

"I'm going to get onto that God-awful motorcycle and pretend I love it, that I was practically born on two wheels. I am going to drive to the compound and demand to see Reign," I whispered out loud to myself as I crossed the parking lot toward my bike parked in the far left corner. There was a small group of truckers standing beside their rigs as I passed, but I had gotten over my fear of what random nobodies had thought about me around the first time K taught me how to get out of an arm-triangle choke.

"What's that honey?" one of them, the one with the biggest beer belly and a huge, bushy mustache, asked as I passed.

"I am going to drive to the compound and demand to see Reign. I am going to get him to give me a chance. I am going to integrate myself into the club. I am going to belong. I am going to be safe."

"Crazy bitch," I heard muttered as I threw a leg over my bike, unclasping my helmet from the bars and slipping it on.

Crazy bitch.

I wasn't offended.

No, in fact, in that moment, I totally agreed with him.

If I thought this plan was going to work, well, I was definitely a crazy bitch.

But it was the plan.

It was K's plan

And I trusted him. I trusted him, quite literally, with my life. If this was what he thought I needed to do to get safe and stay safe, then I had to believe him. And I owed it to him to work my ass off to make sure he didn't have to come up with some backup plan because I failed.

Navesink Bank was, well, an enormous town. It was chopped up into sections from the sprawling, lavish mansions to the 'burbs, the industrial area, then, well, the slums. Growing up in the city where most areas looked like most of the other areas then Vermont where everything was desolate and green in the summer then, well, desolate and *white* in the winter, it was a bit of a culture-shock to be able to, in twenty minutes, drive through such a drastically diverse landscape.

I drove through the 'burbs and into the industrial part of town full of more than a few abandoned buildings along with some that were still operating: namely tattoo shops, bars, mechanics, bail bonds, convenience stores, and the occasional still-afloat despite the shitty economy, mom and pop stores.

I sucked in a greedy breath as I pulled up to the gates in front of The Henchmen compound, shutting off the engine and forcing myself to pull off my helmet and get off my bike, despite my better sense telling me to run screaming.

There were two probates at the gates wearing leathers with no patches. They were brothers by the looks of them.

"You lost, baby?" one asked, giving me a slow once-over that made me feel practically naked despite the obnoxious, hot, disgusting leathers I was wearing.

"No," I said, lifting my chin a little. "I need to talk to Reign."

"Don't know what you heard of the prez, babe, but he's got himself a woman. He don't need another," the other said, shaking his head at me like I was annoying him.

"That's wonderful for him, but I still need to speak to him."

"About what?"

"About it's none of your fucking business," I countered,

making his brother laugh and shove him in the shoulder.

"Listen bitch..."

"No, you listen, bitch," I snapped, my voice low and vicious and nothing like it normally sounded, "I'm here to talk to the president, not some probate on a power trip so get your head out of your ass and..." I trailed off when I saw someone else out of the corner of my eye.

Turning, I saw someone in his mid-to-late twenties, tall, muscular but in a not-too-bulky way, with dark hair and handsome in an almost classic way with a strong jaw, severe brow ridge, and well-proportioned features. His dark blue eyes looked like they were dancing and, judging by the smirk he had on his face, he was amused. Literally the only thing marring his perfection was a scar that ran fully down his cheek, cutting off at the strong jut of his jaw.

He was gorgeous.

Like advertising companies should have used him to sell cologne. Or shaving cream. Hell, the man could make khakis look sexy if that was what they needed.

"Go on," he invited when I looked at him. "He can get his head out of his ass and..." he prompted, smirk getting a little more sinister.

"Get Reign," I decided, pretty sure that was not what I was going to say, but struck just the tiniest bit dumb by how good looking he was.

"That's not a bad idea," he said with a shrug. "Moose, Fox, go find the prez and see if he has a minute."

"You can't..." Moose, the one with his head in his ass, started.

"The fuck I can't," the new guy snapped, his face losing its smirk and looking a little dark, a little scary. "Do what you're told, probie," he said, his tone brooking absolutely no argument. Moose, smartly, shut his mouth, but the tightness in his jaw said he wanted to go a round about it but knew he was the lowest man on the totem pole and that it would get him nowhere but on his ass.

Moose and Fox shared a look and moved to go back into the compound. The compound itself was at one time a mechanic shop, low and windowless. It even had the one garage door left. But out toward the back, there was a new (also windowless) addition that I knew from my research was the sleeping quarters for the patched-in members. If all went to plan, I'd be getting one of those rooms myself.

"Probate on a power trip, huh?" the guy asked, moving over to the gates and pulling them open, but standing in the opening so it was clear I wasn't welcome. At least not yet.

There was something interesting about him. I couldn't quite put my finger on it and that would drive K up a wall when I checked in on Tuesday. He had hammered it into my brain how important it was to be able to size someone up, to get their number within minutes or even seconds of meeting them. For Moose and Fox, that was easy. Moose was a bully and mistakingly thought he was leader-material. Fox was a bit of a follower and a creep.

But this new guy... I wasn't sure.

There was an aura of authority to him when he spoke to the probates. But there was also a sort-of laid-back quality to him as well. He was attractive and carried himself in a way that suggested he was aware of that fact, but not ruled by it.

But that was all I got.

I couldn't tell you if he was an important member of the bike gang. I couldn't tell you if he was attracted to me or if he found my presence amusing just because I pushed the probates' buttons or because he genuinely liked a woman with a little spunk.

"He's an asshole," I said on a shrug.

"True," he said, shrugging. "But this isn't exactly a gentlemen's club, honey."

"Don't honey me," I said, rolling my eyes.

"Why do you want to see Reign?"

"That's my business."

"If it involves him, it involves the club. And club business is all our business."

"What's going on, Repo?" a deep, masculine, sexy voice asked and I looked behind the guy, Repo, to see another man walking up, older, darker and more dangerous-looking. It took all of, say, point-zero-one seconds to realize that he was Reign, the president of The Henchmen MC. Also, a gun runner and a lethal son of a bitch if what K said was true.

Repo waved a hand out to me and Reign's light green eyes fell on me, taking me in quickly in an almost clinical way.

"Hi," I said, feeling dumb, but needing to say something.

"What can I do for you, babe?" he asked, crossing his arms over his broad chest.

I exhaled the breath that felt trapped in my chest.

Here went nothing.

"My name is Maze and I'm your newest prospect."

The silence after my declaration was deafening. Well, save for the pulse that was whooshing as loud as a hurricane through my ears.

Reign's head actually jerked back slightly, taken by surprise no doubt.

I wasn't stupid. I knew women weren't allowed in biker gangs, almost as a rule. It just wasn't done. MCs were about brotherhood. Meaning, no sisters. Meaning, we were, as a sex, relegated to the status of clubwhore or old lady and that was it. We spread for you and fetched you beer and never, ever, interrupted you when you spoke or showed you any disrespect whatsoever.

"You're fucking with me," was Reign's response a couple long seconds later.

"No, I'm not fucking with you. If dipshits like Moose can get a chance, I don't see why I can't."

"Dipshits like Moose, huh?" Reign asked, a sexy grin toying with his lips as he brought a hand up to stroke his cheek.

"Yeah, I..."

The sound of another bike cut off my response as I turned to see the bike park next to mine, two people on top. Driving was a man. He was tall and a lean kind of strong with colorful tattoos and blonde hair that he left long on one side of his head and shaved to a buzz cut up the other. He had dark green eyes and unmistakable bone structure that looked just like his brother's. Cash, Reign's younger brother and also the vice president.

He got up, giving me a charming as all hell smile as he slung an arm around the hips of the woman who had ridden up with him. She was tall and leggy with a killer rack, long blonde hair, and brown eyes. There was something about her. I wasn't sure if it was the way she carried herself or the depth of her eyes or what, but it was as if everything about her screamed: I can handle myself.

"Who is this?"

"This is Maze," Reign said, waving a hand at me. "And she thinks she is going to be our next probate."

*Thinks.*

That didn't slip by me.

And, judging by the way the blonde woman's eyes narrowed slightly, it didn't slip by her either.

"Thinks?" she asked, angling her head toward Reign, raising a brow at him.

"Oh, shit," Repo said, a boyish smile toying at his lips, making his eyes do that dancing thing again.

"Yeah, Lo," Reign said, seemingly unaware or just unconcerned by the way she had straightened and pulled away from Cash.

"Are Janie and Summer in there?" she asked, moving toward the gate, not so much as pausing so that Reign and Repo both had to scramble out of her way before she plowed into them.

I looked over at Cash, maybe a little charmed by the huge smile he had on his face as he watched his woman storm away. "Is it a good or bad thing if Janie and Summer are in there?" I asked him, dropping my voice a little low, not particularly wanting Reign or the Repo guy to hear.

"Depends on where you stand, sweetheart," he said as he tucked his hands into his front pockets. "For Reign... I'd say he's in for a world of shit if the girls club put their heads together about this."

"And for me?" I asked, wondering what the girls club was and how such a thing existed in the testosterone-centric world of outlaw biker gangs.

"For you, sweetheart, I think it means that you will be getting a shot to prove yourself whether Reign likes it or not."

I turned back toward the man in question just as the door to the compound opened and Lo reappeared flanked with two women. One was a gently curved redhead with freckles and gray eyes. The other was an incredibly short and thin woman with long black hair, blue eyes, and arms covered in tattoos. All of them were looking at Reign and each of them looked ready for a fight.

"Oh, shit," Repo said again, lips twitching for a minute as he took a step away from Reign as the women started to approach.

Reign closed the distance, obviously wanting to keep me out of whatever was about to transpire. But, I guess he didn't factor in that this 'girls club' was pissed and therefore not overly concerned about keeping their voices down. And then, I got to stand back and watch as the girls club leashed into not only Reign but the innocent Repo and Cash, each of them their own kind of angry, all of them yelling over one another. Reign stood there stoically while they raged, arms crossed over his chest, everything about him suggesting that he had no plans on bending.

But then the redhead moved away from the other women who were still yelling, got in close to Reign, put her hand on his upper arm and leaned up toward his ear. I swear the second she touched him, his body language softened slightly. His arms fell from his chest, one moving casually to rest on the woman's hip as the side of his face rested on the side of her head as he listened to whatever it was she was whispering to him.

At the display of what was, painfully obviously, some intimate kind of conversation between two people who seemed to love one another deeply, I felt a strange hollow, swirling feeling in my stomach that no amount of denying it could change what it was: longing.

To have that, to have a man as big and scary and stubborn as Reign obviously was lean into you and really *listen* to something that was important to you... what that must be like.

Then she turned her head slightly, kissing his scruffy cheek and moving away from him to rejoin the two other women who were still ranting. Reign watched his woman for a long moment before he looked at the others, shaking his head.

"Jesus fuck, alright already," he said, sounding both angry and defeated at once. "You want her to have a shot, fine. She has a shot. But she's not getting any special treatment. We're treating her just like we treat all other prospects," he said, slanting a look over at me that made me feel a little cold despite the fact that I was literally sweating down my legs underneath my leather pants. It was gross. "Repo, I need to talk to you for a minute," Reign said, not bothering to speak to me as he and Repo moved away back toward the clubhouse.

"Well, Maze," the black-haired tiny slip of a woman said, looking over at me, all traces of her anger gone in a blink, "welcome to The Henchmen MC. And the girls club. You don't need to prove yourself to us though. With hair like that, I'm pretty sure we'll all fucking like you."

I cast an uncertain look over at Cash who gave me another of his charming smiles. "Told you."

Before I could even figure out which of the new two women was Janie and which was Summer, the door opened again and Repo walked back out.

"Maze," he said, waving a hand, "you're with me. Let's go."

I took a breath and moved through the girls club to fall into step with him as he led me around the back of the compound in complete and utter silence.

So, yeah, K would be happy.

I got my spot in The Henchmen MC, notorious one-percenters, arms dealers, killers.

And, though they had no idea, my protectors.

Of course, I was only breathing easy because I had no idea at the time what being 'with' Repo would mean for me.

# TWO

*Repo*

She was hot as shit.

Really, it came down to that initially. Call me a pig, call me a chauvinist, call me whatever, but fuck off if you think people don't notice your looks before they notice anything else about you. So when I walked up to the gates to see Moose and Fox having some kind of conversation with a woman who pulled up on a bike a minute or two before, I noticed first that she was on the tall side and fit, but with a fucking phenomenal ass. Her long, straight hair was dyed the darkest shade of purple possible which, aside from being a huge 'f-you' to societal norms, was hot as hell. Her face, well, it was pretty. She had a somewhat square chin, nice green eyes, and lips that just begged you to get a taste of her.

The next thing I noticed was that she had a killer voice. It was all sex and smoke, a little breathy, a little husky. And wasn't it just perfect that a voice like that was spitting fire?

"No, you listen, bitch, I'm here to talk to the president, not some probate on a power trip so get your head out of your ass and..." her gaze snapped to mine, her mouth closing, her brows drawing together slightly as she did a somewhat slow inspection of me.

I decided right then and there that, once she finished whatever business she might have had with Reign, she and I were going to get acquainted. By 'acquainted' I didn't mean over drinks and bullshit; I meant I was going to get to know what her ass looked like bent over one of my cars while I pulled her hair and fucked her from behind.

Of course, that all got shot to shit once the girls came out and started raising hell, browbeating the formidable leader of a arms-dealing biker gang. See, it wasn't often people ever even thought to do something like try to go toe-to-toe with Reign. One of my earliest memories of him as a probate was him tearing into the shed where one of the bikers, a slimy fucker by the name of Mo, was being held.

Probates weren't exactly allowed to be involved with official club business, but, well, I was on patrol of the perimeter and I had ears. Hell, you could have been almost fully deaf and you would have heard Mo's screams. Reign came out the better part of an hour later, his body literally dripping with blood.

We, as a group, would learn later that Mo, along with being a lousy drunk, a shameless gambler, and a giant pussy, was also the worst thing a brother could be: he was a snitch. And, see, snitches didn't get stitches as the saying went. Snitches got a timely grave.

So Mo was pushing up daisies and I learned real early that Reign was not a man to fuck with.

The girls club, fuck, I don't know what they were thinking. Maybe it was as simple as knowing Reign, for all his ruthlessness, would never raise a hand to a woman. Or maybe it was just because the women were all certified badasses themselves and were no way intimidated by him like most normal people would be.

But regardless of what balls it took the ball-less lot, they were on a tear. See, all being badasses in their own rights, they really had very little (if any) tolerance of things such as sexism. I didn't blame them per say. I understood that shit. Anyone who had ever seen Janie build a bomb or Lo grapple or Summer hold a gun, yeah, they'd know that this particular group of women couldn't be held to any gender norm stereotypes, not even in the criminal underbelly. So when they thought Reign was being unfair to a woman who might very well be a badass herself, they weren't having any of it.

I had to hand it to them, they got what they wanted.

Though I knew from experience it was less about Lo and Janie's ranting and raving and more about Summer going all soft on him and exploiting the one real weakness Reign had in the world: her, and the feelings he had for her.

Regardless, it worked.

Or so we all thought until Reign led me inside the compound.

"This shit isn't gonna fly," he told me, waving a hand out toward the gates.

"You just told them it would," I said, shrugging.

"Oh, I told them she would have a shot. I didn't say it was going to fly."

I knew Reign well enough to know that he wasn't just pulling me inside to casually bullshit and bitch and whine to me. "What do you need?"

"I need you in charge of Maze."

"In charge of Maze?" I repeated, thinking of all the ways that could be a very, very good assignment.

As if sensing my train of thought, Reign's lips twitched.

"Keep your dick in your pants," he said, shaking his head. "I don't care if she has that hot, alternative, 'I don't give a fuck' vibe going on, from now on, she's a probate. And you don't get to fuck her."

I let out a breath that sounded suspiciously like a sigh and nodded. "So what do I get to do with her then?"

"You get to make her life a living hell until she quits or fucks up badly enough to get thrown out."

I paused, choosing not to speak until I resisted the urge to tell him that was kind-of fucked up. Because, fact of the matter was, I didn't get to have opinions like that. Sure, Cash and Wolf and sometimes even older members like Vin would question Reign, push the limits of his patience with their insubordination. But that was a luxury I was not afforded. Not because Reign wouldn't allow it. If anything, I was on Reign's good side. But I learned a hard lesson in loyalty before I happened across The Henchmen and decided they were going to be my life. And that lesson, well, it made me absolutely fucking incapable of behaving even the slightest bit like I didn't fully respect authority.

So I swallowed my objections and nodded. "Alright."

"You sure you got this? I could put one of the older guys on it."

"No, I got it."

I got it for multiple reasons. One, Reign asked it of me. If the prez picked you out for something, you damn sure didn't throw that offer back in his face. Two, I admit that I was curious about Maze. Three, I knew the other guys would do shit that would not only be un-called for, but borderline shitty to her to get her to quit. That would also involve getting the other probates to purposely give her shit, exclude her, make her feel unsafe and unwelcome. And while she was definitely unwelcome if Reign's behavior was anything to go by, she wasn't unsafe. It was a really shitty thing for a man to cross that line with a woman just to make her squirm, regardless of whether they were going to follow through or not.

So I wanted to oversee things to make sure they didn't get out of hand.

As a whole, we weren't bad men. But I knew that it was very easy for decent men to turn downright evil when given permission to do so.

They wouldn't get that chance.

I was on it.

Case closed.

"You already keep an eye on the probates," Reign reasoned with a shrug.

He wasn't wrong. While most of the patched members had rooms at the compound, very few of them took advantage of them. Many of the men had old ladies and kids and houses and shit to take care of. Cash had Lo in a townhouse. Wolf had Janie in his place in the woods. Even Reign had Summer and their daughter, Ferryn, to look after at his place. Not many of the men were at the compound twenty-four seven. I, however, wasn't exactly the settling down type. And I saw no reason to take on a mortgage when I had a comfortable place at the compound.

So I lived there.

I also worked there, rebuilding my cars in the field in the back.

As such, I was around the most and, therefore, kept a close watch on the probates.

"Not a problem, Reign. I'm on it," I said and was rewarded with a whack on the shoulder before I opened the door and made my way back to the small crowd out front.

Why there was a knot in my stomach, well, fuck if I knew. But there was.

"Maze," I called, cutting off whatever Janie was about to

say, "you're with me. Let's go."

To her credit, she didn't bristle or ask any questions or even waste any time saying thank yous or goodbyes to everyone else. She simply nodded tightly, moved through the group, and fell into step, two respectful feet behind me as I led her around the back of the compound where I knew the rest of the probates would be hanging around and talking shit about the chick who thought she had a chance to be in The Henchmen MC.

We had four probates, well, with Maze, five. There was Moose and Fox, the brothers. Moose was as simple as sawdust and as mean as a grizzly. Fox was slightly less stupid, and maybe only half as mean, but he was uninteresting in every possible way. Both were dark-haired with that ridiculous pretty-boy thing going on, but also strong, capable, with impressive juvenile rap sheets and clean adult ones. Duke had long blond hair he generally kept in a bun at the crown of his head. He was on the rough-side looks-wise, tall and solid with deep blue eyes. And, finally, Renny was a fucking redhead. No lie. He was young, around twenty with a thin, scrappy body that he had half-covered with tattoos already. His hair was of the copper-red variety, longish on top, with bright blue eyes. By some miracle, he managed to be freckle-less.

Personally, I favored Duke and Renny as potential members.

But that decision had literally nothing to do with my opinion.

That was all up to Reign with maybe a little input from Cash and Wolf.

"You can't be fucking serious," Moose said as we moved to stand where they were all hanging out around the picnic tables.

"You can't be fucking questioning Reign's decision," I said back with a pointed brow raise that had him shutting up.

"Moose, Fox, Duke, Renny, this is Maze. She's the newest probate."

Moose rolled his eyes; Fox raked his eyes up and down Maze; Duke's brows drew together but he shrugged. Lastly, Renny leaned back on the picnic tabletop, arms behind him, and gave Maze a genuine smile. "Smash that fucking patriarchy," he said, catching her off guard because she made a strange snorting noise before she laughed a little nervously.

"She's not going to be bunking with us is she?" Moose asked.

"That's not going to be a problem is it?" I countered.

Moose shook his head and turned away from us as Fox gave Maze a smile that I imagined he thought was charming or sexy, but even to me it looked creepy as fuck.

"The open bunk is above me," Duke said and, if I wasn't mistaken, he meant it as a comfort. I was left wondering if maybe he picked up on Fox's creep vibe and Moose's animosity like I had. If so, it was yet another thing that worked in his favor.

"Works for me," Maze said, shrugging, slipping her hands into her butt pockets and it made her tits press out invitingly.

I sucked in a breath, reminding myself that Reign said she was off limits, and took a step away. "I'll leave you guys to get acquainted. Meet me at the bar in an hour and we'll discuss jobs. Maze, you should run and grab some of your shit."

Because the first plan of the Maze Takedown was to have her working ungodly hours days in a row, seeing if that was enough to break her before I had to get more creative. She wouldn't be allowed to leave the compound. She'd be lucky if she had time to change her clothes.

--

"You know the wrath of shit you're going to get from the girls if they find out what you are up to?" Cash asked as I moved into the kitchen to grab coffee.

"I don't even want to think of the lecture Janie is going to give me," I agreed, shaking my head. Janie might have been Wolf's woman, but she was one of the best friends I had. She was a genuine pain in the ass with all the charm of a porcupine, but there was something about her foot-in-mouth tendencies, about her spine of steel, about her resilience despite everything she had been through that made you have to like her. It also helped that she was one of the very few people I could count on being awake if I called at three A.M when sleep was a foreign concept and the walls were closing in and I needed to get out. Janie had nightmares too. She understood. And she would meet me for coffee or beer or just conversation on occasion.

That being said, Janie would string me up by my balls and carve a fucking Rosie the Riveter image into my flesh if she knew I was blindly following orders to make a girl's life a living hell so she would quit the MC just for the reason that she was a girl.

"You disagree with Reign?" Cash asked, running a hand up the shaved side of his head.

"That's not my place."

"Chrissake, Repo, you can have an opinion. We all have opinions."

"And yours?" I asked, leaning against the counter.

Cash, maybe because he grew up with Reign, was a lot more free with his thoughts and feelings regarding club business. And Reign wasn't a dick. He was open to ideas and opinions though it was commonly known that the ultimate decision was his and his alone.

Cash shrugged. "I don't feed too much into the sexism bullshit, but I can honestly see both sides here. This is and has always been a brotherhood. Bringing women into the fold could cause conflict with the older members. And Maze will have to put up with the guys being dicks to her all the time. This isn't exactly a gentlemen's club and most the members are used to seeing women just one way."

"Maybe she's okay with having to eke her way up in the ranks."

"Maybe. Maybe not. I guess time will tell. If you do your worst and she still doesn't break, I don't know what the fuck Reign is gonna do," he said, clamping a hand on my shoulder as he made his way back out into the main room.

Yeah. I didn't know what the fuck I was going to do if I couldn't get her to quit.

I'd never disappointed Reign before.

I got on his good side when, as a probate still, I had tried my best to fight off the mother fucker who kidnapped his woman. Then, barely healed, I had charged in to fight her out of a shit situation at his side. I was pushed through to being patched as soon as possible after that.

Since then, I held down shit at the compound. I was there when the bombs went off and blew Reign's torture shed to kingdom come. I kept the probates in line. I made the club money with my car restoration. I went on runs when they needed me to.

It was maybe a little pathetic of me, but I needed Reign's approval. I needed his faith in me.

So, while my opinion was that it was fucked up to haze a probate just because she happened to be a woman, I was going to do whatever was necessary to stay in my boss' favor.

What that said about me as a person, as a man, well... fuck if I knew.

And I was going to do my best to not harp on that.

# THREE

*Maze*

I let out the breath I felt like I was holding as Repo walked away.

"Barbie, you're so not getting a patch before me," Moose said as soon as Repo was out of earshot.

"I dunno. If you can't keep a muzzle on that big fucking mouth of yours, I'm liking my chances."

To that, Duke snorted, giving me a lip twitch that I figured was his badass equivalent of a smile. As per my training, I sized up Duke and Renny as fast as possible.

Renny would be a friendly. He was a kid, laid-back, not overly ambitious. He was either unconcerned about a position in the MC or he had some reason to believe he didn't need to see all of us as competition. If I rubbed elbows with him a little, he could be a good ally to have on my side. Especially since I knew Moose and Fox were going to be an issue.

Moose because he was a dick.

Fox because he looked at me like a piece of meat.

Duke was pretty much guaranteed a patch so long as he didn't fuck up royally and he knew that so my presence wasn't a threat to him. He might not go out of his way to make my life easier, but he wouldn't do anything to make it intentionally difficult either. I doubted I would make a friend of him, but he wasn't an enemy.

And seeing as I didn't exactly have the favor of the president, I needed all the non-enemies I could get.

"Listen, bitch..." Moose snapped, moving toward me in what he probably thought was a threatening way. To anyone else, it would have been scary. But my training had involved being attacked by men a lot bigger and badder than his immature, surly ass.

"No, you listen, bitch," I said, approaching him so fast that he actually went back a step before my hand slammed into his chest and pushed him back another foot. "You and I don't have to be friends, but you're going to learn real quick that I'm not going to put up with your bully bullshit. Get used to me because I'm not fucking going anywhere."

"Alright, alright," Renny broke in, climbing off the picnic table with an odd sort of grace. "Maze, wanna come see where you're staying before you take off to get your shit?"

"Sure," I said, keeping my gaze on Moose for a long minute before turning and following Renny into the back door of the compound.

The door led right into the great room, a big open space with couches, a pool table, a full bar, stereo system, and massive television. It looked like, because it was, a place for men to hang around and have a good time. The couches had stains. The walls had scratches and even the occasional fist-holes. The back bar was full of Jim, Johnnie, and Jose.

"It's really a glorified frat house for grown ass men,"

Renny said, as if sensing my analysis. "Through here is the kitchen," he said, waving a hand toward a room on the left. He kept walking, leading me into a hall with a dozen or so doors. "These are the rooms for the patched members. Obviously off limits. And we, like the lowly peons we are, are relegated to the basement." He flicked on a light switch and started down the narrow stairs, leaving me to follow behind.

The basement was, well, a basement. There were cinder block walls, cement floors, and a marked decrease of temperature. Straight ahead toward the back was a room with a steel security door.

"The gun safe," Renny explained, nodding toward it. "Forbidden except for the top five."

"Top five?" I repeated.

"Reign, Cash, Wolf, Vin, and Repo."

Repo? He seemed young to be considered a higher-up.

I nodded to Renny as he waved a hand toward a dark corner where there was a chair with cuffs hanging off of it. "For obvious reasons," he said, then waved a hand to the right of the room where washers and driers were situated. "Get intimately acquainted with those. They make us do all the laundry," he explained casually. Grunt work, it was to be expected of the low men on the totem pole. I was sure I would also spend a lot of time scrubbing bikes and fetching drinks. "Here we are," Renny said, moving us toward the corner on the left where two sets of metal bunk beds were situated along with an old recliner. "Home sweet barracks."

"There's only four beds," I observed somewhat unnecessarily.

"I sleep here," Renny explained, throwing himself in the chair.

"You sleep in a recliner?"

"It's weird as shit, I know, but I can't sleep when I lay

flat," he said with a shrug. He waved a hand to the bunks that were pushed against the wall on one side. "That's you and Duke."

"Good," I said, eying the other set of bunks that were open on both sides. That was too exposed. Especially in an area that was going to be hostile for me.

"Moose will adjust," Renny said as I looked at the piles of burst-open, overflowing duffel bags full of clothes on the floor.

I leaned back against the bunk beds, crossing my arms, and giving him a small smile. "No he won't."

"Hey, can't blame a guy for trying to be comforting," he said, giving me a sweet smile. He sat up suddenly, kicking in the footrest. "Can I ask you why you want to put yourself through what I think we both know you're going to go through to get in here?"

"Would you ask Duke or Moose or Fox that?"

"No, but they won't be putting up with extra bullshit like you will."

I shrugged a shoulder. "I have thick skin. I'll be fine. I, like the rest of you, just want to be part of something I guess."

"Sure, Violet. Whatever you say," he said, shaking his head at me like he could see right through the lie. "You better get a move on. Repo will boot your ass if you're late for the meeting."

With that, I nodded and tore up the stairs, slowing my pace once I got into the great room as to not draw too much attention to myself.

I walked past Reign, Cash, and Repo as they leaned against the bar. I lifted my chin as I moved past, grabbing the door, hauling it open, and almost running into a giant wall of lumberjack biker.

Yes, lumberjack biker.

That was literally the only appropriate way to describe

the man.

He was six and a half feet tall and about five million feet wide and a thousand pounds of solid muscle. He had dark hair that was neatly trimmed with a long, full beard, and light honey-colored eyes.

His head jerked back for a second before he stepped inside, making me take a step back. "Woman," he said, nodding his head at me and moving inside.

Well, that was Wolf.

I knew from my research that Wolf was a lot of things: The Henchmen MC road captain, Reign and Cash's best friend, a vicious, violent killer, and a man of very, very few words.

I let myself out through the open front gates, got on my bike, and headed back to the motel. Once inside, I grabbed the burner phone I bought the day before and charged up as I moved around my room, and typed in the number for K's office.

"K.C.E Boxing Emporium," Shelly's hospitality-pleasant, but slightly cool voice answered.

"Vermont," I said and there was a slight pause as she looked through paperwork.

"Hold for K," she said and there was only a small silence before the line picked up again.

"Maisy," K's smooth voice met my ear, sounding a little winded and I imagine he had been training. He usually was. "How'd it go?"

"I'm in. Just barely. Reign didn't want me," I said, holding a handful of panties with a feeling of ridiculous insecurity. I grabbed an old tee and stuffed the undies inside, then wrapped them up out of sight then stuffed the whole of it at the very bottom of my bag.

"You convinced him?"

"No. There was a woman there. Cash's woman. And she got pissed that they were going to turn me down and then she went into the compound and got Reign and Wolf's women and they all threw such a fit that Reign got sick of it and let me in."

There was a second of silence. "That won't help you beyond this point. If I know anything about these guys, you're in for a tough ride. They don't want a woman in their ranks so they are going to do everything in their power to get you to quit."

"Yeah," I agreed, feeling a pit of uncertainty settle in my belly.

"Maisy, you need to focus. Stop stressing out. This is what we trained for. This is not a choice. This is a necessity for your safety."

"I know," I said, my voice decidedly defeated-sounding.

"Maze," his voice held warning.

"I am going to do what it takes to gain the trust of the members. I am going to gain the favor of Reign and I am going to get a patch that guarantees my present and future safety," I recited.

"Because if you don't..."

"If I don't, they might find me."

"And if they find you..."

"They *can't* find me."

"Because if they find you, you are going to die, Maisy," he said, his tone even. It was brutal, but it was true. K wasn't in the business of sugar-coating facts or handling you with kid gloves. That wasn't why you went to him. You went to him because there was nowhere else to turn. You went to him because he was who you went to when there was no hope. He was the one person who was willing to take on the lost causes and dedicate his time to giving us a chance.

In return, we were given no softness.

I learned to love the sandpaper sensation of his words.

Because I learned what they were doing. They were scraping away the me I used to be: weak, naive, gullible, clueless and replacing it with the woman I needed to be to survive.

"Okay K. I have to get back. We all have a meeting with Repo in about fifteen and I'm clear across town."

"I want an update in two days. Then we will set up a new system."

"Got it. Thanks, K," I said, feeling the gratitude down to my bones. But K wasn't the touchy-feely kind of guy and I knew that if I went and got all gushy on him, he would make me start repeating my mantras.

"Stay safe and kick ass," he said before the silence told me he hung up.

I slung my bag over my shoulder, feeling the weight of it. Not just the clothes and books, but the fact that it was literally all I had in the world anymore. I had a bug-out bag stashed in a locker at a train station in Pennsylvania in case something happened and I needed to get out of town with nothing but the clothes on my back.

There were no more mementos. I didn't have any of the furniture I had spent months online pinning and un-pinning and re-pinning on Pinterest before finally purchasing. I didn't have the funky street art I had bought when I was walking one evening on my way home from work. I would never see the pair of pearl earrings that had been on my nightstand, a gift from my grandmother on my seventeenth birthday, again.

Ignoring the stabbing sensation in my chest and the burning behind my eyes that threatened tears, I ran across the parking lot and threw myself on my loathed motorcycle and made my way back toward The Henchmen compound.

My home.

"Ugh," I growled at the idea as I pulled up to the gates, parked, and went inside.

"Just like a chick to be late," Moose grumbled as I walked past.

"I still have ten minutes, jackass," I said, swinging into the seat between him and Duke, 'accidentally' hitting Moose as hard as possible with my bag. "Oops," I said, hoping I looked genuinely apologetic.

From the smirk that Repo was giving me from across the room, though, I was pretty sure I failed. But whatever. No where in the 'outlaw MC handbook' did it say we had to get along with fellow probates. If anything, we were encouraged to fight, to show the patched members what we were made of.

No one wanted a new member who was all sugar and honey.

They wanted piss and vinegar.

So that was what they were going to get from me.

"Alright, let's get this over with," Repo said, pushing off the wall and moving toward where we were sitting at the bar. "New work assignments. Moose and Fox, you're on the gates in the afternoons. Duke and Renny, you'll do alternating overnights. Maze, you relieve Duke and Renny at four. That's not a problem, is it?"

"Nope." If anything, it was the ideal assignment. I was part of that point-zero-zero-one percent of the population that was a die-hard morning person. The sun started peeking through the sky and I was wide awake. I was half-afraid he would have stuck me with the overnights.

"She gets to patrol alone?" Moose asked, sounding dangerously close to whining.

"Is that... safe?" Fox asked and I heard, for the first time, a hint of malice there. Maybe he wasn't unlike his brother after all.

"Any of you want to get up and do a four A.M. patrol is welcome to join her. Otherwise shut your fucking mouths and do as you're told."

With that, he left, moving out the back doors and across the field to where three different cars were in various stages of disrepair.

"Fucking bullshit," Moose growled, jumping out of his chair.

"That you're still here after talking back like that? I agree. Bullshit," I said, pushing away from thc bar and moving off toward the basement.

--

I went to bed early. For one, because I needed to be bright-eyed and bushy-tailed to do my patrol. But also because it saved me from having to deal with Moose and Fox without Renny as a buffer. Duke didn't seem overly fond of the two either, but he didn't seem overly inclined to help me deal with them. Not that I blamed him. It was an 'every man for himself' kind of situation and, well, you couldn't exactly expect bikers to be the warm and mushy type.

My alarm beeped once before I shot up and shut it off, looking around wildly, praying it hadn't woken anyone up. Across from me, Moose and Fox were both still passed out. I wiped the sleep out of my eyes and climbed down from the top bunk. My feet had just settled on the ground when I felt a big hand close around my right calf. I opened my mouth to scream, but clamped it shut at the last possible second, spinning with raised fists to find Duke sitting off the edge of his bed, watching me with a tilted head.

"Jesus," I hissed quietly, feeling my heartbeat slam so hard that I felt like I was choking on it. "What's wrong with you?" I whisper-yelled at him, throwing up my hands.

He gave me a small smile and I realized how attractive he actually was. His hair was out of its bun, flowing long and blond and soft-looking around his shoulders. It was dark and I couldn't make out the pleasant deep blue of his eyes, but they were crinkled up slightly with his smile as he reached for something sitting on the surface of his mattress. "Here," he said, holding out a pocket knife, flicking it open to reveal an illegally long, sharp, serrated blade. At my drawn-in brows, he shrugged. "They don't give probates guns. You need to have something to defend yourself. Not being sexist here... we all need something in case..."

Okay, well. Maybe I was wrong about him after all.

With a small smile of my own, I planted my bare foot on his bed beside his thigh, leaning down and rolling up the pant leg of my jeans to reveal the band I had strapped around my left calf with a knife attached. Granted, it wasn't as big and mean-looking as his was, but K assured me it would slice through human flesh like filet mignon. Those were his words, not mine. "Have another in each boot," I added because it was the damn truth. I wasn't walking into a compound full of armed gun runners without something to ensure I stood a chance of fighting out if it came to that.

"Good for you," Duke said, nodding, and I felt a swell of pride inside. I got the impression that Duke wasn't an easy guy to impress, which made his approval all the more rewarding.

"Any tips?" I asked, wanting to engage him.

"Don't fall asleep and don't be a hero. You think you hear or see something, investigate, but don't engage if you don't have to. Get help. You won't impress Repo by getting yourself killed."

At that, I tilted my head a little as I leaned down to slide into my boots and tie them up. "Repo? Shouldn't I be worried about impressing Reign, not Repo?"

Duke shrugged. "Reign has the ultimate say. But he's not here all the time. Repo is and Repo is, for all intents and purposes, in charge of us. So the only way you can impress Reign is to impress Repo."

"Good to know," I said, nodding at him. I didn't need to say thanks for him to know that was what I meant. Along with some self-defense training and the most intense study session of my life about The Henchmen MC and their members, K had drilled it into me that I needed to stop thinking like a chick. He said that if I wanted to get into a boys club, I needed to learn to communicate without having to say much. It wasn't exactly something I excelled in, but I was learning.

"Now get a move on. There should be fresh coffee and you'll want to relieve Renny. He gets cranky when his relief is late."

"Renny? Cranky? I can't imagine that," I said with a small smile as I reached up to settle my sheets back into place.

"Not everyone is who they appear to be, Ace."

I stopped my walk toward the stairs and turned. "Is that a warning?"

"Let's call it a word of advice," he said, jerking his chin at me then falling back into his bed.

With that little nugget to mull over, I made my way into the kitchen that did, indeed, smell like fresh coffee. I found the pot with a sleeve of disposable insulated cups and tops, poured myself a cup, added a sugar, then slipped on the top as I looked over at the clock. I still had twenty minutes. But it was always better to be early than late. Especially if it meant I got to stay on Renny's good side.

"Won't get you far to kiss their asses," a voice said behind me, making me jump on a gasp as I whipped around to find Repo sitting at the table in the corner, hand around a steaming mug of coffee. He was slouched back in the chair, eyelids a little swollen, the skin under his eyes looking purple from lack of sleep. A part of me wondered if he had stayed up to keep an eye on me which I found incredibly insulting. But a bigger part was seriously worried about how I hadn't noticed he was there when I walked in. K would box my ears if he ever found that out. Luckily, I had no plans of telling him.

"I'm not kissing anyone's ass. I'm just an early riser," I said with a chin lift even though it was only mostly true. Yes, I rose early. But early for me was around four-thirty in the morning, not three-thirty. But whatever. He didn't know that.

"Sure, honey," he said, nodding in a way I found condescending.

"Two out of six isn't that bad," I mumbled to myself as I walked toward the doorway.

"Two out of six what?" he asked, apparently having some kind of super hearing.

I turned my head over my shoulder, chin lifted, and told him flat-out. "Two out of six of you aren't close-minded sexists," I said with a brow lift. "In case you were wondering, you're of the six, not the two." With that, I made my way out into the great room then out the back door, my stomach swirling around ominously. I knew I wasn't supposed to talk back to them, but I also had the feeling that I wasn't going to get myself anywhere by being a withering flower either. Especially if they were discounting me on the sole ground of my sex.

Besides, I'd rather be kicked out because I wasn't afraid to speak my mind than be kicked out because I proved myself simply unimpressive.

"Thank God, Violet," Renny's friendly voice groaned as I made my way toward the front gate where he was leaning against a tree.

"Tired?" I asked, taking in the heaviness of his bright blue eyes.

"Hate this fucking shift. Guess that's why they gave it to me," he said with a knowing smirk.

"Well I may or may not have just let on that I am, by nature, an early riser. So I imagine I'll be getting stuck with your shift in no time," I mused.

"Aw, Violet, don't be getting all down on them yet. You just got here," he said, pushing off the tree. "Here," he said, holding out a huge, heavy, black Maglite. "You still have a good hour of darkness," he explained as I reached for it.

He moved to walk past me and I blurted out the question I had wanted to ask someone since I learned about us being the ones to patrol the grounds. "Hey, um, do I just watch the gates or am I supposed to walk this whole thing?"

Renny turned back and gave me a knowing smile, like maybe he knew what it was like to be the new guy. I guess, at one time, he had been as well. "You can stay at the main gates for ten minute intervals only. Then you need to do laps, alternating your route each time in case someone is watching. They had a breach years back because some probies fucked up their watch. Don't want that happening on your shift."

"Right. Thanks, Renny. Get some rest. Dream sweet." I cringed the second it was out of my mouth, knowing it wasn't something a biker would say. Damn it.

"Don't lose the soft," Renny said, as if sensing my thoughts. "It's easy to fold into the mold they all seem to fit into. But don't do it at the expense of who you are." With that, he turned and made his way back toward the compound, leaving me to exhale so loudly that it could maybe be called a sigh.

Because, as a whole, I agreed with him. I didn't believe in squeezing yourself into someone else's mold. But, that being said, this was not a case where I had a choice. By whatever means necessary, I needed to integrate. I needed to become one of them.

If I didn't, well, like K said earlier... I would die.

On a deep breath, I gripped the Maglite tight and started my first round of the night, taking the enormous fence at a clockwise path.

Eight and a half incredibly long, incredibly boring hours later, completely out of new ideas of how to switch up my rounds, Moose and Fox finally came ambling out of the clubhouse, laughing at something until their eyes landed on me.

"You look like shit, Maze," Moose informed me.

I would have taken offense, but I was pretty sure his assessment was nothing but accurate. As soon as the sun rose in the sky, it started pelting down on me in a way that made the sweat start to bead up on what seemed like every freaking inch of skin. I had tied my hair up with a band I kept around my wrist, putting into a messy knot at the top of my head. My tee was sticking to me with sweat and my face felt sunburned.

So yeah, I looked like shit.

So I didn't even bristle at the comment.

"Don't worry," Fox said attempting (and failing) to give me a charming smile, "I'd still do 'ya."

"Lucky me," I deadpanned, moving away from them, snagging my discarded coffee cup off the ground as I went.

"Hey babe," Reign's distinctive voice called to me as I stepped into the great room, almost crying the air conditioning felt so good.

"Yeah?" I asked, attempting to push the misery out of my voice as I turned to find him standing at the bar with a sweating beer in front of him.

I totally didn't wet my lips at the thought of a nice, cold beer. Nope. Not me.

"Bring this out to Repo, will you?" he asked with a smirk that I knew meant he knew it wasn't something I could turn down doing. It was normal for probates to have to run drinks to members. But, that being said, Duke was sitting on the couch and from the looks of it, had been there a while. And Renny had just walked out of the kitchen with a cup of coffee. So... me getting the job? Yeah, it was because I was the girl.

*Assholes.*

"Sure thing," I said, giving him a saccharine smile as I reached for it. "Do you need me to make everyone a sandwich too? Maybe vacuum the carpets in high heels and full makeup?" I asked, but in such a sweet tone that there was no way he could call it insubordinate. I swear to Christ, I made it sound like I was just tickled at the prospect of being subjugated.

From behind me, I heard Renny chuckle and Duke snort. In front of me, Reign's lips were totally twitching. He might not have wanted me there, but he respected my spirit. I couldn't really ask for more than that.

I took the beer and made my way back outside to where I heard the music blaring in the back field.

Repo had made his way out to his cars sometime around eight in the morning. I could occasionally feel his eyes on me, but I did everything in my power to not return the favor.

The metal music was blaring from a dock propped up on an overturned garbage can and clanging was coming from under the hood of the faded red old school muscle car. That was about as specific as I could get. Cars mattered to me about as much as high school trig, meaning not at all. I skirted around the car to find Repo leaned into the hood, his shirt discarded, sweat beaded on his skin, all the muscles from his hand to his shoulder tensing as he used it to screw or unscrew something inside the engine. I swallowed hard against the unexpected stab of desire at the sight.

It wasn't that Repo wasn't attractive; he was. He was actually one of the best looking men I had seen in a long time. And it wasn't helping that he was half naked and that I got to see all the ink he kept covered with his shirt. There was something across his chest I couldn't quite make out given his position, but his back had a huge piece in the American traditional style. There was a giant red and black snake with a jeweled knife stabbed through its head, blood dripping down from it. There were words above and below it spelling out: "snakes and snitches get it where they slither".

"Honey..." Repo's voice called, sounding amused and I jumped, eyes shooting up to his face to find his lips twitching. He'd totally seen me staring at him. Great. That was just wonderful.

"Snakes and snitches get it where they slither?" I asked, trying to keep my eyes on his face though I did notice that he had "Henchmen" written across his chest in a huge, bold font.

His head cocked to the side slightly as he turned and leaned against the car, a wrench still in his palm. "Words to live by," he said, his tone a little guarded. There was history there, meaning. "That for me?" he asked, jerking his chin toward my hand where I was still holding the beer.

"As per orders," I said, giving him a humorless smile as I held it out.

"Thanks," he said, reaching for it, tipping it back, and taking a long swig. I felt my own throat go dry as I watched him swallow.

I coughed awkwardly, not sure what the hell was wrong with me. "Um... anything else?" I asked, shifting my feet slightly. How was it that I was somehow more at ease with Reign than I was around Repo? That made no sense whatsoever.

Repo shrugged a shoulder. "How was your first patrol?"

"Uneventful," I said, leaving out the fact that it was quite literally the most boring eight hours of my entire life.

Somehow reading between my words, Repo smirked. "Yeah, I remember those days." Then suddenly he pushed off the car, taking a big step in my direction, surprising me enough to forget to take a step back and therefore allowing him to be all up in my personal space. There was barely a breath of air between us, his beer hanging down at his side actually touching my thigh over my jeans. His hand moved out, brushing the sensitive pad underneath my eye. "Might want to remember sunblock next time," he said as I felt a shiver work its way up my spine at the light, sweet contact.

"Ah, yeah," I mumbled, looking up into his deep blue eyes and feeling a heaviness settling on my chest.

And through the heat and the pressure of trying to fit in and the ever-present worry about what could happen to me at any moment if *they* found me or The Henchmen found me out, I felt another realization dawn on me- Repo was trouble.

First, because he was in charge of me.

Second, because he was attractive and I wasn't exactly unaffected.

Third, because he was definitely willing to take me to bed.

Normally having a really hot, somewhat alpha badass you were attracted to who wanted to take you to his bed would be a good thing. But for me, yeah, it was another major complication. If he decided to act on his attraction, I was in for some deep shit. Because I would have to turn him down. And turning him down would bruise his ego. And bruising his ego could be enough for him to want to kick me out.

Shit. Shitshitshit.

"Maze," Repo's voice called in a way that was almost... soft. When my eyes found his again, he exhaled a little heavily. "Relax. That's not a line I'm crossing."

I swallowed hard. "It's not a line I'd *let* you cross," I countered, but a part of me was pretty sure it was bluster.

"So we understand each other," he said, taking a step back. I was getting ready to step away when he quirked a brow. "Did I say you could leave?"

I felt myself jerk at the chastisement, biting my tongue to keep from lashing out. "No," I said, my tone clipped.

"Right. Because you're going to keep your ass right here and hand me tools."

"Hand you tools?" I repeated, my tone a little dumbfounded.

"Yeah, probie," he said, his tone going so dead that I felt a sliver of cool rush through me. "Forget your place already?"

My place.

Nope. I definitely didn't forget that.

And I got the distinct impression that if I ever did so, for even a second, someone would be right there to remind me.

# FOUR

*Maze*

For the next week, Repo decided to tick off me and, by extension, all of my fellow probates, by switching up patrol rounds daily with no notice. One day I was working the early morning shift, then I was informed only minutes after completing it that, surprise, I was pulling the afternoon one. With Fox. The next day, I had the overnight with Duke. The next, I was back on my early morning. Then the overnight with Renny. I was getting the impression that the overnight was too important to The Henchmen to screw with it. For whatever reason, Reign, Cash, Wolf, and Repo trusted Duke and Renny more than the rest of us and therefore always wanted one of them on the shift.

By my ninth day, I was sick.

Literally sick.

Over a week of a weird sleep schedule and being out in the unyielding heat or rain at any given time with no protection from the elements, I woke up from a short sleep to start my early morning patrol to realize that every single inch of my body was sore. I groaned as I rolled off my bunk, not realizing how weak my muscles were and collapsing into Duke's bed, my hand slamming down hard on his stomach.

He flew awake on a grunt, hand automatically moving to my throat before his eyes focused and released me. "What the fuck?" he whisper-yelled at me as I pushed myself up.

"Sorry, I... my legs gave out," I admitted, each word like swallowing glass to my sore throat.

"You sick?" he asked, taking in the croaking weirdness of my voice.

"No. Nope," I said, shaking my head and ignoring the dizziness brought on by the motion and my clogged sinuses.

"Billy, don't be a hero," he said, moving to follow me out of his bed. "I'll take your..."

"No," I snapped, wincing at how loud the word came out. It was loud enough to make Moose's snores stop as he rolled around in bed. "It's fine. I got it," I objected, biting my cheeks to keep from groaning as I bent to tie my boots.

"Ace, come on," Duke said, reaching out as I straightened and putting a hand at the side of my neck. "You're burning up..."

"I'm fine. Go back to sleep. Sorry I woke you."

With that, I made my way up to the stairs, cringing when each step made me feel like I used to at twelve, lying in bed with growing pains bad enough to prevent me from walking.

It was okay. I just had to make it a couple of hours and then I could take a handful of medicine and crash. Plenty of people had to do worse jobs feeling a whole lot shittier than I did right then.

I grabbed a bottle of water from the kitchen and made my way outside to find Renny. "Violet, you look like hell," he said as I approached at my grandma pace.

"Gee thanks," I grumbled, taking the Maglite and waving him away.

"You sure you..."

"I'm fine!" I snapped, my voice echoing across the empty night.

I wasn't exactly fun when I was sick. It wasn't that I liked to wallow in it, but I damn sure never forced myself to go into work when I felt like I was going to pass out at any moment. I always would just hole up in bed with orange juice and a heating pad and wait it out.

"Alright," Renny said, holding up his hands and nodding. "I get it. You're as capable as all of us. But don't forget, Maze, you don't have to make yourself sick to prove a point either." With that, he walked away and left me to drown in my misery as I walked the grounds.

I was pretty sure I finished my first round. See, I say pretty sure because at one point, I sat down to give my screaming leg muscles five minutes of rest... and then I must have either fallen asleep or passed out.

Because the next thing I knew, I felt a cool hand touching the side of my face and a annoyingly smooth voice calling my name over and over. My eyelids felt weighted and I had to struggle to force them open. It was still dark out. I noticed that first. All around, it was still pitch black out. There was a hand underneath my head and another rested at the side of my face. And those hands belonged to Repo. He was kneeling down beside me on the ground, his brows drawn together and his mouth in a firm line. "Hey honey," he said when he noticed I was awake. "Scared the shit out of me," he admitted.

"Shit," I gasped, trying to push myself up, realizing what had happened. I had fallen asleep while on duty. Fuck. There was no way...

"Easy," Repo demanded in a soft voice, his hand landing

in the center of my chest and pushing me back down on the ground. "It's alright."

"How long..." I started to ask, my heart slamming in my chest so hard that I felt nauseated.

"Not long. Duke told me you were sick. Then Renny came in and said you looked dead on your feet. Figured I should check on you. Good thing I did. You were out fucking cold. What were you thinking?"

"I had a job to do," I objected, moving to push myself to a sitting position, my arms shaking under the pressure.

"If you can't take care of yourself, you can't take care of the compound. Part of being a good member is knowing when you should lean on one of your brothers, Maze."

I noticed movement from behind Repo and reached for the Maglite beside my body, lifting it by the light end to strike with the heavy side if need be. But then Duke came into view, holding up his hands palms-out. I felt my eyes lowering at him in accusation and he shrugged a shoulder. "Sorry, Ace. There's no way you should be out here when you couldn't even get out of your bunk. It's not a chick thing. If it was any of the guys, I'd have gone to Repo too." Somehow I doubted that and I felt my eyes rolling at him. "So fucking stubborn," Duke said, shaking his head, but smiling like he approved as he reached down, snagged the Maglite, and moved off to do his rounds.

"Come on, honey," Repo said, slipping an arm across my back and moving to bring us both to our feet. To my absolute horror, I had to give him almost all of my weight, my own body completely giving up on me.

Now, I was pretty sure I made it to the back door to the compound.

I say 'pretty sure' because I remember seeing the back door. And then all I saw was the back of my eyelids.

The next time I woke up, I was in a bed.

There wasn't much I noticed aside from the fact that my ears were so clogged that I could barely hear anything, my sinuses were painful they were so full, my throat felt like I swallowed acid, everything hurt from the neck down, and I was both a ball of sweat and so cold that my teeth were chattering.

But I did notice this one other thing. The bed I was in, it wasn't my own.

The room itself was not mine.

I knew this because *my* room was a cold, damp, dark basement that always smelled like laundry detergent and men's feet. This room, while windowless like the rest of the compound, wasn't cold, damp, or dark. The walls had black and white wallpaper of a foggy forest, making it seem cozy and relaxing. There was a white dresser with a giant television across from the bed I was in and a door to the side where I could make out a shower stall. The bed itself was huge and covered in white sheets and a fluffy white comforter which I was tucked tightly into... and had dampened with my sweat.

As I was looking around with curious eyes, the door to the hall opened and in walked Repo with a tray in his hands. His eyes landed on me and he gave me a tight smile as he skirted around the bed and put the tray down near my shoulders as he sat down by my hip. His hand moved out, pressing into my sweaty forehead and I wanted to swat him away, but my arms were trapped under the blankets and it was too cold to pull them out. "Heya honey," he said, shaking his head slightly. "Still burning up. Open," he said, reaching for two pills off the tray along with the glass of orange juice and bringing them to my lips. "Come on, Maze," he begged quietly, tiredly, as if maybe not-so-conscious me had been giving him trouble. I opened my mouth and the pills slipped inside as his hand went behind my neck to angle my head up so he could bring the juice to my lips. Swallowing felt awful, but I knew better than to try to refuse medicine that might help. "How ya feeling?"

I made a whimpering sound as he placed the glass back on the tray and pulled out a thermometer. "Open up," he demanded, slipping it beneath my tongue and I closed my mouth around it. "You've been sleeping for almost sixteen hours," he told me as we listened to the thermometer bleep out the passing seconds. I felt my eyes bug and he shook his head. "Relax. Reign was in here. He's not mad you're out of commission for a while," he said, pulling out the thermometer and cursing. "Fuck," he growled, tossing it on the tray and suddenly reaching for the comforter and ripping it off me.

"Cold," I cried out, trying to grab it and cover myself up again with achy arms.

"I know honey," he said, reaching for me and hauling me off the bed against his chest. He stood, taking me with him, as he went into the bathroom. He turned on the light with his shoulder, revealing an average-sized bathroom that boasted a simple vanity, the shower stall I had mentioned earlier, the pre-requisite toilet, and a soaking tub. Before I could even ask what he was doing, he sat down on the bath platform, reached out to turn on the water, then sat me beside him. His hands went to the hem of my tee and before I could register his intention, he pulled it up and off me. My mind may have been a little sluggish, but I was present enough to squeal and reach up to cover my bra. "Sorry, Maze. No room for modesty. We need to get this fever down," he said, his hands going to my button and zip and making short work of them.

"Repo..." I said, my head shaking at him as I felt a mortified blush creep up on my cheeks. Not only was it bad enough that I was being stripped by my boss, but I had on a hideous cream-colored bra and my panties totally had little red and pink hearts all over them.

Seeing the blush, his face softened as he stood, kicking off his shoes, reaching for his shirt and discarding it. "Let's even it up then, yeah?" he asked as he went for his button and zip, then stepped out of his pant legs, leaving him in a pair of dark blue boxer briefs. He leaned down, his arm going around my back and picking me up a couple inches so he could drag my pants down. My breath caught at the contact, my eyes going to his face as the flip-flop feeling moved through my belly. Hearing my indrawn breath, his eyes found mine as his fingers dragged the material down my thighs. He took a deep, slow breath and looked deliberately away.

The next thing I knew, I was in the tub, Repo holding me down as I fought to get back out of the too-hot water.

"I know," he said as one of his arms crushed into my hipbones and the other pressed in hard to my ribcage. It was so hot that the water was already enveloping the entire bathroom in steam. "Jesus Christ," he grumbled and I turned my head to look up at him, finding sweat beading up on his forehead. I watched, as if not attached to the traitorous appendage, as my arm rose slowly, rubbing the sweat away, leaving a trail of the hot bath water in its wake. Repo's hand closed around my wrist, holding it aloft for a second as his eyes pierced into me, before slowly lowering it back into the water. "You gotta sweat out this fever," he explained to fill the awkward silence.

"You don't need to be here."

"You're too fucking stubborn to be trusted to stay in the tub by yourself," he said, sounding amused as his arms lessened up their pressure.

I took as deep a breath as my stuffy nose would allow, closing my eyes and trying to force myself to relax. "I feel awful," I admitted and Repo's hand moved up and down my side gently, soothingly.

"I know, honey."

"You shouldn't call me that," I said, feeling sleep start to tug at my brain again.

"I know that too," he said, exhaling slowly as his hand settled high on the side of my thigh, his fingers grazing the material of my panties that covered my ass.

The last thing I was conscious of thinking before I fell asleep again was that it felt nice to be close to him.

# FIVE

*Repo*

She wasn't just sick. When Duke and Renny said she wasn't feeling well, I figured she just had a cold or something. But finding her passed out in the yard, then dealing with her fever dreams for fifteen troubling hours afterward, I realized she wasn't just under the weather, she was seriously fucking sick.

I was trying to hold her down in bed when the door to my room opened and Reign walked in, his dark brows furrowed as he took in the scene. "Heard she was sick," he explained, shutting the door. "Should we call someone?" he asked as he moved closer to the bed as Maze cried out in her sleep.

"If it doesn't break soon, yeah. This is fucking insane," I said, my stomach tied in a knot as I felt the skin of her arms underneath my palms. It was hot, almost to the point where it felt uncomfortable to touch.

"Any of the others sick?" he asked, meaning the probates.

"No, but none of the others have had their schedules

fucked with as much as she has. She had to have been bone tired. Her immune system didn't stand a chance after being stuck out in that thunderstorm the night before last."

"It's not your fault, Repo," Reign said, drawing my attention. He was right, but he was also wrong. Technically, it was his fucking fault. But I couldn't say that. Hell, I felt guilty for even thinking it. But it was also my fault because I had been the one to change up her schedule, to deprive her of sleep, to send her out in a torrential, freezing cold downpour that lasted almost the whole duration of her shift. As if something in my gaze gave me away, Reign's lips twisted up slightly. "Yeah, I know it's my fault," he said, shrugging his shoulders.

"She's not quitting," I said, looking down at her as she writhed against my hold. "Can't have gotten more than six or seven hours of sleep all week and she's shown no signs of giving in."

Reign sighed. "Yeah, I know."

"Is it really that important that she fails out?" I asked, my voice a little quiet at questioning him at all.

"Have you seen the way Fox corners her when he catches her alone?" Reign asked, knowing I had, knowing very little slipped past me. "And the way Moose is constantly on her case? You see the way the old timers ogle her?" He paused, shaking his head as he looked at his feet. "I'm not saying that I can guarantee the safety of my brothers, Repo. That's not the life we live. Some of us get hurt. Some of us get killed. That's the choice we make when we join. But I can give my men some comfort that they are safe from one another under this roof. I can't give that to Maze. Much as I'd like to think that all my men are good and have a moral compass and would never cross that line, I can't fuckin' promise that. We all have darkness and fuck if I know if some of the old timers hadn't done some awful shit under my father's leadership. Especially to women who, we all know, those men didn't exactly place a high value on. I know for a fact that more than one or two of the club bitches got roughed up back in the day. I know she's not a clubwhore and I know that she seems at least somewhat capable of taking care of her shit, Repo, but fact of the matter is... she's smaller, she's not as strong, and she is out numbered. I could try to lay down the law and threaten the men, but that would be problematic..."

"Because you're choosing a probate over patched members," I guessed.

"That, yeah, and because even that isn't a guarantee. They get drunk, they get mean and stupid. Something could happen. And while there would be fuckin' repercussions, swift and fuckin' permanent, it wouldn't take away the damage. I can't have that shit on my conscience, Repo. Neither can you. She doesn't belong here. The sooner she sees that, sees that we aren't doing it to be assholes, but for her best interest, the better."

And, again, I saw his point.

There was no denying the logic there.

The old ladies, they were protected out of a need to respect your brothers. No one would so much as look at Summer, Lo, or Janie sideways for fear of getting their eyes gouged out by their men.

Maze didn't have that kind of protection.

If someone got a couple too many in them, got turned down by one of the bitches, or were the sick kind of fucks who liked a fight, liked to take what wasn't freely offered, Reign was right... there was no way to promise that couldn't happen. And while there would be consequences, he was also right about it not taking away the damage. Maze would be left to have to deal with what happened.

I could see that Reign wished he had the ability to trust all his men implicitly. And while he did trust the ones he had appointed himself: Cash, Wolf, myself, and about three or four of the other guys... there was nothing he could do about the other men, the ones who had been around when he was still biting ankles. He couldn't kick them out because of something they *might* be capable of. And because he couldn't do that, he couldn't tell Maze she was as safe as any of the other men.

It wasn't right.

It was unfair.

It sucked.

But it was how things were.

"Get her better," Reign broke into my thoughts. "Then get her out. The sooner, the better."

With that, Reign left me alone with Maze.

Every few hours, I got her conscious enough to shove some fever reducers and pain medicine in her before she passed back out again. She didn't eat. She barely drank. And by the time I opened that door on the sixteenth hour, I was seriously worried I'd have to wrap her up and drag her to the hospital to get some fluids in her. But I walked in to find her on the bed, somewhat alert, and I felt a weight slide slightly away.

Her fever was still around one-oh-four so I dragged her to the bathroom and got her in the tub. Tired, weak, sore, and miserable, her defenses she wore as a impenetrable shield slipped away. Once she was done fighting me in the water, she curled up on her side, her hand holding onto mine as she passed out. She slept peacefully for half an hour as I tried to drain water and refill with hotter water three times over until her skin stopped feeling like you could fry an egg on it. But even after that, I stayed there with her for another twenty minutes, stroking my hand up her side or through her long purple hair.

See, the problem was, I fucking liked Maze.

It was easy in my lifestyle, *our* lifestyle, to start to view women as nothing more than pieces of ass. For men like me who spent the majority of their time at the clubhouse, most of the women we came into contact with were clubwhores, biker groupies, women who just wanted to fuck a bad boy. And while, in recent years, the arrival of Lo and Janie brought and their own brand of gender-bending badassery, they weren't around nearly enough to make a big change in everyone's ways of thinking.

Having Maze around constantly as she slaved around the compound on next to no sleep and did whatever one of the members asked her to do, which included: getting drink refills, cooking dinner, cleaning sheets, scrubbing floors, changing television stations, scrubbing bikes, and fetching fucking darts, and doing so without so much as a whimper of complaint, it was easy to be reminded how sexy it was to have a strong woman around.

Being obedient, however, did not mean she was meek. Far from it. I couldn't walk past the group of probates without overhearing her saying some smartass, well-crafted rib to one of the men, doing so mostly in good-nature toward Duke and Renny, dismissively toward Fox, and maliciously toward Moose. And while she was extremely careful to never be disrespectful to patched members, there was an air of defiance, of quiet rebellion. Hell, I'd even heard her address a demand from Reign himself with a sharp tongue but a huge, fake ass smile that made it impossible to call her out on her behavior.

And despite her staying far away from any of the physical altercations between the members and her fellow probates, I'd once caught her screwing around with Renny in the yard one night and damn if she didn't best him twice.

Whoever Maze was, whatever her background, there was one thing that was clear: Maze had some kind of training. And it wasn't just a self-defense class at a local fire station. It wasn't all solar plexis, instep, nose, and groin. Renny had moved to grab her from behind and in the space of a blink, he was over her shoulder and on the ground. She anticipated his advance before he even moved. She blocked, deflected, then advanced herself. And she did it with a sort of practiced ease that made me wonder if maybe she grew up with some kind of martial arts.

It was a fucking shame she had to go, because to be perfectly honest, she would have taken a patch over Fox or Moose by a long, long shot.

Duke had a place because Duke had some secrets. He had some information we very much valued. He had led the kind of life that meant he had absolutely no childhood, every moment of his time on Earth being about hard work, fights, blood, money, business, and evading police.

Renny got a place because, while he was young and maybe a bit too laid-back for a typical biker, he was whip-smart. He hadn't had a normal upbringing by any accounts. On the surface, there was nothing even mildly criminal about his parents. In fact, they were both really renowned psychologists back in Maine where he was from. Which likely explained his ability to read people fast and accurately. But some dark, twisted, awful shit went on in his house and when he was seventeen, he ran away, found himself in Navesink Bank, fell into a rough crowd, found out about The Henchmen, and wanted in. We had all been ready to dismiss him until he had been at the compound for about a week. After that, well, it was clear he was on a fast track for a patch.

Maze was a wild card. When we ran her name, not much came up but some brief employment history at a few bike shops and bars. She had no record and no social media. We didn't know shit about her.

I sighed as I shifted her up and out of the water, cradling her against my chest and making water pool all across the bathroom as I walked to get a towel. She woke up enough to lean against the counter so I could dry her off. I grabbed a tee, slipping it over her head then reaching up under and pulling off her wet bra and panties, saving her vanity. She probably wouldn't remember the whole encounter, but that wasn't the point. Seeing some unconscious girl's tits seemed creepy as fuck, no matter how sick she was. No matter how much I may have been wondering about said tits in private.

As I reached around her to dry her dripping hair, she leaned forward, resting her head against my chest and nuzzling into my neck, making a low, contented sound in her throat. I paused slightly in the drying of her hair, looking at my reflection in the mirror and seeing the confusion in my own eyes. Confusion because as I felt her snuggle into me, there was a strange warm sensation spreading across my chest that felt comforting, right.

"Fuck," I said, shaking my head and focusing back on my task.

So, yeah, Maze was fucking hot. There was no denying it. She was tall and fit with those great hips, thighs, and an ass a man would kill for. She had incredibly long and soft hair. Her lips were just begging you to taste them.

It was shallow of me, but the second I saw her, I wanted in. Meaning, inside. Her. And every day that followed, watching her step up to the plate, never waver in her tasks, and doing so with a lifted chin and a smile (or alternately, a giant 'fuck you' on her forehead), yeah it only made the attraction grow.

Aside from doling out jobs and riding her ass about doing or redoing some task, I spent very little time with her. Actually, I spent less time with her than I did the other probates. I'd shoot pool with Renny or let Duke lend a hand with my cars. I even bullshitted with Moose and Fox on occasion. I didn't do any of that with Maze. Part of that was because I knew that being close to her was dangerous. It would be an unnecessary temptation. It was also because she avoided me almost as a rule. Even when she was around me, she seemed to shut down. While

I'd seen her laughing and joking about with Renny or having seemingly serious conversations with Duke, when I was around, she shut her mouth and only spoke when spoken to. And even then, her answers were clipped.

I wondered if that was because she was trying to avoid fucking up or because she also had an issue with the lines between us. I wasn't stupid. I knew she was attracted. If I didn't know from the jump, I definitely knew when I caught her checking me out while I was working on my car that day.

Or maybe she was quiet because she was keeping secrets.

Fuck if I knew.

All I knew was that being around her, even when she was out of her mind sick, was a problem.

I put her back down on the bed, tucking her in even though she wasn't chattering anymore, grabbed the tray and headed out of the room.

Maybe I just needed to get laid. That could be the problem. Fact of the matter was, the clubwhores didn't, and never did, do it for me. It wasn't that I necessarily got off on the chase, but I didn't exactly want pussy thrown in my face either. And I certainly wasn't thrilled at the idea of being the third cock in someone's hole on any given night. No thanks.

So if I didn't get out and hit the town, I didn't get any. And, quite frankly, I'd been pretty fucking busy lately with working on the cars, club business, and keeping an eye on the probates. It had probably been the better part of a month. Which, by normal standards, wasn't bad. But for me, it was probably a record. I wasn't a slut, but I enjoyed my fair share. I was young and single. No one could blame me for enjoying the company of women.

I closed my bedroom door, leaning against it in the hall, deciding that as soon as she was out of my bed, I was bringing someone else into it.

That would definitely help the attraction to Maze thing. I hoped.

# SIX

*Maze*

I woke up the next morning fever-free and mortified.

Mortified.

Because there was no blissful blanket over my brain shielding me from the reality of what had happened over the twenty-four hours that I was burning up. Oh, no. It was all bright, vivid, sharp. Obnoxiously so. First, he'd carried me to his bed. That wasn't so bad. He'd removed my boots and tucked me in then went in search of medicine. When he came back and tried to get it in me, however, I screamed and flailed. I was pretty sure I whacked him across the face during the second dose of medicine. By the third dose, I was mostly conscious. He'd undressed me and bathed me. Then I, *good lord,* snuggled him.

He left after getting me back into bed and I slept. He came back sometime later, kicking out of his shoes and getting into the empty side of the bed. I woke up from a bad dream, of which I generally had very few if any, rolling to face him to find him watching me aptly with his tired-looking blue eyes. "Don't let them get me," I begged in a quiet voice, knowing my eyes were pleading.

His head had tilted, his brows drew together slightly. His mouth opened, then closed, like he thought better of what he was going to say. He slumped down further into the bed and rolled on his side to face me, draping a strong arm over my hips and hauling me against him.

"I won't," he said, the words almost sounding like a promise, like a vow.

"Good," I said, moving closer and resting my forehead against his chest and falling back to sleep.

So, yeah.

I'd snuggled him.

Twice.

I sat off the side of the bed in what I assumed was one of his tees, and nothing else, cradling my head in my hands and trying to figure out how the fuck to get out of such a messed up situation. True, I could blame the fever. People did weird stuff when they were delirious. I was no exception. In fact, my grandmother used to say she dreaded when I got sick because I always tended to run way too hot and then hallucinate and act weird until it broke. It wasn't unusual for me to be not like myself when I was sick. I could easily blame the sickness.

But, fact of the matter was, I knew better.

Usually, I hallucinated about being chased or trapped in small rooms.

I didn't randomly snuggle my grandmother or the doctors who would treat me.

Oh, no.

That was all me. Well, me and my libido.

There was really no denying it anymore, it wasn't just

that Repo was hot and had that bad boy thing going for him. It wasn't even as simple as having the hots for your unattainable boss or authority figure.

Because when his hands touched me as he took off my clothes, it wasn't surprise that made me gasp. It was desire. The chaste, two-second contact sent off a shock through my system, culminating in a strong clenching between my thighs. Then when I was nightmare-scared and only half awake and he vowed to not let them get me, well, I felt a strange fluttering feeling in my belly.

K was going to have my head.

"Shit," I said, straightening.

K.

If I lost an entire day, that meant I missed check-in.

You did not, *ever,* miss check-in.

You missed check-in and K started to worry.

If K worried enough, he'd drag his ass down to Jersey and come looking for me.

And that, well, it would not be good.

I jumped out of Repo's bed, finding my boots and slipping into them, then running, literally running back toward the basement. The longer I let pass, the more shit I would be in for. It was early morning and Duke's bunk was empty so I figured he was on patrol. I rummaged through my bag and found the burner, turning it on. I threw on jeans then made my way back upstairs, taking in the quiet compound with a sense of relief as I went into the kitchen and typed in his number. This time, to his cell. It was too early to call the boxing emporium like I was supposed to.

"K," his voice grumbled into the phone, sounding half-asleep.

Half-asleep was good. Half-asleep meant he wasn't in his car flying down the highway to try to figure out what happened to me.

"Vermont," I said quietly into the receiver.

"What the *fuck* Maisy?" he exploded, suddenly fully awake.

"I know. I know. I'm sorry. I was sick. Literally delirious with fever for a full day. I was barely conscious. I'm sorry."

There was a short pause. "Okay," he said, calm again. "So your cover is still good?" he asked and I felt myself smiling. No asking if I was alright or how I got sick. Still no softness. Just some more sandpaper. I almost forgot how much I needed it.

"Yeah. Solid. Nothing to report really. All is par for the course."

"All the probates still in?"

"Unfortunately."

"Distinguishing yourself?"

"Haven't had much opportunity to prove myself. It's all grunt work."

"Alright. Check-ins on Tuesdays by midnight. If you can't sneak away to call me, send me a text with an eighty-six. I'll know all is fine and that you'll contact the next Tuesday."

"Sounds good."

"Stay safe."

"And kick ass," I finished for him, smiling as his line went dead.

I was still smiling at the wall as I put the burner down on the counter. Talking to K always helped. It always made me focus. Fact of the matter was, it was easy to forget why I was doing what I was doing. It got easy to fall into the lifestyle and let it eat at me, to lose sight of how necessary it was for me to make it work. K reminded me of that. He reminded me of the countless hours of him telling me just that. All the hours that he sat with me and told me that if they...

"Whose ass are you planning on kicking?" a voice said

from the doorway, making me jump and turn, arm already cocked back before I placed the voice. It was almost the same instant that my eyes found Repo leaning against the doorway in black jeans and a white v-neck tee, arms crossed over his broad chest.

I felt my eyes go wide for a second, feeling caught, before I forced my features into a mask of indifference, reminding myself that I hadn't really said anything incriminating. In the future, I needed to be a helluva lot more careful.

"Anyone who gets in my way," I said casually with a small smirk.

Repo answered my smirk with one of his own. "Somehow I don't doubt that at all," he said, pushing off the doorway and moving into the small room.

He walked past me toward the coffee machine and started the process of making a fresh pot. His attention elsewhere, I watched him, taking in the paleness of his skin, the heaviness of his eyelids, the bruises under his eyes from tiredness. It struck me that while he had gotten into bed beside me the night before, I was pretty sure he hadn't slept. In fact, he seemed almost perpetually awake. It didn't matter what time I pulled a shift, he was always mulling around. And he always looked exhausted.

"Do you ever sleep?" I heard myself blurting out without thinking.

"Not often," he surprised me by answering honestly, hitting the button on the machine and turning to me. "How are you feeling? You probably shouldn't be up and moving around already."

"I'm fine," I said with a shrug. It was half-true. I still felt pretty crummy. My sinuses were clogged and I had a headache. But with the fever, chills, sweats, and body aches gone, I felt a heck of a lot better than I did. At his raised brow, I smiled a conceded, "I'm starving and dehydrated," I admitted.

"That's more like it. Sit," he said, waving a hand toward the small table. He turned away and went to the fridge as I sat, grabbing a bottle of water and a carton of orange juice. He walked over to the table and put them on the surface. "Drink," he instructed and turned away again.

"Bossy much?" I asked, unscrewing the water and taking a long swig that I swear I could feel sliding along all my dried-out organs.

Repo turned over his shoulder at me, giving me a small smile. "Hey, it's not my fault you're dehydrated. I think it would be easier to get fluids in a crocodile than you," he said, turning back to grab items out of the fridge.

I pressed my lips together, trying to figure out the protocol. He took care of me when I was sick. For that, I felt like I needed to thank him. But did badass bikers thank other bikers for being nice to them?

In the end, I figured, to hell with it. I was raised with manners. Regardless of the weird lifestyle I was in, I was going to use them.

"Thanks for looking after me," I said, my voice a strange, strangled sound. "I know I'm not a good patient. My fevers get out of control." I paused, biting into my lower lip as I prepared to do a little lying. "I get completely delirious and do things that I never would normally do."

To that, Repo didn't look over his shoulder at me. No, he put down everything in his hands which had to be half the contents of the refrigerator, and turned to me fully. One of his dark brows were raised, his lips teased up at one corner. "Honey, if that is what you need to tell yourself, knock yourself out. But don't fucking lie to me."

I looked down at the bottle of water cradled between my hands. "I don't know what you're talking about," I mumbled.

I didn't see or hear him moved but the next thing I knew, his fisted hands caged in mine on the table and I looked up to see him leaning over the table at me. "Can we cut the shit, Maze? I'm good with us ignoring this. In fact, I'm gonna have to insist on it. But don't pretend it doesn't exist."

I swear there was an alarm going off in my brain screaming "danger, danger, danger!" but I wasn't sure exactly what was more dangerous: acknowledging it or keeping up the charade. In the end, I chose to stick with the latter. "Repo, seriously, I have no idea what you're talking about."

That was, apparently, the more dangerous choice.

I knew this because he was no longer leaning across the table, but around it, right in front of me. His hands grabbed the sides of my face. Not held, not cradled, grabbed. He simultaneously pulled me upward as he leaned down and his lips took power over mine, crashing down hard and demanding. He pulled me onto my feet as his tongue traced the crease of my lips until they slid open and he slipped inside. My arms grabbed his forearms, holding on as a shiver ripped through my system. Against my mouth, Repo growled, dropping my face. His one arm went around my lower back, hauling me against his body. The other traveled into the hair at the crown of my head, sinking in, curling, and tugging slightly.

Another shiver worked through me and my hands went up and around the back of his neck, pulling him closer, holding on tight as his tongue teased mine, retreated, then teased some more before pulling away as his lips took mine again, softer, deeper. I whimpered against him, feeling the desire like a white hot bolt between my legs.

His teeth bit into my bottom lip hard, holding and pulling, making another whimper escape me. "Fuck," he hissed, releasing my lip, but not my body or my hair. He used the latter to drag my face back several inches so he could look down at me. "That's what I'm talking about," he informed me, releasing me so quickly that I actually faltered a step, slamming my hand down on the back of my chair to keep my feet.

His back was to me as he grabbed all his items off the counter by the fridge and moved beside the stove, giving me a long minute to pull myself together. I needed it. Actually, what I needed was a cold shower, an hour long session with a powerful vibrator, and about fifteen miles between me and Repo at all times in the future.

Pretty sure all three options were out for me, I lowered myself down at the table again and focused on drinking the rest of my water and ignoring the frazzled, electric sensation to every inch of my skin, most especially that of my sex.

I slanted my eyes to look at Repo, his back still to me, as he steadily chopped something on the cutting board. His shoulders seemed more tense than usual and the knife seemed to be slamming down with way more force than necessary to chop an onion. Not able to see his face, I couldn't tell if he was affected at all by the kiss that had pretty much just thrown my whole world off its axis.

I'd kissed plenty in my life.

I'd had sweet, gentle kisses and hard, demanding ones.

But never, as in ever, had I ever felt like someone had owned me with a kiss. But that was how I felt when Repo's lips were on mine; I felt owned. For the duration of it, there was nothing but him. The entire compound could have come in and started cheering and I wouldn't have noticed. He kissed like he was going off to war, like a dying man, like he was sure it would be his last and he wanted to make sure it was a good one.

"You alright, Ace?" Duke asked, walking in, his shirt sticking to him with sweat so I assumed he was coming in from his shift.

"What?" I asked, shaking my head a little.

"You alright?" he asked, snagging a mug off the counter and coming to sit across from me, grabbing the orange juice container and pouring himself some. "You're all spaced out."

"Oh, um," I said, chancing a look at Repo whose chopping had stopped. It had stopped because he had turned to look at me, brow raised, waiting to hear the next lie out of my mouth. "Yeah. I'm just all stuffy," I said, waving a hand dismissively.

"Yeah," Repo said, his lips twitching, "that must be it." With that, he went back to doing whatever the heck he was doing that required so much cutting.

"You back on tonight?" Duke asked, sitting back in his chair the way only men did: legs wide, upper back against the chair, the rest detached, chest puffed out slightly.

"Ah I don't see why..."

"No," Repo cut me off.

Both Duke and I looked over, but Repo wasn't facing us. "I'm better now," I pressed.

"For what? An hour? Don't get cocky, probie. We need men on guard who can stay conscious for their shift. Until we're sure that's you, you're grounded."

I straightened, opening my mouth to object when Duke's raised hand caught my eye. When I looked over, he shook his head at me. I didn't need all that man-training K put me through to know he was warning me to shut the fuck up before I said something to get myself kicked out. Knowing he was right and there was nothing I could do, I stood up fast enough for my chair to turn over, drawing Repo's attention. But he said nothing and I stormed out of the kitchen. I ignored the presence of Wolf and Vin in the great room and threw myself outside, tearing across the field until the fence stopped me. I turned to the tree, taking a deep breath and jumping up to grab the lowest branch, pulling myself up.

It was a weird habit I picked up after my grandmother took me in as a kid. Growing up in the city, there generally weren't many trees around, let alone ones strong enough to climb. But when my mom was in a mood and I couldn't take it anymore, I climbed out the window and took up the fire escape until I hit the roof of whatever apartment building we were living in at the time. At my grandmother's in Vermont, there weren't fire escapes. But there was still an adult on my case about something every once in a while and my desire to run away from it. Given that we lived in a little Victorian in the woods, there were plenty of old, sturdy trees around. So when my grandmother started in on me, I would go out in the yard and climb a tree, often not coming in until it was dark and my growling stomach made me finally come down and find food.

Maybe it was immature.

But, the fact of the matter was, I had no privacy anywhere else at the compound. Someone always seemed to be in their bunks. Or in Renny's case, his recliner. The great room was always packed. And we weren't supposed to leave without permission. I knew I'd never get that. So the only thing I could do was get up and above it all for a little bit. I needed time to calm down and get my head together. Seeing as I was apparently 'grounded' until I proved I wasn't some pansy-assed weakling, there was no reason for me to even be in the compound. Technically, if we weren't directly given a job to do, we were free to do whatever the hell we wanted as long as we stayed on the grounds. I was on the grounds. So no one could say shit about it.

So what if Repo kissed me? And so what if it rocked my world a little bit? It was a *kiss.* A kiss was nothing. We were both adults. We also both understood how things were. He had even said it was best that we ignored what was between us.

I needed to stop being such a girl about it.

It was nothing.

The only reason it happened was because he was on some mission to prove I wanted him. It was an ego thing. Which, the more I thought about it, the more angry I got. What a shitty thing to do. The jackass.

I had worked myself up into what I thought was a righteous anger by the time I heard a throat clearing beneath me, surprising me enough to make me jump and almost pitch forward before my hands slammed down to steady myself.

It was him.

Of course it was.

Who the hell else would it be?

"You done sulking, Maze?"

Oh, the bastard.

"I'm not sulking. I'm sitting up here so I don't rip your fucking head off."

Repo's brow raised but he didn't call me on the threat. "You're kinda cute when you're offended."

"You're kind of an asshole all the time." That was another lie. In general, he was actually a pretty nice guy. I mean he'd nursed me when I was sick. How many women could claim to have a guy do that for them?

Repo exhaled a loud sigh, shaking his head. "Well this asshole brought you some food," he said, waving a plate I hadn't noticed him holding outward. "So you can go ahead and sit up there and starve to prove some asinine point or you can hop down and get something in your stomach so you don't fucking pass out again."

"Did you cook for Duke, Renny, and the assholes too?" I asked, crossing my arms over my chest.

Repo shook his head, looking back over his shoulder for a minute before tilting his head to look up at me again. "Maze, can we just... fucking not do this? You're pissed at me. I get it. Hell, I probably deserve it. But do you really have to throw it in my face anytime I do something halfway decent?"

"Tell you what," I said, my words way harsher than they needed to be given that he was, yet again, being a good guy, "you keep your fucking hands off me and we won't have a problem."

"Fair enough," he said after a long pause as he bent to put the plate down on the ground before turning and walking away from me.

I gave it about two minutes after he disappeared inside the compound before I climbed down and dug into the freaking perfect, fluffy omelet stuffed with tomatoes, spinach, onions, mushrooms, bacon, and cheddar cheese.

So he was a gold-medal kisser, a caretaker, a verifiable badass biker, an all-around good guy... and he could cook?

Great.

That was just *fantastic.*

# SEVEN

*Maze*

Exactly one week later, The Henchmen were having some kind of giant BBQ. As such, the night before, the members got a real kick out of running all of us probates freaking ragged. We cleaned. We cooked. We set up tables. We ran to the food store. We stocked the back bar. We washed the sheets to all the beds because all the patched brothers knew they would be way too wasted to drive themselves home afterward.

By the time the darkness came down, we were bone tired. Moose and Fox had gone down to bed before anyone else could demand anything of them. I was still in the great room with a bottle of Pledge and the orders to make every single wood surface shiny enough to see a reflection in. This order came from some jackass named Murry who was old enough to be my grandfather and a real mean son of a bitch. But it was an order from a patched member and I had to do what I was told.

Cash, Wolf, Repo, and Reign were all gathered at the bar,

sharing a round of beers and bullshitting when the back door flew open and Renny came in, his usually open and smiling face set in hard lines, his hands curled into fists at his sides.

Duke was on his heels, his hair free, his entire body practically sparking with anger. "We're not done, mother fucker," he shouted, the sound so unexpected and loud that I actually dropped the bottle of Pledge as I turned and pressed back against the wall just in time to see Renny whip around and land a right hook to Duke's jaw.

The patched members started hollering, clapping, smiling, cheering it on as Duke plowed into Renny bodily, sending them both flying, landing hard on the coffee table that gave way under their weight and crashed to the floor.

I just stood there completely dumbfounded.

From what I had seen over the past few weeks, Duke and Renny got along. Well, as well as anyone got along with Duke. He wasn't exactly the kind to sit around and crack jokes and bullshit. But he was friendly enough to me and Renny. I'd certainly never seen even a hint of animosity between the two of them.

But Duke was, quite plainly, pissed. It was in the tightness of his movements, the way he was holding nothing back despite outweighing Renny by a good fifty pounds of solid muscle. To his credit, Renny was fast and scrappy. He took his blows with grunts then slipped away before another could be landed. He looked a little bit like a punching bag, but he had gotten some good shots in himself which impressed the hell out of me.

They both crashed to the floor again, both fighting for dominance as they kept throwing furious fists.

I looked across the room to Repo who caught my eye and raised a brow. I held my arms up at my sides, a silent 'are you going to do anything about this?' To that, he only shook his head and turned back to watch the show.

Alright. So I knew it technically wasn't my place. First, because it was a source of entertainment for the patched members. Second, because it was really none of my business. And third because it was probably stupid to wade into a fight between two worthy opponents. But the fact of the matter was, I liked the both of them. They were good buffers between me and the douchebag brothers. I didn't want one of them heading to the hospital or getting kicked out over what I was sure was some nonsense.

I wiped my Pledge-greasy hands on my pant legs then moved over toward where they were still rolling around on the ground. Duke was on top, giving me a slight advantage as I moved behind him.

"Maze..." Repo's voice called out a warning to me.

Which I promptly ignored as I reached out, grabbed a handful of Duke's abundant hair and yanked viciously back. He came up ready to keep fighting. Before he even registered it was me, his hand was at my throat. He reminded me of a dog that way; he always went for the throat instinctively. I brought up both hands, grabbing his wrist and twisting until his hand loosened, taking the advantage and swinging it behind his back. It all happened in a matter of seconds and his body went slack as he saw through the red of his anger and realized it was me. At about the same time, Renny gained his feet and tried to charge again. Tried, because I slammed a hand into his solar plexis as he tried, cutting off his advance and knocking out his air. "Enough!" I growled, looking between them. "Enough," I said more quietly. "Now I can't stop you from fighting it out like boys, but I strongly suggest you talk it out like the fucking men you are instead," I snapped and Renny had the decency to look sheepish as he wiped blood from his lip.

Duke was still sparking with anger, but he just gave

Renny a hard look and stormed out the back door. Renny gave me a shrug and went toward the bathroom to clean up. Me, well, I grabbed the Pledge and a rag lest I get lectured for leaving a mess, then did another thing that was totally not my place. I walked past the bar on my way to the hall, and mumbled just loud enough for Repo to hear, "Was that so fucking hard?"

"You just cost me fifty bucks, bitch," one of the older patched members called as I passed.

"That must suck for you," I said, sending him a sweet smile despite the bile rolling around in my belly. "Maybe next time you should put your money on a winner. In case the inflection there is lost on you, I meant *me,*" I added with a chin lift before walking away.

I was sick, sick, sick of the shit in the compound.

It wasn't just the hard work. I could live with that. It wasn't even the sleep deprivation. My body was adjusting. It wasn't even Moose and Fox. They were jerks, but they were, for the most part, pretty predictable and easy to avoid.

No, mostly, my issue was with Repo.

See, since him dropping off the food beneath the tree, something had changed. I wasn't sure if it was because of my surly demand for him to keep his hands off me or what, but he went from being a good guy I could count on to at least be fair... to an outright asshole. He ran me ragged. He put me on patrol with Moose and Fox. He picked on everything I did, no matter how careful I was to make sure I did everything perfectly. He would invite all the guys to have a round with him while demanding I go cook them all food.

And on top of that, the bastard seemed to use any excuse to get close to me. When he was giving me an order, he would get in my face. When he was chastising something I did, he got up behind me and spoke over my shoulder.

He never out and out touched me again, but he got close

enough that he might as well have.

It was a problem because, one, he was doing it because of my request to keep his hands off me. And, two, because while my brain was beyond annoyed with him, my body didn't get the message and any time I felt his body near mine, my skin flushed, my breasts felt heavy, my sex clenched, a sense memory of his kiss pressed into my lips.

So I had been, for a week straight, in a state of absolute anger and constant sexual frustration.

It was an issue.

It was especially an issue because it was making me forget my mission and causing me to lash out in small ways when I knew that the littlest thing could get me thrown out. I needed to get a grip. I needed to remember why I was there and what it would mean if I got kicked out.

So still fully clothed and in a sour mood to end all sour moods, I went to sleep.

--

It was hard to hold onto my anger the next day. Granted, we were all still called on to do all the menial tasks. But all the members were around. Most even brought their old ladies and children. Reign's wife, Summer, was hanging around. Their daughter, Ferryn, toddled around us while we talked about the food and who was going to be at the BBQ.

I had to admit, it was nice to talk to a woman for a change. Being around so many men had, in a way, been almost refreshing. There was a lot less of the cattiness, the back stabbing, the bullshit. But that being said, sometimes it was just nice to hear someone complain about the humidity making their hair get crazy.

Duke and Renny mulled around, both of them giving the other a wide birth. Renny was uncharacteristically quiet, barely even saying good morning to me. I wondered if I would ever figure out what had made two reasonably friendly men go HAM on each other.

Considering this was supposed to be a job of sorts, I found myself getting a bit too invested. K wouldn't approve.

"Probie," Repo's voice called, making me stiffen and turn. He didn't call me by my name anymore. That was apparently part of his newfound asshole-ness.

"What's up?" I asked, giving him a wholly fake smile that actually hurt the muscles in my face.

"Reign needs you out front," he said, turning and expecting me to heel like an obedient little dog.

I stared daggers at his back as we went out to the front where Wolf had pulled his mammoth truck up, Moose and Fox already up in the bed working on untying the kegs. "Hey what do you need?" I asked Reign before Repo could announce that he'd brought me to heel.

"Kegs," Reign said, jerking his chin toward the bed of the truck.

Fuck. Of course.

See, after all my training with K, I knew that there wasn't much a man could do to best me unless he had even better training. It wasn't about strength per say, it was about technique and instincts. But, that being said, it wasn't sexist to admit I was weaker. Physically, I was simply not as strong as my male counterparts. I didn't like it. It chafed every time I needed help lifting something that one of the guys could lift by themselves. But it was just how it was. I wasn't as strong. Kegs, well, they were about one-hundred and sixty pounds. There was absolutely no way I could lower one to the ground by myself.

But fuck if I let anyone know that.

"On it," I said on a shrug, walking past Janie and Wolf and hopping up into the bed.

"You guys are *assholes*," Janie hissed and I bit into my lip to keep from smiling. I liked Janie. I think it was impossible to not like her. She was a certified badass and completely unconcerned about speaking her mind and even pushing around the members of the club. You had to respect her balls. I envied her ability to speak her mind.

After yelling at the guys, she hopped up in the bed to help me, evening up my odds.

"Ass looks great in those jeans," Fox said, giving me one of his trademark creepy smiles as I walked past.

Honestly, his comments were so frequent and, for all intents and purposes, innocent seeing as he never tried to act on any of it, that I had long since learned to ignore him. Janie, of course, was not of the same mind. That just wasn't her style.

"Funny, I don't hear you telling Cash or Reign or Wolf what nice asses they have," she snapped, reaching for the handles on the keg I was untying.

"Don't want to fuck theirs," Fox shrugged. And, well, it was the wrong thing to say around Janie.

"Are you fucking serious?" she asked, straightening and advancing him across the bed. "You do realize this is a brotherhood right? You're not supposed to..."

"Have to deal with a sister? And her fucking mood swings

when she's on the rag like you obviously a..."

I felt my stomach muscles tense, knowing there was no way she was going to let him get away with that. See, Janie worked for Lo at Hailstorm and aside from being a good hacker and pro bomb-maker, she was really *really* good at Krav Maga. So when I saw her plant her legs wide and bend at the waist, well, I knew that Fox was going to be in a world of pain.

One second he was standing there on the truck bed. The next, he was flat on his back on the ground.

"Hey, bitch..." Moose growled, slamming his big palm down on her tiny shoulder.

And, well, he just signed his metaphorical discharge papers with that one move. Because down on the ground, Wolf was actually fucking *growling* and Cash and Reign had both stiffened. You did not, *ever*, touch another brother's old lady. No matter what.

In K's words, it was time to distinguish myself.

I turned, grabbing his wrist and twisting it, planting the palm of my other hand on his shoulder so he couldn't whip back at me and turning him fast, shoving his chest down on the top of one of the kegs.

"Apologize," I demanded as he tried to throw his weight back at me and I brought my knee up to press into his back, holding him in place.

"Fuck you," he spat.

"With what? While we're talking about our *brothers'* body parts, I've seen you changing, Moose. You don't have anything a woman wants in those pants."

"Maze," Repo's voice called. It wasn't just my name; it was a warning.

And, well, I had hit my limit of shit I was willing to take.

"What?" I almost screamed back, every last drop of frustration spilling into my voice. "Last night Duke and Renny got into a knock down drag out and all you did was stand there and place bets! But because it's me you're going to pull the fucking 'boss' card a-fucking-gain?" I asked, still yelling, slamming Moose against the keg hard then pushing away from him. I moved across the bed, focusing all my anger on Repo. "He put his *hand* on someone else's old lady. He's lucky it's still attached to his body!" His hands dropped down by his sides, his hands curling up into fists as a muscle ticked in his jaw. But he stayed silent.

"She ain't wrong," Wolf declared, reaching for his woman and pulling her down on the ground with him so he could wrap a protective arm around her.

"Maze, you need to calm down," Repo said, his voice sounding tired.

Calm down? *Calm down?* The bastard...

"You need to stop..." I started, but was cut off by Reign's bark.

"Alright, enough," Reign said, obviously done with the situation. "Moose," he said inclining his head toward him in the truck bed, rubbing his wrist where I had twisted it, "Maze is right; you don't put your hand on a woman. Ever. And you certainly don't put your hand on your fuckin' road captain's woman. What the fuck were you even thinking?"

"She could have broken my brother's bac..."

"Then your brother should show a little more respect. You're out," Reign said in a lethal way that brooked no argument. "Your brother can stay if he shapes the fuck up. Now you've ruined enough of this party so get the fuck gone so we can all enjoy the rest."

Moose turned an almost comical shade of red as he fought to keep his mouth shut, knowing damn well that the last thing he wanted to do was start some kind of argument with Reign. He moved past me, slamming so hard into my shoulder that white sparks of pain made me grit my teeth to keep from hissing. He wasn't going to get a reaction out of me. He was out. He wasn't my problem anymore.

I hopped down off the bed, storming back toward the compound. I needed a minute to get myself together, take some deep breaths, repeat my mantras. Hell, even call K if I couldn't get myself under control. All I knew was I needed to get the hell away from Repo.

"Maze..." he said, his voice almost soft like I remembered it being when I was sick, as he tried to reach for my arm as I passed.

"Don't you fucking touch me," I hissed under my breath as I passed, trying to keep my eyes off him because if he looked at me, he would see the nonsensical cocktail of anger, sadness, betrayal, frustration, and defeat. And, well, I'd be damned if I let him see any more weakness from me.

I stayed clear of the basement, knowing Moose or Fox would be down there collecting Moose's stuff eventually and hung out instead in the bathroom, pacing the small space, murmuring the plan to myself under my breath.

Regardless of how Repo got down on me, I knew I had done the right thing with Moose. I also scored a point because he was out. He was out and that meant one less person riding me. It also meant I was one step closer to getting a patch.

So long as I could swallow my pride, bite my tongue, and just... deal with whatever else Repo and the others might throw at me.

Twenty minutes later, deciding I had wasted enough time of a good party on a bad mood, I made my way back out to the yard where a few of the men had congregated around the grill. The smell of hamburgers and hotdogs filled the air, making my stomach groan in protest of its emptiness.

"Sugar, honey, darlin'..." a smooth voice called from

behind me, immediately making me stiffen.

"What?" I growled as I turned, brow raised, ready to take more sexism crap from whoever it was and knowing there wasn't much I could do about it.

And there was a guy. Really, it was hard to describe him. He almost had a greaser look with his thin face, slicked back hair, tight black pants, and white tee. But that wasn't exactly right either because he was literally covered in tattoos up to his neckline and had an eyebrow and tongue piercing. His deep green eyes didn't so much as drift below my neck and his smile seemed open and friendly.

"You belong to someone here?"

"I don't *belong* to anyone," I bristled.

"Shoot, this is Maze. She's a probate," Cash said, walking up, slamming a hand on Shoot's shoulder and holding out beer bottles for us to take.

"No shit?" Shoot asked me, smile getting wider. "'Bout fucking time you jackasses got progressive," he remarked, giving me a wink as he sipped his beer.

"Says the lone gunman," Cash laughed, shaking his head.

"Hey you find me a skirt who can shoot fifty yards in a dense fog and hit their target, I will happily take them on. I could use some vacation time. Thinking 'bout taking Amelia down to Al'bama in the shit part of winter here."

It started to click then. I'd heard of Shoot, better known as Shooter. He was a hitman for lack of a better term. Amelia must have been his woman. Legend was, he was the most charming man in fifty miles in any direction. Somehow, I believed that. There was obviously just something wrong with me that he had no impact on my mood.

I again blamed Repo.

I chanced a look over to where he was talking to Janie by the picnic tables. Janie looked angry, Repo kind of dead-eyed.

"Maze," Cash called, drawing my attention.

"Yeah?"

"I know you're having a shit time of it here and I'm not gonna disrespect your intelligence by saying it hasn't been planned that way, but I have to say... you're bearing it like no one else would."

"I'm just as deserving as the rest of them," I said, lifting my chin a little.

"I'm not saying I don't agree with you, sweetheart," he said, giving me an almost sad smile. "But I'm not going to be giving you any false hope either. The odds aren't in your favor and you were really close to fucking it up for yourself out front. Not because of that shit with Moose. The fucker had it coming. But if Reign didn't cut you off, I'm pretty sure you would have crossed a line with Repo."

"Why are you telling me this?" I asked, shrugging my shoulders.

"Because if I don't, Lo is going to tie me to the headboard and chop off my balls for not warning you. Now," he said, his smile going a little wicked, "I'm okay with some kinky rope fun, but I'm pretty attached to my balls. I'd like to keep it that way."

At that, I felt my lips curve up slightly. "I didn't really need the warning. I've known how it was from day one," I said, my eye automatically catching the movement of Repo from the picnic tables to the far end of the yard where his cars were situated. Why my eyes always sought him out despite my strong aversion to him lately, I had no idea. They apparently had a mind of their own.

"Oh, pumpkin," Shoot said, bringing my attention back to him and making me realize that Cash had walked away without my noticing.

"What?" I asked, feigning innocence.

"Oh fuck off," he laughed, shaking his head at me. "You

want on your boss-man."

"Don't be ridiculous," I said, rolling my eyes for good measure.

"What's the problem?" he asked, ignoring my objection because he saw right through my bullshit. "Take him for a ride. It'll certainly help."

"Help what?" I asked, smiling a little.

"Well, this borderline psychotic attraction you are feeling toward me right now," he said with such a straight face that I felt a laugh get caught in my throat then burst out, making me throw my head back and laugh. "Really helping my ego here, darlin'," he said, smiling.

"Oh, I think your ego can withstand a few knocks, Shoot."

"His ego could withstand a category nine earthquake," a woman's voice said as she walked up, giving Shooter a warm smile. She was short and curvy with long dark hair and deep brown eyes. As soon as she was within arm's length, he hauled her up against his side and gave her cheek a wet, smacking kiss. "I'm Amelia," she supplied unnecessarily.

"Maze," I said, giving her a smile.

"I heard all about you from Janie, Lo, and Summer. Welcome to the girls club. Have you met Alex yet?" she asked, waving a hand across the lawn to where a tall, leggy, brunette with delicate bone structure was standing beside a blond giant with a beard and piercing light blue eyes.

"No," I said, shaking my head. "She's in this... club too?"

"We have to stick together. All these boys around," she said, lowering her eyes at Shooter who leaned over and bit into her earlobe, making her laugh.

"Speaking of," Shoot said, nodding at Wolf. "We have to go make a round. Think about what I said, darlin'."

"Or completely ignore him depending on how ridiculous what he said was," Amelia called over her shoulder as he led her away, one of his hands slipping into her back pocket as she frantically tried to swat it away. To no avail.

I made my rounds too, talking to Lo and Janie, meeting Alex, sharing a picnic table with a still too-silent Renny. As the night went on, things got rowdier and louder, making me feel like a buzzkill for not being in a partying mood. Seeing no one across the field, I made my way toward the back and found my tree. I climbed up, watching the party rage on as I enjoyed my solitude, feeling a calmness settle down on me for the first time in weeks.

At least that was until I heard rustling and looked down to see Repo move around the tree to stand under me.

"Fuck honey," he said, shaking his head, his eyes sad. "Don't look at me like that."

"Like what?"

"Like you fucking hate me," he said, jumping up and grabbing the limb I was sitting on and hauling himself up, moving to straddle it and lean back against the trunk as I swung my legs like a kid on a swing.

"I don't hate you," I said, looking off at the party, wondering if they could all see us or if we were lost in the night. Either option terrified me in their own unique ways. "That's the problem," I whispered.

# EIGHT

*Repo*

*Tell you what, you keep your fucking hands off me and we won't have a problem.*

That was what she said to me perched up in her tree like a sullen nine-year old.

And, well, I couldn't even be mad about it. She was right; I needed to keep my hands off of her. But to be perfectly honest, the only way to pull that off was to get her the fuck out of the MC once and for all. If she was hanging around, I was going to want to put my hands on her. So she needed to go. To make that happen, I had to stop trying to be fair, trying to keep the guys from riding her. I had to be on her all day and night. I needed to encourage her exclusion and hazing. So I did that, with a lump the size of a boulder in my gut the whole fucking time.

Fact of the matter was, I didn't have it in me to be a fucking asshole all the goddamn time. That wasn't me. It especially went against pretty much everything I had learned and believed in life about treating women. And every time her face fell when I called her or lectured her or excluded her, I felt like the worst kind of scum.

That thing in the truck with Moose and Fox and Janie and Maze? That was seriously fucked. There was no way I should have been giving her a hard time, but I had my orders and Reign was standing right the fuck there. But her jerking away from me, hissing at me, then getting lectured by Janie as I watched Shoot and Cash try to cheer Maze up, yeah, none of that sat right with me.

Most especially because I wanted to be the one to make her throw her head back and laugh like she did at something Shooter said.

Don't ask me why, but that was where my mind went.

So when I walked underneath her and she looked down at me with a mix of anger, resentment, sadness, and hurt... I just couldn't fucking keep up the act anymore.

"I don't hate you," she said, avoiding looking at me. I didn't blame her. I made her not want to look at me if she didn't absolutely have to. "That's the problem," she added, her voice barely above a whisper.

"You should."

"Yeah," she agreed, not bothering to spare my feelings.

"Then why don't you?"

"You know why," she said, ducking her head, watching her feet swing.

"Honey..." I said and I watched her profile as her eyes closed for a second before she turned her head to look at me.

"What?"

"It's my job."

"What's your job?"

"Making your life miserable. It's my job. I don't want to do it."

"Then don't."

"That's not an option."

"Bullshit," she said, shaking her head at me. "There is always a choice."

"Not for me."

"Why not?"

Little did she know, that was a loaded fucking question...

I grew up in a violent shithole.

Was there really any other way to describe the part of Detroit I came from? All there was was abandoned buildings, job scarcity, corrupted law enforcement, and crime. That was it. There was really no chance of turning out a good, upstanding citizen unless you got the fuck out of there before one of the gangs sucked you in.

I was not one of the lucky few who had parents always searching for a way to make their lives better for their kids. My dad was an irregular child-support check and my mother smoked crack. Had child protective services not been completely overwhelmed with actual physical and sexual abuse cases, my ass would have been hauled out of that roach-infested apartment in a heartbeat. But fact of the matter was, my mom was always too high to smack me around and I never got molested. So I was left where I was with empty cabinets and a mother who disappeared for days on end, sometimes coming home beat to shit, sometimes bringing men with her that I wasn't stupid enough to even try to pretend they were anything other than Johns.

When I was twelve and my mother got pulled into the

hospital for an OD, there was a knock on the apartment door. I ignored it, turning up the TV, fighting the swirling uncertainty in my belly I always felt when someone was at the door. In my experience, the only people who showed up at the door were cops and bill collectors. Neither were people I wanted to see.

"Rye, open the fuck up, kid," a deep, masculine voice called, making me start.

As far as I knew, bill collectors didn't know my name and the cops didn't curse at innocent kids.

I made my way toward the door. "Who is it?" I asked, reaching for the bat in the umbrella stand.

There was a pause and a sigh. "Ain't got no one to blame but myself that you don't know your own fucking uncle, huh?" he asked through the door, leaving me to pause for a moment before I reached for the chain.

I pulled open the door to reveal a tall, dark-haired, blue-eyed man in a blue tee and jeans stained dark in places. If my mother wasn't thin to the point of starvation and her hair wasn't perpetually greasy from her forgetting to wash it, you might have been able to see the similarity between the two. Hell, he actually looked a lot like I imagined I would when I grew up.

I didn't know much about my mother's family. Her parents were dead and no one else was close. I did know from one of her manic moods that she did, in fact, have a brother. His name was Seth and they had been estranged since teenagers when he moved out.

"Christ," he said, shaking his head at me. "When the fuck was the last time you ate anything?"

"Mom has been in the hospital two days," I said, shrugging.

"Was there food before she went in?" he asked as if he somehow knew how screwed up she was.

"Not usually."

"Alright," he said, looking into the apartment with distaste. "Go pack your shit."

"Pack my shit?" I parroted, not even tripping over the curse. No one lifted a brow to a kid cursing where I was from.

"Yeah, pack your shit. Can't imagine you got much. What you do, throw it in a bag. You're coming with me."

"Until Mom gets back?" I asked, not moving out of the doorway.

"Until your mother gets her fucking shit together," he said, pushing inside, making me move out of his way. So then, with what seemed like very little choice, I went and collected my shit. Of which there really wasn't much, just a couple outfits, a skateboard I found abandoned in a park, and a couple books the library was selling for nickles one afternoon. That was all I had.

"Jesus fucking Christ," my uncle said as he stood in the kitchen, holding open one of the kitchen cabinets where I knew from experience that we had an impressive infestation of roaches. He turned back, hearing my footsteps. His eyes fell to the bag in my hand. "You overly attached to any of that crap?"

I looked down at the bag and shrugged. "Guess not."

"Leave it the fuck here. We'll get you new shit."

With that, I left my childhood apartment.

I never went back.

And I got a boatload of new shit.

Because he made a fair amount of money.

My Uncle Seth was a lot of things: a strong, alpha masculine personality, a moderate drinker, a vintage muscle car enthusiast, a fucking phenomenal shot, and a drug dealer. Not the illegal stuff, the heroin or meth, the crack my mother smoked. No, my uncle, better known as Doc Seth, peddled prescription drugs. You needed some Benzos or Percs, he was who you saw. Reds, yellows, blues, Poor Mans PCP, Schoolboys. You fucking name it, he fucking sold it.

"Just not that Special K or Mexican Valium shit," he told me one night as we put pills into baggies at his dining room table, referencing Ketamine and Rohypnol. "I might be a real son of a bitch, but I ain't selling shit some pussy-ass mother fuckers are going to use to rape little girls with."

My Uncle Seth, the drug dealer with a conscience.

For the next five years, he stepped up to the plate. He taught me how to avoid the good cops, pay off the crooked ones, know when a deal was going to go south before it did, how to pick men for their particular brands of skills to add to the 'team'. He showed me how to rebuild an engine, paint a car like a goddamn pro, drive a stick, appreciate good music, charm a woman, take a hit, then throw a devastating one back. And, last but certainly not least, he taught me how to shoot. Well. He made me into a man. And, granted, I wasn't a *good* man just as he wasn't a *good* man. But I was strong, smart, capable, skilled.

By fifteen, I was helping him deal alongside all his other men.

By sixteen, I was a part of his team just as any of the others. Not because of nepotism, but because I fucking earned my place.

Two days after I turned seventeen, I walked into our apartment to see him lying in a pile of his own blood on the living room floor. He wasn't dead, his chest rising and falling in a weird, unnatural strobe-like motion. His eyes went to me as I froze, and he tried to lift his hand to indicate something to my side. I missed the meaning though and the next thing I knew, I felt a knife slice through the skin of my cheek from my eye to my jaw.

Then there was pain.

A lot of it.

Until there was none because I passed out.

I woke up to a cop kneeling over me checking my pulse.

I didn't have to ask. I just read the grim reality in his face. My uncle was dead.

Me, I was taken to the hospital to treat my face with thirteen stitches, my busted ribs, my concussion. I was released the next day and had to go back to Uncle Seth's apartment and clean up his blood and plan his funeral and try to figure out what the fuck I was supposed to do from that point on. He was all I had in the world. He was the only person who ever gave a good goddamn about me.

And he was gone.

He had a lavish funeral four days later, all of his men showing up. My mother, not surprisingly, never showed. I hadn't expected her to. Hell, I had never actually seen her again after she showed up fresh from the hospital looking for me. Seth had given her an earful, a wad of cash, and pushed her out the door.

It wasn't long before the shit hit the fan with his men. Everyone was vying for his position, trying to lead the others, trying to control the trade.

But, fuck them, that was my fucking legacy.

"You really slithered into his role," Wayne, my Uncle's second, said, nodding his head at me. Wayne was Seth's oldest friend and, in a way, became another uncle to me over the years. He taught me to play pool and tie a tie as my uncle was a staunch advocate for never wearing anything other than jeans and tees. He was big and reasonably fit with a taste for bourbon and dime store cigars, black hair, and eyes to match. I nodded at his comment, shrugging away what I thought was a compliment. "Like a snake," he added, drawing my attention from the pills I was sorting.

"A snake?"

"Yeah. And you know what they say about snakes and snitches," he went on and I felt myself stiffen as the unmistakable click of a pocket knife filled the quiet room. I knew. Oh, I knew. It was his fucking favorite phrase. I'd heard it hundreds of times over the years. "They get it where they slither."

"You mother *fucker,*" I shouted, pushing away from the table so hard that I pinned it, and therefore him, against the wall.

"Clueless little shit you always were. Never meant for fucking leadership. All loyalty, no fucking brains of your own," he seethed, pushing the table away and making his way toward me, knife still in his hand as his words landed hard, settling somewhere on my soul.

"Here's the thing about loyalty," I said, taking a step back, letting him think I was scared, like I was scarred from being worked over the night of my uncle's death.

"What's that, Rye?"

"It extends beyond the grave you fucking backstabber," I yelled, charging suddenly and sending us both flying to the ground. My hand grabbed his wrist, squeezing until I heard a crunching sound that was a sick sort of music to my ears. I grabbed the knife out of his useless hand as I straddled his center. "Is this the same knife?" I asked, knowing it was. The bastard was oddly attached to his pocket knife. His father had given it to him on his thirteenth birthday. "Say it!"

Wayne's face twisted. "Yeah, that's the knife I plunged into your uncle's heart when he told me that he was moving you into second when you turned eighteen. Same knife I carved into your face, boy. See, Seth was made for leadership. Until your ass showed up and softened him. Me and the men, we'd been seeing it for years. We'd been planning on pushing him out. We'd come over that night to talk to him about stepping down. But then he pulled that shit about forcing me down a peg and pushing you in my place. And, well, me and the boys, we had no patience for that shit."

All of them.

All of his men had turned their backs on him, had been

plotting his demise.

Then all of them had taken a part in his murder.

And then my beating.

No fucking wonder I'd had so much damage.

I felt an odd calmness settling over me as I looked at the knife, twirling it in my hand, imagining my uncle's blood all over the blade, my own blood mingled with it.

"Give it up, Rye," Wayne said, rolling his eyes. "You ain't never spilled blood beyond a busted nose in your life. You aren't going to use that on me."

He was right about one thing and wrong about the other.

It was true I'd never stabbed or shot anyone before. I had never needed anything more than my fists.

But I'd also never needed to avenge the death of the only decent man I'd ever known.

So I was, abso-fucking-lutely going to use the son of a bitch's knife on him.

Then I did, pulling back and stabbing the blade into his heart like he had done to my uncle, then pulling it out and slicing it down his cheek like he had done to me. And then I sat there, watching as he choked on his own blood, watching his chest hitch in the same unnatural way my uncle's had for a long couple of minutes before he died.

Hell, his body was almost exactly in the same spot Seth's had been when he'd died.

I got up, washed my hands, tucked the pocketknife into a bag along with whatever shit I could, including a huge supply of cash Seth kept to pay his suppliers then stored it in my uncle's piece of shit, only half restored Chevy Chevelle.

But I didn't leave. Not yet. Oh, no.

Because Wayne wasn't the only man who needed to pay.

They all did.

That night, briefly, I stopped being me.

All the grief, the love, the betrayal, it swirled together until it became a bigger part of me than I was anymore.

That night I took off on foot and I exacted revenge.

For my uncle.

For myself.

For the dead sense of loyalty inside me.

The second man got the same treatment as Wayne. The third got stabbed ten times as the rage started to surface. The next was missing the things he had used to betray my uncle with when I was done with him: his tongue, his hands, his balls. He'd died before I even got to the part where I was removing his body parts like a medical school cadaver. By the last man, I was pretty sure all that was left was a bloody pile of meat, nothing recognizable as even human anymore.

Done, dripping blood and reeking of death and sweat, I climbed in my uncle's car and I got the fuck out of the town I knew would only let me be the monster I had become that night instead of the man I knew I was underneath it all.

I got out of Detroit with a scar on my face and some dark marks on my soul that wouldn't let me sleep at night, images of my uncle taking his last breaths as he tried to warn me of the snakes in our grass and images of my hand shoving a knife into the heart of a man who had been family to me and watching him choke on his own blood, eyes popping out of sockets, tongues slicing off, insides becoming outsides, and death becoming nothing but sport were memories always sticking to the inside of my eyelids when I tried to close them. But I figured that was a fair penance to pay.

The Chevelle died on me in some shitty part of town in Jersey.

I figured it was fate, got a crummy apartment over a liquor store with the money I had, and started working at an auto body shop. That was how I met Cash. We hit it off. He brought me around the club. Reign gave me a nod when I showed interest in being a prospect. From there, it was all history. I had a new family. I had men who were loyal to death and beyond.

The day I got patched-in was the day I went to the tattoo shop and got my back piece started- the snake and the obnoxious, ostentatious gilded pocketknife stabbed through his head. As soon as I could, I got the quote as well, forever marking myself, reminding myself that there was nothing in life more important than loyalty.

*Snakes and snitches get it where they slither.*

So when Reign gave me an assignment, I did what I was fucking told, no questions, no hesitations, no lip.

It wasn't an option to not do it.

There was no choice.

I didn't tell Maze that though.

"It's just how it is, honey," I said instead.

"I don't think I need to tell you how screwed up that is," she said, her voice still soft. "To not have a mind of your own. That's so messed up."

"Maze..." I said, my tone begging her to understand. "Look at me," I demanded when she just kept looking at her feet. She had too much pride to keep her eyes averted. She sucked in a slow breath and turned her head.

"What now?"

I watched as my hand rose and reached out to her, stroking down the slightly sun-burnt skin under her eyes. Her eyes closed for a second as her breath rushed out of her. I wasn't stupid. Maze wanted me. When I had fucked up and kissed her in the kitchen, she had been just as needy and lost in it as I had been. The only reason it stopped was because I stopped it and when I moved away from her, her legs weren't strong enough to hold her weight.

I exhaled, my gut twisting as I knew I was crossing a line, as one of my hands went to her hip to steady her and the other grabbed her under her knee so I could lift it and move it to the other side of the limb we were sitting on, so she was straddling it facing me. Her hazel eyes went to my face, her brows drawn together as my other hand went to her hip as well and I used them to pull her toward me. My fingers traced down her thighs to her knees again, lifting them enough to drape them over mine so I could pull her against me.

She didn't pull away. She didn't flinch.

"Now this," I said, my voice soft as my hands went to frame her face as I lowered my head toward hers.

"You're breaking the rules," she whispered, eyes still on mine.

"Fuck the rules."

# NINE

*Maze*

The kiss in the kitchen had been rough, primal, demanding. But in the tree in the dark, our bodies illuminated only by the moon and stars and serenaded by crickets and the distant thrum of rock music from the party, his lips landed on mine soft, so soft that I felt my belly flutter hard for a moment at the contact. My eyes closed, my hands moved up and out and twisted into the material of his tee. My legs tensed over his, pulling me closer until my pelvis pressed against his. Finding him hard against me, a small moan escaped my lips.

His hands slipped from my face, sliding down my back until his palms landed high on my ass, using it to drag me upward onto his lap so his cock pressed against my sex. My legs tightened around his hips as I dragged myself against him, trying to ease the sudden and overpowering heaviness in my lower stomach. Repo grunted against my lips as I stroked him again before his teeth nipped into my lip hard and he pulled backward.

I made some sort of whiny noise in my throat that had him chuckling gently. "Honey, we'll fall out of this fucking tree if we keep it up," he murmured, brushing my hair behind my ear then trailing his nose up the column of my neck before planting a kiss just below my ear.

"Worth the risk," I said, turning my face down and into his neck to bite into the skin hard enough to smart.

"Be kinda hard to explain why we both broke our legs," he said, still sounding amused. I heard myself grumble again, sliding off his lap, so turned on it was practically painful.

"Fine," I said, ducking my head and moving away from him, trying like hell to ignore the insistent throbbing between my legs.

Out of the corner of my eye, I saw Repo's legs move out toward the front of the tree limb. A second later, he was swinging himself down to the ground, landing into a squat before turning back to face me, arms up in the air.

"What?" I asked, shaking my head at him.

"Come on. I got you."

At that, I felt a smile pull at my lips. "Um... no."

"I'll catch ya, Maze. I promise."

"Yeah... no."

He sighed but didn't drop his hands. "Come on honey, you got to learn to trust someone sometime."

"Yeah except I always end up trusting the wrong people," I admitted before I could think to censor myself.

His head tilted to the side. "So a couple jackasses fucked you over. You can't use that as an excuse to never trust someone again, Maze. Take a leap of faith. I'll catch you."

"And be in the perfect position to drop me on my ass," I said quietly to myself, knowing it was the truth. But I took a breath and pushed off the tree, enjoying the dropping sensation in my stomach as I free fell for a few seconds before Repo's arms closed around me, holding me up against his chest so his face was just barely above my breasts.

"Was that so hard?" he asked, smiling up at me and I had that feeling I felt a couple weeks ago: he was trouble. He was so, so much trouble.

"So what now? Are we just gonna stand here all night?"

"Now we get to remember what it's like to be teenagers," he said, his hands suddenly releasing me, making me automatically slam my hands down on his shoulders to keep from crashing down on unsteady legs. But his arms just went under my ass, forcing my legs around his hips. With that, he led us several yards back toward the party. My heart started pounding frantically in my chest the the idea of being seen. "Relax honey," he murmured and then I felt his hands squeeze my ass then drop it. I dropped my feet to the ground and turned.

"Seriously?" I asked, smiling at the car he had been working on for weeks.

"Hop in," he said, rocking back on his heels, hands tucked into his front pockets, looking very much like a teenager trying to talk a girl into his backseat.

"Oh, gee, I don't know. I have a curfew," I said, looking up at him from under my lashes. "And I don't know what you heard, but... I'm a good girl," I teased.

A wicked little smile toyed at his lips. "Come on, it'll just be our little secret," he grinned.

"Really, I'm..." I started, but before I could finish speaking, he came at me, pinning my back against the car with his chest as his hand moved between us, slipping between my thighs and pressing hard against my sex, dragging out an unexpected moan.

"What was that about a curfew?"

I pulled in a breath, my hand curling into his shirt near the waist of his jeans. "Really I..." his fingers curved in, hitting my clit with perfect pressure and making me face plant against his chest.

"Get in the car, Maze," he commanded softly, doing one more stroke before pushing away from me and reaching to open the door.

And, well, with a tingling between my legs and a shaky feeling in my belly, I turned, ducked behind the front seat and fell into the back. "Ow, fuck," I yelled, something stabbing into my side.

Repo chuckled as I straightened, pointing to the metal seatbelt receiver. He reached out, rubbing my side where it had stabbed me. "Forgot how problematic cars can be."

"Spent a lot of time in back seats, huh?" I teased, trying to ignore the fact that his incredibly chaste touch was sending off tiny sparks of desire through my system.

He gave me a sheepish little smile. "Kinda cramps your style to try to bring a chick home to your uncle's apartment, ya know?"

"Why doesn't it surprise me that you were charming even as a teenager?"

His head tilted as he planted one hand beside my hip, leaning over my body, as his other hand slid down my side and sank into my hip. "Think I'm charming, huh?"

"Oh please," I said, rolling my eyes. "You do that eye-dancing thing and the panties get flung across the room."

"The... eye-dancing thing?" he asked with a confused smile, completely unaware that he was *doing* the eye-dancing thing right then.

"Yeah," I said, feeling my cheeks warm a little, embarrassed by the admission.

"My eyes dance?"

"Sometimes," I shrugged.

"And this... pantie-flinging thing," he said, his hand on

my hip moving up toward the waistband of my pants and slipping in slightly to toy with the band of my panties. His fingertip slid under and stroked across the lowest part of my pelvis. "When they get... flung... out of curiosity, are the panties going to have pink and purple hearts all over them again?" His lips twitched as he tried to hold back a smile. "Gotta say... pink and purple hearts just scream outlaw biker..."

"Shut up," I laughed, swatting his chest. "You're killing the mood."

"Am I?" he asked, brows drawing together, suddenly seeming all-business. "You sure about that?"

"Pretty damn sure."

"Really? Huh, then why..." he started, and before I could realize his intention, his hand moved completely inside my panties, stroking up my slit and making my whole body jerk back, hitting the side of the car in surprise, "is your pussy still wet for me?"

"Must be..." I started to try to make some witty comeback, but his fingers promptly slid up and started working over my clit, the motion small and hard, my still-fastened jeans limiting motion.

"Must be what?" he asked, eyes getting heavy as I let out a small whimper. I shook my head at him, my hand curling into the sleeve of his tee. "Lie back, honey," he commanded softly. I slid back on the leather as he towered over me, one knee between my open thighs, the other at the edge of the cushions. He pushed up and used his other hand to finally unfasten and unzip my pants. His thumb moved out to work my clit as his other fingers slid a path downward, pausing at the opening to my body and pulsing his fingers there until my hips were rising up, begging for him to sink inside. The tip of one finger did, just the smallest bit for a long minute before plunging all the way in.

Then he was done teasing, his finger thrusting for a

couple of strokes before turning and scraping up against the top wall and hitting my G-spot with the same relentless precision as he was working my clit.

My free hand moved to the collar of his shirt, using it to pull him down toward me and claiming his lips as my own as his fingers drove me up hard and fast, making every inch of my skin feel electric. The pressure in my lower stomach felt almost oppressive as my hips rose upward to meet his touch, begging for release. His tongue slipped inside to claim mine as my greedy hands roamed his body, stroking up his arms, up under his shirt to feel the strong muscles of his back, stomach, and chest, before moving around and back down, grabbing his ass.

"Fuck," he groaned, releasing my lips and letting his forehead rest on mine. "You're killing me, Maze," he murmured, his voice thick and when he shifted his weight, I could feel his cock press into my thigh. "Come," he demanded as my breath got caught in my chest, feeling my sex clench tight around his fingers as my orgasm threatened to break. "Come honey," he demanded again, running his nose down the length of mine to take my lips gently as his fingers did another sweep of my clit and G-spot and I cried out my climax against his lips, my body jolting upward as I dragged his down, a tremor running through me as the waves of pleasure crashed hard and constant.

When I was spent, relaxing against the seat, his finger stayed inside me, his palm flattening against me, refusing to let go of the intimacy. My hands went to the sides of his face, holding him to me as he kissed me slow and deep until I could feel it through my entire system, until all there was in the world was the two of us.

"Repo where the fuck are you?" Reign's voice called, making my entire body stiffen as I pushed his face from mine. The sound was still from a distance, but I was sure it was getting closer.

"It's okay," Repo murmured, no doubt taking in my huge eyes. Hell, they felt like they were popping out of my skull.

"It's not o-fucking-kay," I whisper-yelled, pushing hard at his chest until he rose off of me. His finger slipped out of me then out of my panties and I had the almost overwhelming urge to cry over the loss of the intimacy. But through the want, the desire, the urge to continue what we had started, my survival instincts kicked in. Reign couldn't find out about us. Repo would probably get a slap on the back and I would be out on my ass. That couldn't happen. If that happened...

"Christ," Repo said, drawing my attention. He was looking down at me. In the dark, it was hard to make him out entirely, but there seemed to be a tightness around his eyes that I took for either frustration or anger. His air sighed out of him and he moved completely off of me. "Fine," he said, shoving the front seat forward so he could slip out, then slamming the door so hard behind him that I actually jumped with a quiet yelp.

So yeah... angry or frustrated or both.

I flattened myself further against the seat, still childishly worried someone would come up and look in. I listened to the sound of conversation for a second before it started to fade as they moved away. I put my hand over my hammering heart and pressed my knees tightly together, still feeling the tingling aftermath of my orgasm.

And the first clear thought that crossed my mind after the panic wore away, was: shit.

Shitshitshit.

I stayed there a long couple of minutes, deep-breathing before finally zipping my pants back up and climbing out of the car. I made my way back to the party with weighted feet.

"Violet!" Renny's voice called and I slowed my pace when I saw him running toward me.

"Hey, what's up?"

"This fucking phone has been ringing off the hook for almost an hour straight. Literally," he said, holding out my burner I used to call K. Panic gripped my chest, making my air feel caught in my throat as my heart started to slam underneath my ribcage. He didn't call. K never called. That was my job. I did the calling. He knew that calling was something that could blow my cover. And no one else had that number. "I know I shouldn't have, but I tried to pick up. I was worried maybe something was up with your family or some shit. But there was nothing on the other end. And then they just kept calling."

I reached for the phone, making a point of trying to seem casual. "That's weird. I'll have to call them..."

"Give it ten seconds, they'll call back again," he said, shrugging then moving off to rejoin the party.

I wasn't going to wait the ten seconds. If K was calling, something serious was going on. But even as I moved to swipe into my contacts, the phone started ringing again. "Hello?" I said somewhat tentatively into the phone as I moved further away from the dock that was pounding out rock music, the guitar rift raking over my already sensitive nerves.

"Fucking hell, Maisy," K's voice called, sounding worried. "I've been calling for an hour straight."

"The BBQ was today. I wasn't by my phone," I hedged, leaving out the fact that I was busy because I was getting finger-fucked by my boss in a broken down car, not because of actual club business. "What's going on?"

"They're gone, Maisy."

In that moment, the entire world fell away. The music muted to my ears, the smell of food and booze disappeared, everything became colorful blurbs to my eyes.

"Gone?" I repeated, my voice hollow as I leaned back against the fence protecting the property, not trusting my legs.

"I keep tabs. Did a drive-by earlier and saw no cars. It

was weird so I parked up the block and took a walk. Maisy, the doors are bolted, the windows boarded from the inside. I went around the back and jimmied off one of the boards facing the alley, everything inside is gone. Desks, lights, filing cabinets. Everything. It's all gone."

"What does this mean?" I asked, needing to hear it from K. If I was left to let my mind wander, I was pretty sure I'd be checking the buildings across the street for gunmen. I had a tendency to run toward paranoia. Not that anyone could blame me.

"I don't fucking know," he admitted, the frustration evident in his tone. K wasn't the kind of man who settled for not knowing. He knew everything. He knew all the good guys, the bad guys, what the bad guys have done, where the bodies were buried, who the weakest links were, how to exploit their Achilles' heels. For a man as powerful, as all-knowing as K to be in the dark, well... it wasn't good. "This doesn't fit their M.O. They've been in the city for a decade."

"Maybe because of..."

"The cops don't have shit anymore. They were paid to bury it. You know that. I know that. It's something else, but fuck if I know what that is. And the not-knowing, that's not fucking good."

"Did you go to their places?"

"'Course I did. Empty too. Cars cleaned out of the garages. Went to their favorite dinner spot and pretended to be an old friend and asked around about them. They haven't been in in a week."

"A *week*?" I squeaked, the panic in my system turning to outright hysteria. They could have made it anywhere in a week. They could be in New Jersey. They could be in Navesink Bank...

"Maisy, breathe. We don't know anything for sure. Right now, there is no reason to believe they know where you are.

We've been careful."

"But," I prompted, knowing there was one coming.

"But we can't be sure they haven't sniffed out a lead either."

"What do you need me to do?"

"I need you to stay inside those gates. Whenever possible, try to take a shift with another probate. Try to avoid the overnight and early morning ones alone. Be alert. If anything feels fucked, chances are, it's fucked. And if it's fucked..." he prompted me.

"If it's fucked, I need to make sure I have a safe way out. Then I need to get to the train station and head to Pennsylvania. I need to get my bug-out bag, power up the burner, and call you."

"Then I will point you in a new direction," he said, sounding calmer.

There was an unexpected, nauseating swirling sensation in my stomach at the idea of leaving. I didn't even need to consider it to know that it was Repo that put that feeling there. Shit again. The last thing I was supposed to do was get attached. K had been specific about that. He told me that, chances were, I would have to find more than one cover. He said most of the women he 'disappeared' had to move at least once every two years. And while it was in my best interest to stay with The Henchmen, to integrate into the lifestyle, chances were it wasn't going to be somewhere I could stay indefinitely.

"Maisy..."

"Okay, K," I said, taking a deep breath as I scanned the trees, the darkness not letting me see anything.

"Stay vigilant, but don't get paranoid. I want to hear from you verbally every two days and I want a text with the word 'pineapple' every single day by noon. If I don't see that by noon, I am in my car. You with me?"

"I'm with you," I agreed.

"Stay safe and kick ass, Maisy."

The line went dead and I curled the phone into my hand so hard it hurt my palm.

I closed my eyes as I took a deep breath, wondering how the hell my life had come to this. Everything had been so normal, so tame, so certifiably boring until...

# TEN

*Maze*

Moving back to the city after my grandmother's death and the volcanic explosion known as my relationship with Thato had been a culture shock. Granted, I had been born and raised there for the first ten years of my life, but that had been under the shelter of my mother. She was there to bring me to the right subways and lead me down the right streets, to slam into the people who were too busy with their lives to notice they almost trampled me.

And then I had been in Vermont where I could walk just about any sidewalk and never run into another soul or drive without seeing more than a handful of cars on the road.

So the crowded sidewalks, the constant squeal of taxi brakes, the honks of horns, the shake of the subway beneath your feet at all times, the never-ending brightness... it had been off-putting.

But that being said, I thought it was what I needed. I

needed to disappear. I needed to not be that naive, gullible girl who had lived above a chop shop for months and never realized it, despite the fact that I had seen the men taking doors off of random cars or removing the stereos and that the supposed car owners never seemed to come by to pick up their vehicles.

I was happy to be a nameless, faceless person in the crowd, to be just another cog in the wheel that was the city that never sleeps.

I took some of my grandmother's money and I got myself an apartment that was so small that I couldn't walk more than ten feet in any direction without hitting a wall. But it was in a not-so-sketchy area and it was all I felt I could afford. I took my unfinished degree and finished it online while working the counter at a pharmacy. Then, Kinkos-printed degree in hand, I started applying for jobs that would allow me to have a little extra change in my pockets after rent and utilities were paid.

That was how I came across Kozlov Inc.

It was like any of the other offices I had interviewed at. There were desks and chairs and office equipment. The decor was a fair bit nicer than the other offices however, sleek, modern, maybe expensive though I had no eye for things like that.

Viktor Kozlov himself had been in the office to interview me. He was exactly what one might expect from a man named Viktor Kozlov. He was tall and brawny with a strong, low brow ridge over his brown eyes, a prominent but not unpleasant nose, and a square jawline. He was attractive and somewhere in his thirties with a booming voice that, even when speaking softly, seemed to reverberate through your entire system. In all the time that I knew Viktor, I had never seen him in anything other than a perfectly tailored suit.

Viktor had a brother, Ruslan, who was similar looks-wise and that was about it. Where Viktor favored nice suits, expensive watches, and Cuban cigars, Ruslan preferred jeans, heavy-knit sweaters in winter and simple tees in the summer, cheap vodka to the point of excess on Fridays during work hours, and his old beat-up pick-up truck. Where Viktor commanded the room, Ruslan owned it with his easy laid-back charm. Both had the lilt of their motherland and I always enjoyed when they would come into the office and I could listen to it. Though the rough Russian accent was wholly unlike the smooth, polished sound Thato had, I always just loved to listen, to occasionally close my eyes and let the sounds wash over me.

Needless to say, I got the job.

And I actually liked the job.

It was mostly solitary work, just keeping the books, occasionally answering a rogue phone call about one of their businesses. The Kozlov brothers owned a restaurant, a pawn shop, and a small gastro pub.

Some days, Ruslan would drop in and hang out at his brother's desk, propping his dirty shoes up on the polished wood like he had absolutely not a care in the world that his brother was anal about things like tidiness and appearances. He'd sip the vodka he kept on the drink bar and bullshit with me about any topic from the latest homicide to stories about the winters in his homeland.

"Girl like you, blondie, you'd have had men falling to their knees to claim you, keep you warm through the winter," he'd tell me, forever flattering my vanity in a way that I often wondered if it was just his flirtatious nature or if he actually meant it. Either way, it was nice to hear and I maybe developed the tiniest of crushes on him. "Know how they'd keep you warm?" he asked, dark brow quirked up, lips twitching.

"I can imagine," I'd said, blushing slightly as I shuffled papers on my desk.

"Ever had a Russian lover, kotyonok?" he asked, his voice low, seductive.

Later, I would ask Viktor what 'kotyonok' meant. He had given me a scrunched-up face, then a head shake and told me it meant 'kitten'.

"No."

"No?" he asked, rounding my desk, tilting his head to the side to watch me in such an intense way that I had to fight the urge to squirm in my chair. "You won't regret," he said, giving me a smile and going toward the door. It hadn't exactly escaped me that he hadn't said "you *wouldn't* regret", but "you *won't* regret", as if doing so for me was an eventuality. Like, maybe, he wanted to be that first Russian lover.

So maybe a part of me blamed my cluelessness on my girlish crush on one of my bosses.

But, truly, it likely wasn't even my fault.

It was all so well hidden.

If maybe I was less of a perfectionist about work, I might have missed it.

Later, I would figure the reason Viktor hired me was because I 'just' had an online degree, that maybe I wasn't as educated or as observant of details as someone who went to a university.

He was obviously wrong.

And one snowy, miserable January morning alone in the office that I couldn't seem to get warm enough, I first started noticing the inconsistencies. It was just small things at first that I had always just written off as unknown income, cash register miscalculations or unaccounted for business expenses. That was until I started to see that each month, each of those amounts was exactly the same. And, granted, I knew enough about finances to know that, hey, freak similarities happened on occasion. But not every single month for a year.

So then, trapped in the office during what turned out to be a blizzard, I started digging.

It didn't take long until I felt a pit get planted in my belly, heavy, foreign, uncomfortable.

Most of the inconsistencies were wholly unexplainable.

It wasn't the registers.

It wasn't pay back for money owed.

It wasn't anything but cash deposits of unknown origins.

I loaded up the coffee machine and went looking through the filing cabinets, praying to find something that pointed to something other than some sort of illegal transactions.

That's when I found them: the files that changed my whole life.

With shaking hands, I reached for my cell, opening an incognito window so there would be no history of my search, and I looked up the Kozlov brothers. And, let's just say, it didn't take me long to figure out that the people I was working for weren't just some successful Russian businessmen. Sure, they truly did own legitimate businesses like their restaurant and pub and pawn shop. But they owned those to launder the dirty money that they got through other means, namely bringing in poor, hopeless women from their homeland and auctioning them off to the highest bidders. It wasn't, in the traditional sense, human trafficking. Granted, the women were promised things they generally didn't get, namely rich husbands who could help them support their families back home, but the women weren't exactly unwilling. They just had no other options. But still, in the law's eyes, it was the sale of human beings and completely illegal. Apparently, law enforcement had been trying to nab them for years. But they never screwed up.

That was, until they hired me I guess.

See, there was a lot of things I could still claim to be: a little unobservant, too trusting, not much of a two-step thinker, but I was not, and promised myself I would never be, gullible or naive ever again.

And I damn sure wasn't going to be involved with even more criminals.

Hell, I had kind-of, in a way, been helping them conduct their money laundering while I worked for them.

I was not, was abso-fucking-lutely not, going to get myself wrapped up in another sweep when the cops eventually did have something to come after them with.

So with a sweat breaking out over my whole body, I made two sets of copies of all the information I had. I placed each set in separate manila envelopes and sealed them. I tucked one into my purse and held one against my chest under my jacket as I made my way out of the office on shaky legs and trudged through eight inches of snow all the way to the closest police station.

I was met by a one Detective Conroy Asher who was tall and fit and way to freaking good looking for a cop. He took me into a room and took the folder from me, looking over the contents with a furrowed brow. When he looked up at me, though, instead of seeing the glee I expected for finally giving them a piece of information they needed to finally nab the Kozlov brothers, I saw concern.

By this point, I was smart enough to know things had just taken a turn for the worse.

"Tell me," I demanded, sitting up straighter, my spine suddenly feeling like it was made of steel.

"Christ, kid, you just signed your death certificate," he said, shaking his head as he tucked the information away.

For a second, I sat there, stunned silent as I tried to sort my racing thoughts so I could grab hold of one of them. "My... death certificate?"

"The reason the Kozlovs haven't been incarcerated has nothing to do with a lack of incriminating evidence, and everything to do with some friends in some high places. This," he said, lifting the folder, "is going to disappear. And then, say, twenty minutes later after it does, so will you."

"But... but how will they..."

"Come on, kid. Don't be stupid," he said, shaking his head at me. "I have no choice but to sign this into evidence. Someone between here and the evidence locker will find it, flag it, call the Kozlovs, and then it's all missing evidence and missing persons reports."

"I thought I was doing the right..." I started, feeling stupid, useless tears sting the backs of my eyes.

"Unfortunately, you are doing the right thing. But the Kozlovs run a tight ship and they will trace this back to you in a matter of minutes and then you will either be dead or wishing you were. It was the *right* move, Miss Mckenzie, but it wasn't the smart one." He moved to stand and I jumped up too. "I hope I don't have to read about you in the paper anytime soon, or see your body in the morgue."

"But... no. *Fucking* no!" I shouted, slamming my hand down on the metal table. "Don't talk to me like I'm a walking target," I demanded, angrier than I had ever been in my life. He was a *cop.* His job was to serve and protect. In this case, his job was to serve and protect *me.* He couldn't just walk around issuing condolences for my seemingly inevitable bloody murder. No fucking way.

"Kid, there's nothing I can do. This evidence will go missing and then I have no cause to offer you protective custody."

"What if I had... copies?"

His face got serious. "Then I suggest you hide them in a good place until you find a cop you know you can trust in a force that has no connections to the Russians or any of their allies."

"How am I supposed to do that if I am apparently going

to end up with a bullet in my brain in some alley somewhere?"

"Garroted," he corrected automatically.

"Excuse me?"

"Garroted. The Kozlovs, they aren't much for guns, though I'm sure they have them. They like the close contact kill, feeling you take your last breath at their hands."

"Great," I said, my hand raising to stroke over my throat as I thought of Viktor's and Ruslan's strong, capable hands holding a piece of wire between them and around my neck as I struggled for breath.

"Hey, look," he said, coming closer, lowering his voice. "I can't offer you protection, but I can offer you a lifeline," he said, his serious brown eyes on mine.

"And that is?"

"K."

"K?" I repeated.

"He's... well, I don't know what exactly he is. But word is, he helps women like you, women who have nowhere else to turn. He disappears them."

"He... disappears them?"

"Yeah. I know it doesn't sound great, but what other option do you have?"

Well, I figured I had better options than having some random whackjob 'disappearing' me that was for damn sure.

"K.C.E Boxing Emporium," he said, his words a little firm. "When you get your head out of your ass and see it's your only option, haul it over there."

"Right. Well, um... I know I should say thanks, but..."

"I get it," he said, nodding as he opened the door for me. "Don't get yourself dead, Miss Mckenzie."

With those ominous words, I walked back into the blizzard. The eight inches was steadily making its way to ten as I trudged my way home, the streets hauntingly empty save for the occasional plow. It took the better part of an hour both because the sidewalks were impossible, but also because I took my time, trying to straighten my thoughts, weighing my options. By the time I punched the code into the outside door, my nose, fingertips, and everything under my waist and unprotected by my heavy winter coat was frozen.

I needed to leave town.

That much was obvious to me.

If some badass cop was telling me to run for my life, well, only an idiot didn't follow that advice. My plan was to grab a bag, throw the essentials inside it, like the pearl earrings my grandmother gave me and the ring I bought myself when I finished my degree, then just... head out. There was nothing for me in the city anyway. Not really. I had a few casual acquaintances, but no real friends and no family. It wouldn't be a hardship to leave, to move on. It was a big country; I could settle anywhere.

I was actually almost a little excited over the prospect as I rounded the corner to my apartment. But as I did so, I found my neighbors from across the hall, a gay couple that I counted as my acquaintances, along with my super standing in front of my open apartment door. You could say my excitement promptly plummeted.

"Hey Maisy," Kurt, the giant African American ballet dancer with the kindest eyes I'd ever seen, greeted me, his tone soothing.

"What's going on?" I asked, but I knew. Of course I knew. Hell, Detective-Mc-Hottie had said that within minutes that the Kozlov brothers would know of my treachery. Shit.

Shitshitshit.

"Everything is alright," Andy, Kurt's boyfriend, a blond, blue-eyed model said, holding up his hands. "Kurt and I heard a commotion," he explained as I moved to stand beside them, looking into my apartment. "Kurt came out while I called the super and found a man in your apartment. He scared him off," he said, rubbing Kurt's belly as he looked up with him with a mix of awe and arousal. "He chased him clear down the street," he went on with a smile.

But I wasn't paying too much attention.

Because all I could see was everything in my apartment in shambles. Pictures were ripped from the walls, couch cushions sliced open, foam everywhere. The contents of my kitchen cupboards were all over the counters. My loose floorboard was even torn up.

"Hey, hey, Maisy," Kurt said, sounding worried. "It's okay. We're going to get this all settled. I got a good look at the guy to give to the police."

"Let me guess," I said, my tone hollow. "Six-three, broad shoulders, broad everything. Dark hair, dark eyes. A distinctly Russian accent..."

"You know who..."

"I have to go. I... thanks, but I have to go," I stammered, turning and running.

As I jogged down the stairs, I grabbed my phone out of my pocket and spoke into it. "K.C.E Boxing Emporium address," I said clearly, hearing the bleep as the search worked its magic. The address came up and I tucked the phone away, grabbing the lone cab I found outside and barked out the address with a hammering heart.

The taxi was all over the road on the slushy aftermath the plows left behind, but that had nothing to do with my flip-flopping belly.

When the cab pulled over in a shoddy area in front of a renovated, expansive building of deep gray stucco with K.C.E Boxing Emporium in perfect, bold letters above the door, I started to question Detective-Mc-Hottie's judgment. But with no other option, I paid the driver and climbed out, scaling over a huge pile of snow to get to the sidewalk. I fell forward, slamming hard into the glass door and letting out a grunt. By the time I was back on my feet, brushing snow off my legs, the door swung open, drawing my attention.

And then there was a man there in the doorway.

He was tall and broad, but in a compact way that only boxers were. He had dark skin and keen eyes and, even during a snowstorm that had obviously kept his business closed, he was in an immaculate suit. An expensive-looking gold watch was around his wrist that led to heavily scarred hands. My eyes drifted back up.

"Are you K?" I asked, my teeth chattering from the cold and the adrenaline and fear.

"Yes."

"I'm in trouble."

"Yeah you are," he agreed immediately, as if he somehow sensed my desperation. Hell, maybe it was seeping out of my pores. "Come on in," he said, stepping inside and holding the door open so I could move through.

The inside of K.C.E Boxing Emporium was sleek and modern, but in a very masculine way with exposed stucco walls and cement floors. There was an office area to the left when you walked into the door and to the right there was a seating area in the front by the picture window with a long black leather couch in front of a low black coffee table. There was a small beverage station with a single-cup coffee machine. Forward and toward the back was, well, a boxing emporium. There was a black ring complete with ropes. On the left side of the ring was a line of punching and speed bags. On the right side were jump ropes hanging on the wall and a huge collection of weapons, only a third of which I recognized.

"Coffee, tea, hot chocolate?" he offered, moving over

toward the beverage station. "Pick one. You need to warm up."

The last thing I needed was caffeine; I was wired enough. "Hot chocolate."

"Alright. Now what kind of trouble are you in? I don't see any bruises so I doubt your boyfriend is beating you."

"I don't have a boyfriend."

"Okay," he said, slipping a hot chocolate pod into the machine and hitting the button. "Look, if you want help, you need to fill me in. If not, there's the door," he said, gesturing toward it. "I don't have the time for evasions or half-truths. If you want my help, you need to be honest with me.

And that, well, that sounded fair enough. I nodded, putting down my purse and reaching in for the envelope. I handed it to him. "I have been keeping the books for the Kozlov brothers. I had no idea what they were into until today. I took that," I said as he flipped through the papers, his face expressionless, "to the cops."

"And?"

"And the detective I talked to pretty much told me I was fucked and said they would come for me. He gave me the name of this place, and you, and sent me on my way. I went home and... one of them had already been there so I just... ran."

"Here."

"Yeah."

He nodded, tucking the papers away, but not giving them back to me as he exhaled. "You know what I find more and more often in this job?" he asked oddly, leaving me very little room but to ask.

"What?"

"Men fuck up and women are left with the damage."

I paused, watching him with drawn-together brows. "Is that a round-about way of saying you'll help me?"

"Love, I was going to help you the second I heard you

slam into my front door."

"Just like that?" I asked, my big-city distrust rearing its ugly head.

"Yeah, just like that."

"Why?"

"Because it's what I do."

"But... why? I can't pay you..."

"I'm not asking you to."

"So this is just out of the goodness of your heart?"

"Maybe we can call it penance."

I felt myself straighten as he moved to retrieve my cup of hot chocolate. "Penance? You've fucked up and left damage for a woman to clean up?"

"Not in the way you're thinking," he said, handing me the cup which I cradled between my hands, the heat making my frozen fingers tingle in an unpleasant way. "I've never intentionally hurt a woman or put her in harm's way. But I'm no saint. I've done some bad shit and I owe it to the world to put some good back into it. I grew up with a mom who used to get her face bashed in every few months by the son of a bitch she fell in love with when I was too young to do anything about it. When I was old enough, I did. Doing this, helping women, it felt like a natural way to make amends for the wrongs I've done in my life."

Not sure what to say, I took a sip of my hot chocolate.

"The detective said something about you... disappearing women..."

To that, he gave me a small smile. "Something like that, yeah."

"How something like that?"

"Chances are, if a woman is coming to me it is because she is literally out of all other options. I take that desperation and mold it into something I can work with."

"And that is?"

"Determination. I need you to feel the will to survive down to your bones. It's easy to give up. It's simple to just fall into the hopelessness of the situation. But I can't do shit with that. I need you to want whatever help I can give you the way you want to keep breathing. Because, quite frankly in your situation, my help is the only way you will keep doing that."

"I don't want to die."

"Then you're going to have to prove that to me."

I didn't know just how much he meant that at the time.

That night, I was given a cot in a panic room at the emporium.

Yes, a panic room.

When standing, if I threw my arms out, I could touch both sides of said room. It was stark white and had a plastic container in the side with a supply of water, power bars, granola, and peanut butter. Thankfully, I wasn't forced to eat that, being given a decent enough portion of leftover Chinese food and another big cup of hot chocolate before I was handed a big, fluffy blanket and pushed into the room that was impenetrable from the outside. And, while it was weird and a little creepy and eerily silent, it was safe. There was even a camera feed from the outside of the door that gave a one-eighty degree view of the outside so I could be sure it was safe before I opened. And I was given strict orders to never open for anyone but him and even instructed to never open if he showed up with anyone else at the door. Because if that was the case, it was against his will.

I would learn that K was incredibly precise about the small details like that.

The next morning at five A.M sharp, there was a rapping at the door. I had been up for half an hour, staring at the white ceiling. The sound made me bolt upright, my heart slamming in my chest, before I looked over at the TV and saw K standing there, in gray slacks and a black, tucked-in dress shirt, his sleeves rolled up to reveal another nice watch in silver. His hands were holding out two steaming cups of coffee. I rolled out of the bed, tidying the blanket, then spinning the giant wheel. With each spin, I could hear the metal bars click until the door opened with a quiet hiss.

I was given coffee, force fed some plain oatmeal because I needed it for fuel, then informed my first phase of training involved assessing my fitness level. I tried to inform him that was completely unnecessary, that I was about as fit as a Basset Hound, meaning not at all, but he wouldn't hear it. He made me change into some of the monogrammed clothes the gym offered then put me through a punishing workout. Until I threw up. Then I got a short reprieve and he set me back to it. Until I cried. Then I was pulled over to the ring and made to sit down in a corner and he crouched down in front of me.

"It'll get better, but I won't lie to you. It's going to fucking suck for a long time. But, fact of the matter is Maisy, these men are taller, wider, stronger, and well trained. You can't get taller or wider; you will never be as strong. But if you can suck it up, I can train you better than them. You'll puke, you'll cry, you'll bruise and bleed. It's the only way to get better. So I'll give you five minutes to pull yourself together after puking, crying, bruising, or bleeding. But that is all you will get. I can't afford to let you be soft. I need to harden you up if you're going to be able to go on living. Take your five minutes. I'm going to go call Faith."

Faith, as it turned out, was a friend of K's. She was tall with long dark hair, almond-shaped dark eyes, a perfectly-shaped womanly body and a 'I'll never be a fucking damsel in distress so don't you fucking dare try to save me' aura about her. She was also, apparently, a kickass Krav Maga instructor.

She was phase one of my self-defense training.

K told me that I needed to practice with someone close to my size before I moved on.

Moving on meant I got to finally see K out of dress clothes, wearing black basketball shorts and a tight black wifebeater that put his perfectly toned arms, chest, and back on display. And if I had been getting a sense of pride or self-confidence after my training with Faith, even getting her on the ground a time or two, I lost every single drop of it in the ring with K.

Then when I started to get comfortable with K, not that I ever really bested him, he brought in Gabe. Gabe was a pretty boy blond with a compact, long-legged, but deceptively strong body. When K brought him in to fight me one morning, I'd actually snorted a little like he'd lost his mind. He certainly didn't seem like he would be harder to fight than K. I would learn to stop underestimating people really quickly after that. Then, finally, I met Xander who was a private eye slash security guy slash anything that paid. He was a giant with black hair and dark eyes. I practically peed myself at the idea of fighting him.

What I learned from all the different opponents was that none were particularly better than the other, but had different fighting styles. Faith had very skilled, very practiced and precise moves from all her martial arts lessons. K had the quick feet and lightening-speed fists of the boxer he obviously was. Gabe had a tight, but smooth style that made me think of law enforcement. Xander had a quick, languid, scrappy style of a street fighter.

So in by forcing me to spar with all of them, I was prepared for just about anything.

And K had been right.

I puked. I cried. I bruised. I bled.

But I got tough.

My soft edges were sanded into sharp points.

By my fifth month, K declared I was almost ready.

Then he told me about the plan.

I was going to go prospect at The Henchmen MC compound. I was going to become a probate. I was going to do whatever it took to get patched in because my only hope for safety long-term, and not have to run every few months, was to integrate myself into a group who would stand shoulder-to-shoulder with me against my enemies. There were many groups to choose from, of course. But K trusted the morals of The Henchmen MC. They also had the added benefit of animosity toward the Russians who, in Jersey, were forever trying to steal the arms trade from them.

So then I studied the top three members: Reign, Cash, and Wolf.

I learned about biker lifestyle. I learned the rules and the taboos.

I learned how to ride a bike.

K taught me to stop being such a girl.

Then came the absolute hardest, most gut-wrenching part of my training: leaving K.

I'm not going to lie; I cried like a baby.

It was pathetic, big, ugly, snot-crying.

He'd surprised me by wrapping me up and holding me tight while I bawled until there were no tears left. It was the only softness he'd ever really given me and it made it all the harder to turn away from him when he drove me to the lot in Staten Island where we practiced my motorcycle riding, handed me the keys, and told me to stay strong and kick ass.

But I couldn't run back to him. If I ran back to him it would scream desperation, and that was something he thought he had beaten out of me months before. So I bit into my lip hard and forced my legs to move forward. I climbed on the bike I hated more than I hated getting thrown onto my back in the ring and I turned it over and drove away.

Toward my new life in The Henchmen MC.

# ELEVEN

*Maze*

The next day, despite K's warning and my own better judgment, I was paranoid as all hell. So when Repo came downstairs and dragged us all, sans Moose of course and Fox who quit too due to pressure from his brother no doubt, out of bed to force us to clean up the yard while he, Reign, Wolf, Cash, and half of the other members sat around and watched us, I was frazzled and distracted.

From the looks of Duke and Renny, they had eventually stopped being ragged on the night before and indulged a bit too much on the very abundant alcohol. Both were sluggish, swollen red-eyed, and cringed at every loud noise.

I had taken off to bed after my phone call, forcing myself to sleep to keep my mind from racing any more than it already had.

While the guys took a water break, I sneaked my phone out of my pocket and texted 'pineapple' to K before he got worried.

"Alright," Reign clapped loudly, drawing everyone's attention. "Probies, it's time to get out of the compound for a bit."

At that, I felt dread well up strong, almost overpowering. And, apparently, it must have been written all over my face because Repo's brows had drawn together.

"I'll be staying behind to pull the patrol. These fucks," he said, waving to Wolf, Cash, and Repo, "will be taking you out and testing you whatever the fuck way they see fit. We will do this three times until they each get a feel for you and your potential as members. Make your choices and roll out."

With that, Cash immediately went for Renny for reasons unknown. And Wolf, unsurprisingly went for Duke, leaving me feeling very much like a third grade leftover after choosing sides for dodge ball.

"That means you're with me," Repo said in a very bored, very disappointed way leaving me to wonder if he genuinely was unhappy with being stuck with me or if he was just putting on a show for everyone else. Either way, it stung a little bit.

"Oh joy," I said with an eye roll that made Reign chuckle slightly.

"Wear your cuts but you leave all your knives here," he said, pointedly looking at Duke and I like he somehow knew we both carried them. He turned back to his men, "Try not to kill them. It's a bitch to find good probates." With that, he walked out toward the front gates.

"Cuts," Repo barked. "Two minutes to the front gates or you're out on your asses."

We all ran off toward the compound, each grabbing the cuts from wherever we had them stashed. Duke took his knife out of his waistband. I took the one off my calf and one out of my boot, but left the other in my other boot. When I straightened with the two knives, Duke had a raised brow, but said nothing.

When we got out front, our bikes were all lined up beside Repo's, Wolf's, and Cash's. The sky had darkened to the point of definite rain clouds and I hoped whatever we were doing involved being indoors. Repo inclined his chin at me and I got on my bike, clipped on my helmet, and we waited until they all took off in different directions. I looked around the streets carefully, looking for any familiar faces in cars or alleys. "Where did they all head?" I found myself asking when Repo just continued to sit on his idling bike, not pulling out.

"Wolf probably took Duke hunting on his land. Cash likely took Renny to Hailstorm to suss out some of his... unique skills."

I fought the urge to ask what Renny's unique skills were, and asked instead, "Where are you taking me?"

To that, he lifted the back of his shirt, revealing two guns in his waistband. "Target practice." With that, he'd dropped his shirt and peeled off, leaving me to follow behind, my stomach twisted into knots at the punishing speed he kept.

I'd shot guns before. It had been part of my training, courtesy of Gabe who was the most skilled with them of K's colleagues. I couldn't claim to be good, but I usually managed to hit the chest cavity even on moving targets.

We drove thirty minutes out of town until we hit a more rural area, pulling off and parking in an abandoned field. "Here? In city limits?" I asked as I pulled off my helmet, my hair sweaty from the heat, watching a bit of heat lightening flash across the storm-dark sky.

"Nothing around for a good five miles. This is private property. No one will hear shit," he explained, moving off his bike and ambling off toward the tree line. I took a deep breath and followed behind, still a little off-put by his oddly distant behavior. I mean... we had made out the night before. He had *fingered* me the night before. We would have done a lot more had we not been interrupted.

Ugh.

I was thinking like a girl.

K taught me better.

Even if we fucked in new and inventive ways, chances were a man was going to treat me no different the next day than he did before we fucked. That was just how men were. I needed to stop putting my thoughts and feelings on him.

"Alright," Repo said a long, hot, disgusting twenty-minute walk later, coming to a halt in a clearing where there were targets already set up, human shaped ones, the cliched bottles and tin cans on a downed tree limb, actual point targets. You named it, he had it there.

"Come here often?" I asked, slinging my sweaty hair out of my face.

"Some of the men practice at the compound, but you can't get the distance there," he said with a shrug.

"The distance?" I repeated, tilting my head to watch him load bullets from his pocket into his gun.

"I'm a good shot," he said simply, no real pride behind the words, just a relaying of facts. "What about you?" he asked, looking over at me for the first time since we left the compound.

"I'm fair. I'm better with..."

"Hand to hand," he finished for me, surprising me. How the heck could he have known that?

"Saw you fucking around with Renny. And then you were quick, practiced breaking up the fight between him and Duke. People without training don't move like you move. Where'd you learn?"

"I had a, ah, team of instructors. Boxing, Krav Maga, street fighting, you name it."

"It shows."

"Is that... actually a... compliment?" I asked, giving him a teasing smile.

"Oh fuck off, Maze. You know you're a good probate. You have your own unique set of skills. You don't need me stroking your ego left and right."

"Need it? No. But it's still nice to hear. Especially seeing as everyone else is really fond of pointing out my flaws."

"If you were looking for cheerleaders, you tried out for the wrong team, honey."

"Cheerleaders? No. But maybe I was hoping for some teammates. But whatever. I get it."

"You get it?"

I felt my lips turn up slightly. "Repo, this is nothing new. This sexism shit? It's old and familiar. It's the sneers from the boys on the playground when I wanted to play cops and robbers with them instead of hopscotch with the other girls. It's the middle school bra snapping. It's the high school pressure to be both a virgin and a slut somehow at the same time. It's the men who tried to take the jumper cables from me when I stopped to help them on the side of the road because they thought that, while I had the common sense to actually buy and keep cables in my car, that I was somehow too stupid to know how to use them properly. Believe me when I say I am familiar with all of this crap. If anything, I think it is worse now that women are becoming stronger and more independent. It's like it makes men even more aggressive and violent toward us. But they're all just going to have to buck up and deal with it because now that we all have a taste of power, we aren't going back to the fucking kitchen. The Henchmen are just going to have to adjust because I am not going any-fucking-where."

"I believe you," he said, nodding a little. "And I respect the determination, Maze. But I'm not sure it will be enough to get you a patch."

"Maybe. Maybe not. We'll see. So are we going to gab like

chicks all day, or are we shooting?"

"Gab like chicks?" he repeated, lips twitching.

"You seem awfully interested in my thoughts and motivations for a guy," I said, shrugging, trying to be casual.

"You're a fucking piece of work," he said, shaking his head and turning toward the targets. "You'll go first," he said, taking my gun and replacing it with his since it was loaded.

I nodded, taking a deep breath as I moved out a couple feet. "From here?" I clarified.

"Yeah, that'll do for now," he said, sounding distracted, but I could feel his eyes on me.

I took a breath as I set my feet wide and raised the gun, holding the handle in my right hand with my left hand cupped around the front of the handle to steady it. On an exhale, like Gabe taught me, I slowly squeezed the trigger. The shot echoed across the empty area, making the birds scatter from their hiding places in the trees as my bullet buzzed and landed in the center of one of the human targets.

"Can you do a head shot?" he asked, moving in behind me, looking over my shoulder so that I felt his breath on my neck and, despite the sweltering heat, I felt a shiver move through me.

"We'll see," I said, taking aim and hitting just outside the left ear.

"Again," he instructed, but as I held my arms out, his hand moved to the inside of my elbow, putting pressure until I bent it. "Don't lock your arm, keep it loose." I nodded tightly and pulled the trigger again, hitting where the eye would be, cringing a little at the visual I got in my head. "That'll do it," he said moving away from me, taking the gun from my hand. "Go stand in front of the target."

I'm pretty sure my blood went immediately cold at that instruction. "I'm sorry, what?" I asked, turning to face him, brows drawn together.

"Go stand in front of the target," he said, checking the clip before looking up at me.

"You can't be fucking serious."

"Are you questioning an order?"

"I'm questioning your marksmanship and sanity."

To that, he chuckled. His hand raised, his thumb stroking gently down the side of my jaw. "Do you really think I'd tell you to do it if there was even a chance of my fucking up this face?"

I ignored the fluttering in my belly at him sort-of calling me attractive because, really, standing in front of a target was a much bigger priority. "Um, Repo, this isn't a carnival. The bullets aren't going to come in from the back of the target like a knife throwing wheel. And I may not have the most exciting life in the world, but I still very much like being alive to live it."

"Maze... trust me, okay?"

I closed my eyes on an exhale as his finger stroked down my cheek again before dropping. Then, every cell in my body screaming not to do it, I turned and walked toward the target.

"Hey," he called as I moved away, "tie up your hair," he commanded. Then, figuring there must have been a good reason for the instruction, I grabbed the band off my wrist and tied my hair up.

I took a deep breath as I pressed my back to the target, tucking my hands behind my ass, pulling my shoulders in, trying to shrink myself as best I could. Across the field, I watched Repo check the clip again before raising his arm. Yes, arm. Singular. He didn't even spread his legs to distribute his weight. He did none of the things I was taught were integral to a precise shot. Then I stood there, frozen in absolute horror as he squeezed off a succession of six bullets faster than I could draw a breath. The bullets whizzed past my body almost simultaneously, so fast and close that I could feel them move the air around me before they stabbed into the target behind me.

When he dropped his hand, I slid down the target on shaky legs until my ass hit the ground, pulling in my legs and wrapping my arms around them as I tried to stop the way my insides were shaking.

A minute later, Repo crouched down in front of me, resting a hand on my knee. And, well, I felt the anger well up as my head snapped up to look at me. "Did I pass your stupid fucking test?" I hissed, my jaw so tight that my teeth hurt from clenching them. "Out of curiosity, this hunting Wolf is doing... is Duke the deer? And this assessing of Renny's skills up at Hailstorm, does it involve being strapped to a chair with his eyes taped open while being injected with LSD ala Mel Gibson in *Conspiracy Theory*? You guys are so fucking twisted."

"Hey," he said, his voice doing that obnoxious soothing thing as his thumb moved under my chin and tilted it up, "stand up and turn around to look at the target."

"Oh yay, another order."

"Maze, just fucking do it okay?" he asked, his voice still calm.

"Fine," I grumbled, pushing up onto my feet and turning to look at the target. And there were the six bullet holes: one on either side of my head, one above, one at each side of my body and one down near where my feet had separated.

"See," he said, moving in right behind me, his hands stretching out on either side of my body and sticking his fingers in the holes on the sides of my head.

"See what? How close you were to shooting me?"

"See how close I can get without even grazing you," he corrected, not moving away though his hands dropped. "Shooter is the best shot I've ever seen, Maze, but I'm a damn close second."

"I don't understand what the purpose of this was," I said shaking my head a little and I could feel the back of my skull brush against his chest. He was way, way too close.

"Maze, I'm a lot of things, but I'm not stupid or unobservant," he started. "You trust the lot of us just about as far as you can throw us which, with those little arms of yours, is not very far. And, well, a trust fall is just too Goddamn cheesy."

"Seriously? This is just trying to get me to trust you? Will you do the same thing to Renny and Duke when they get their turns with you?"

"No. But the difference is, I don't need to with them."

"Why bother with me when you guys are obviously doing everything in your power to get me out?"

"Maybe this doesn't have anything to do with them, Maze. Maybe this is about you and me."

I felt myself stiffen. "There is no you and me," I said, my voice quiet.

"Sure there fucking is," he said, his breath in my ear, his words emphasized by a rolling of thunder.

"There can't be," I objected, shaking my head as I watched one of his hands slide up my thigh then up and across my belly, folding over it and pulling me against his chest.

"And yet," he murmured, his head ducking. His lips found the sensitive spot just below my ear, pressing in gently and making a shudder pass through me.

"Repo," I whispered, hearing a pleading in my tone, but not sure that I was asking him to stop, or to give me more.

His nose tilted up, teasing the edge of my ear before his tongue moved out to tease the lobe. "Tell me you don't want this and I'll stop," he said as the first few fat drops of rain landed on our heads and shoulders.

Of course I wanted it.

I wanted it like I wanted The Henchmen to accept me, like I wanted K to be proud of me, like I wanted to keep on breathing.

It no longer felt like something as simple as a want, a desire. It felt like a need, like something necessary to keep going.

So I swallowed the lump that was trying to get me to stick to the plan, follow the rules, do the right thing, and admitted the truth. "I want this," I sighed as his arm squeezed my belly, his teeth nipped my ear, and the sky finally opened up.

"Turn around, honey," he said in a deep, rolling way that made my belly flip over as I turned in his arm. His one arm settled low on my back, the other raised to brush across my neck until it grabbed my ponytail and pulled my hair free, slipping the band over his own wrist for safekeeping, before cupping my jaw.

Above us, the thunder roared again loud enough for the ground to shake under our feet. "Should we take that as a bad omen?" I asked, eyes seeking his as the rain poured down our faces. To me, it was welcome, cooling my overheated body, washing the sweat away.

"Probably," he agreed, tilting his head a little as he closed the space between us, "but it's not gonna fucking stop us."

With that, his lips crushed into mine, hard, desperate, not a hint of restraint in him as he slanted his head, bit into my lower lip, claimed my tongue. His hands didn't stay where they were. As soon as my arms went around his neck, his hands started roaming, both moving down my back and slipping up under the wet material of my tee, sliding up to my bra strap and making short work of the clasps.

"Arms up," he said, pulling his lips from mine and dragging the material of my tee and my cut and pulling them upward. My arms went straight up and the material was gone in seconds. His hands moved out, brushing the straps of my bra off my shoulders. They slid down my arms until they disappeared, leaving me topless in front of him, the cold rain and heavy dose of desire making my nipples harden almost painfully. To my surprise, his hands didn't immediately go to cover my breasts, instead they moved to the sides, teasing over the skin that was usually looked over, then stroking down my sides to the waistband of my pants. They tickled across my belly before they moved to unfasten and drag the material down. As he was exposing me, he lowered down onto his knees in front of me, planting a kiss right below my navel before he reached down to untie and remove my boots, then slip my pants and panties off my body.

His face was almost level with my pussy and he angled his head up to look at me, his chin brushing up the triangle above my sex. "Beautiful," he said as I reached out to brush the rain off his forehead. His palm moved up and around my calf, snagging the back of my knee and yanking it up and open, forcing my hands to slam down on his shoulders to keep my balance as his head ducked then angled up so his tongue could slide up my slick cleft. A tremor ran through the muscles in my thighs as one of my hands left his shoulder and sank into his soft, wet hair, curling in and holding on tight as his tongue worked slow circles around my clit.

I watched him for a moment before tilting my head up to the sky, feeling the rain splash down on my face, watching the lightening crash across the sky. I'd never done anything sexual outside before, let alone during a storm. Something about it felt right, natural, primal. Rain slid down my body as Repo's lips closed around my clit and sucked hard, making me double over.

His arms went out to my waist, grabbing me as I went down on my knees in front of him. My hands went automatically to his shirt as my eyes held his, pulling the wet fabric up and tossing it to the side. My hands moved down his chest, moving over the bold Henchmen tattoo with guns, roses, and stocking-clad ladies' legs, then down over his firm abs, until I found his hard cock through his jeans and stroked my hand over it.

Leaning forward, I kissed up the column of his neck as his hands moved down the skin of my back, landing on my ass and sinking in, using it to pull me forward until I was flattened against him.

My hands worked his button and zip then grabbed the waist of his jeans and boxer briefs, fumbling with the heavy, wet material until it pooled around his knees.

"Condom. Wallet. Back left pocket," he demanded as his hand slipped down my ass then between my legs to tease my clit again. I shook my head slightly, trying to work past the overwhelming need for release he was creating and I fumbled for his wallet, finding the condom foil, then discarding the wallet to fall with a slap onto the sopping ground. His finger left my clit. He grabbed the condom and his hands went between us for a long minute, protecting us, the task made harder by the ever-increasing rain.

He pulled back, giving me a wicked smile. "What?" I asked, my hands sliding down his belly and closing around his cock.

"This is gonna be filthy," he declared and I took the double entendre for all it was worth for all of, say, two seconds before his arm went around the center of my back and we were both falling to the ground, my entire body slapping down in the grass that was no longer really grass, but a puddle of water and mud. It coated my body from ankles to the back of my head, slick and slippery.

But I only had a second to consider that before Repo pressed up and moved down my body to nip his teeth into my hardened nipple as his other hand went between my legs again, thrusting two fingers inside me with no pretense at teasing. I arched up into his mouth, my legs going up on either side of his hips so I could move with his thrusts, fast and insistent. I felt myself tightening, getting close quickly.

It had been so long, too long.

My body was desperate for release.

"Nuh-uh," he said, pulling his fingers out of me, giving me a sinister little smile as he moved his hand upward and pushed them into my mouth. "You're gonna come around my cock this time," he said, sliding down onto his forearm as his cock pressed up against me. His fingers pulled from my mouth and moved between us until his cock pressed up against the entrance to my body, pausing for an impossibly long minute until I was squirming against him.

He leaned down, claiming my cold lips and warming them immediately. Then and only then, he thrust hard to the hilt in one smooth move, landing deliciously deep, his mouth muffling the sound of my moan. There was a vibrating, rolling sound in Repo's chest as he stilled inside me for a moment, his lips ripping from my lips and his forehead landing on mine.

When he lifted up, he started thrusting. Slow, but hard, each stroke forward sending us sliding slightly across the slick ground. My hands went to his back, digging in, as my legs crossed around his lower back, allowing me to take him as deep as possible on each stroke.

"Fuck, Maze," he growled, suddenly throwing his weight to the side, pulling me with him until I was lying over him. I laughed as I pressed up, planting my knees on the sides of his hips and taking over, my grinding a lot less practiced and smooth than his, my movements fast and frantic with no real rhythm. "Push up," Repo demanded, pushing at my shoulders until I sat back on my heels to look down at him. His hands slid up the fronts of my thighs, over my belly, moving to cup my breasts for a second before sliding back down to my hips and digging in, using them to force my hips into a quick, but steady pace as I felt the pressure low in my belly build, threatening oblivion as the sky kept raining down on us. "Faster," he demanded, thrusting upward into me as I stroked forward and back, hitting my G-spot each time. I leaned forward, planting my hands on his chest and worked my hips faster, every inch of my body tensing as I got closer.

Repo knifed up suddenly, one arm around my hips, the other under my ass, as he got back onto his feet. My legs wrapped around his back, my thigh muscles clenching hard to try to hold me against his slippery body. I felt my back slam into the trunk of a tree, both of his hands holding me under my ass as he started thrusting fast. One of my arms went around the back of his neck, the other went up above my head, curling around the tree trunk behind me, trying to hold myself in place as Repo pistoned relentlessly, offering an end to the coiled, almost painful pressure inside.

"Maze, come," he commanded as my moans became whimpers, my nails digging into his neck enough to leave marks.

Then, as if my body had been seeking the permission, I exploded, crashing louder than the thunder, exploding brighter than the lightening as I cried out his name.

One of his hands left my ass, taking away my support and making my leg fall and land numbly on the ground as he pounded harder, faster through my orgasm, getting closer to his own. His free hand moved to cup the side of my jaw as he planted deep, jerked hard and came, his deep blue eyes on mine the whole time and I felt a tremor in my belly at the intensity I found there.

As he came down, he rested his forehead to mine, taking deep breaths as my body trembled slightly from both aftershocks of my orgasm and the cold rain pelting my body.

"You alright?" he asked, pulling back to look at me. I felt the smile toying at my lips and he gave me an almost vulnerable-looking smile back. "Cold?" he asked, running a finger down my cheek.

"We just had sex in a thunderstorm," I observed, letting out a weird, strangled laugh.

"Hell fucking yeah we did," he grinned devilishly at me, looking way too proud of himself.

"Can I put some clothes on now?" I asked when he just stood there, one hand squeezing my ass, the other tracing up my side from hip to the side of my breast and back again.

"You can try but wet skin and tight clothes, honey, I don't see that working out for you."

"So I should just... stay naked you're saying?" I asked, head tilting to smirk at him. "It's almost like you planned it this way."

"Yep. Put in an order to the universe for a well-timed thunderstorm so I could have slip-n-slide sex in the woods just to be able to look at your body." He paused mid-smile, eyes dancing a little. "Though, I did miss something."

"Missed something?" I asked, feeling him slide out of me and sad at the loss of intimacy.

"Your ass, Maze, is a result of Divine design. Been having real impure thoughts about it since the first day you showed up."

"What kinda impure thoughts?" I teased, sinking my ass against the tree as he tried to turn me. It was too nice, too rare to experience Repo in a light, carefree way without fear of being found out for me to let the moment go so quickly.

"The kind that made me think about how it would look as I fucked you doggy style or..." he tapered off, brow quirking.

"Or?" I prompted.

"Or fucking it while working your clit and G-spot until you come so hard you're convinced nothing ever has, or ever could, feel as good as my cock inside your ass."

I swallowed hard against a second wave of desire overtaking my system. Then, lost for anything to say because I was pretty sure he was fully capable of making good on that promise, I turned slowly. There was nothing for a long minute, making the twisting feeling of insecurity coil in my belly. But then his hands moved out, stroking down from my shoulders, pausing at my hips, then whispering over my ass.

It felt like it went on forever, but was probably only seconds before his hands moved back up and slid around my lower belly, pulling me backward against his chest. Above us, the downpour became a trickle, the rain clouds slowly moving on to other pastures. My head tilted back to rest on his shoulder and his face moved into the crook of my neck. The was a long pause where he was just holding me, both of us lost in the silent perfection of the moment, before Repo finally spoke and washed it away.

"We won't get this again."

"Get what?" I asked, feeling a small guard move back up over my heart, horrified that I had let it slide down for even a moment.

"This. Privacy. No one sniffing around, no one to give a fuck what we do with our personal lives. This is the first and last time."

I closed my eyes against the crippling truth of that statement, swallowing hard against the bitter taste in my mouth.

It was time to stop letting myself be, well, me.

It was time for Maze to make an appearance.

"Works for me," I said, shrugging a little as I pulled away. "We had an itch; we scratched it. We can move on now," I added as I moved off toward my sopping wet puddle of clothes and slipped into my panties. I had just pulled my tee over my head when Repo's hand snagged my wrist as I lifted my hands to free my hair from my shirt. He used it to turn me roughly.

"What the fuck, Maze?"

"What?" I asked, jerking my wrist from his and pulling out my hair, reaching for his arm and slipping the band off his wrist to tie it all back up.

On a sigh, he reached for his pants, turning away from me as he jumped into them, tying off the condom and wrapping it up in his still-discarded boxer briefs. I took the opportunity to shimmy back into my pants, balling up my bra and shoving it into my back pocket. It would be impossible to try to get the damn thing on with damp skin. Repo snagged his shirt, squeezed it out, and stuffed it into his waistband and I really, really wished he would put it on. Trying to keep my defenses (and libido) in check with him half-naked in front of me was going to be a challenge.

"Are we heading back?" I asked, feeling squirmy with the silent awkwardness between us.

"Maze..." he said, shaking his head as he stepped into his boots.

"What?" I asked, careful to keep my tone hollow.

"Oh, fuck this," he growled, storming over toward me, both his hands going to the sides of my face and using it to hold me still as his lips claimed mine, hard, angry, crushing. I stayed resistant for all of two seconds before I melted against him, my hands grabbing him at the biceps as my tongue pressed forward to tease his. He pulled back just as suddenly as he pulled me in, his hands still crushing into my face. "You want to bullshit everyone else and make them think you're all barbed wire and steel, go right the fuck ahead. But you can't fool me so stop fucking trying."

With that, he pushed me back a step, turned, grabbed his boxers and guns off the ground, then started moving toward the tree line we had entered the range through.

Not having much of a choice, I slid into my boots and rushed to follow, keeping a safe couple of yards between us at all times.

We made it back to the bikes a while later, both of us

mostly dry and the heat was starting to bear down on us, making me miserable once again. Well, the heat and the reality of getting a taste of Repo only to know it was the only one I would get, making me miserable.

Repo pulled his tee out of his waistband, wiped my seat then his own before slipping it back on. Even pissed at me, he was still sweet.

The bastard.

We made it back to the compound. We both parked and Repo tore off before I could even get off my bike.

With a shrug that I didn't feel, I made my way inside and down to the basement, planning to grab a change of clothes and going to take a long, cold shower, praying that would settle my frazzled nerves.

That was the plan until I heard footsteps behind me and I turned to find Renny standing there, hands tucked into his front pockets, his normally carefree face looking uncharacteristically serious.

"What's up, Renny?" I asked, dropping my hand with my fresh clothes to my side.

"Why the fuck are you getting called dozens of times from K.C.E Boxing?"

Shit.

Shitshitshit.

# TWELVE

*Repo*

The drive back to the compound, quite frankly, sucked.

I was wet and dirty and hot.

But it had absolutely nothing to do with any of those things.

Oh, no.

It did, however, have every goddamn thing to do with a hazel-eyed, purple-haired, spitfire who had shown me more of her softness back in that field. Whoever Maze really was, it wasn't the hardened badass she worked so hard at portraying herself as. The badass, she was a mask, a defense mechanism, big nasty thorns to protect the soft, delicate flower.

Being with her, kissing, holding, being inside her, it had been the best experience I'd had in a miserably long amount of time.

And I had no idea what the fuck to do with that information.

"You fucked her, didn't you?" Cash's easy voice asked as I walked into my room, causing me to stop short for a second.

"Did you seriously break into my room?" I asked, shaking my head.

"Yeah. Now stop trying to change the subject. You fucked her, right? I mean, I think we all knew it was gonna happen after the car incident."

In my chest, my heart started thrumming in a sickening beat. "Car incident?" I repeated.

"Fuck off," Cash laughed, crossing his arms over his chest while an easy grin spread on his face. "Steamed windows and you come out of it grumpy as all fuck? We've all been teenagers with blue balls before, Repo."

"Reign knew it was her?" I asked past the lump in my throat over him possibly knowing I had disobeyed a direct order.

"Repo, man, come on. Reign might be a lot of things, but he's not stupid. I think when he told you to keep your dick in your pants, he knew damn well that wasn't going to happen. Especially not when you're stuck with her night and day, always on her case. Hate can make a great aphrodisiac. And today when you got stuck with her, taking her out to that field no doubt..."

"Fuck," I said, shaking my head as I sank down at the foot of my bed. "I screwed up."

"Like I said, Reign knew you couldn't have..."

"But I should have been able to," I objected. "It was an order. What the fuck does that make me that I disobeyed it?"

"Fucking human? A pain in the ass biker like the rest of us. We have all done something that Reign wouldn't like before."

"Not me."

"Well," Cash broke in and I could hear the smile in his voice, "that's not so true anymore, huh?" I brought my hand up to my face, raking it across my brow. "Christ, Repo, chill the fuck out. It's not a big deal."

"Yeah, sure."

"Unless," Cash broke in, his teasing tone making me stiffen.

"Unless what?"

"Unless you have feelings for her that might get in the way of your assignment."

"Don't be ridiculous," I rolled my eyes at him.

It wasn't a lie. Not exactly.

Because it *was* ridiculous to have feelings for her.

But, that being said, there was no denying that they were there.

I didn't know exactly what they were, but they were something, something more than what they were supposed to be: probate to member, boss to subordinate.

"Wouldn't be the first time one of us ended up with a woman over something we first thought was ridiculous."

Yeah, well, that was the fucking truth.

Reign and Summer got together after she escaped the people who had held her captive and tortured her. He protected her. He fought for her. The whole thing was insane.

Then Cash and the leader of fucking Hailstorm got together. Hell, if someone would have told me that Cash, shameless manwhore, would end up with anyone, I would have said that was ridiculous. Let alone the female leader of a bunch of lawless men and women.

And Wolf and Janie, yeah, who the fuck wouldn't think it was ridiculous that a man who could barely rub five words together would end up with a woman who was never lacking something to say?

But it was different.

"Yeah, man. But none of you were in charge of literally making your womens' lives hell and killing their dreams."

"Yeah, I can see that complicating things," Cash said,

moving to sit down at the other end of the bed.

"She can barely bring herself to look at me half the time she hates me so much."

"I think you underestimate her capability for understanding. She knows you don't want to screw things up for her."

"And she thinks it's pathetic of me that I can't say no to something that I am adamantly against."

Cash sighed. "I don't know what to tell you, Repo. The situation is fucked. Eventually, she's gonna be on her ass and she's going to resent you for that. But I think you underestimate how forgiving women can be if you make it worth their while."

"You have met Maze, right?" I asked, turning to look at him with a smirk.

"You've met Lo, right?" he countered. "And Janie? And Alex? Fuck, even Summer can be a stubborn pain in the ass at times. They're all strong and take-no-prisoners. And me, Reign, Wolf, and Breaker ain't ever been boy scouts. We fuck up. We stick our feet in our mouths. We piss them off. But they forgive us. You know... after they hand our asses to us. But, hell, all that conflict makes for some fan-fucking-tastic make-up sex so you won't hear us complaining."

"I'm sure there is a point in there somewhere," I mused, shaking my head at him.

"The point is, man the fuck up. You got a job to do, do it. You got a woman you don't want to lose in the process, fucking make that clear to her. She'll be pissed. She'll resent it. She'll take all that out on you, but you'll deserve it and you'll take it on the chin and then, when all is said and done and this is over, you can make it up to her."

"You make that shit sound easy and you fucking know it won't be."

"No," he said, standing, slamming a hand into my

shoulder hard enough to make me lurch forward slightly, "but it'll be worth it, don't you think?" he asked as he let himself into the hall, closing my door with a click.

Fact of the matter was, it felt premature to decide if it would be worth it.

I didn't know much about Maze. Out of all the probates, she was the most tight-lipped about her life before prospecting. True, Duke and Renny weren't exactly big talkers about their lives before either, but we knew their stories. I knew their ghosts, their demons, their reasons for their guards. I didn't have that advantage with Maze. I didn't know anything about her upbringing, about what led her to seek out inclusion in a biker club instead of being a normal person. It wasn't a move that made sense for a normal, well-adjusted person. So what had she been through to send her our way?

That being said, I was under the belief that what someone came from meant a hell of a lot less than what they became.

If our pasts really defined us, I was a vicious, violent, horrifying, soulless mutilator and murderer.

True, I'd done that shit.

But that wasn't who I was.

Who I was was the person who never wanted to be that way again.

Aside from the nightmares it gave me and therefore my perpetually tired mind and body, it had very little weight on my daily life.

I felt the same way about Maze.

I didn't particularly need to know what made her into a stubborn, hardass, trash-talking, sarcastic, determined, but also sweet and soft and vulnerable person. I didn't need to know how she learned to fight and shoot and ride a bike. All I needed to know was that was who she was. She was all those things. She was smart and capable. She was guarded for reasons she had that I didn't need to know to understand.

It didn't matter what her favorite color was.

It didn't matter what her earliest childhood memory was.

It didn't matter if she thought tomatoes and avocados were too squishy and disgusting to eat.

What mattered was the woman I worked beside and trained beside and spent time with daily.

And that woman? Yeah, I was thinking she might be worth all the hassle.

Sure, some day, I'd like to know all the other shit. But I wasn't delusional enough to believe she would offer up that kind of personal information to a man who could and would need to use it against her.

Fact of the matter was, I needed to be in it for the long game if I wanted more than a fuck in a field. Though, that fuck in the field was easily the best fuck of my life. It was raw and primal and just fucking... honest. That was what it was. There were no guards between us, no lies, no nothing but bodies enjoying bodies, just the acknowledgment of the connection between us.

So if I wanted a chance of a repeat, I needed to stop playing the tug-of-war with Maze and be upfront. I needed to tell her how it was. I was planning on getting her kicked out, but that didn't change the fact that I wanted a shot with her.

True, it was a risky hand to play.

But if you wanted to win big, you had to be willing to take chances.

I sighed, grabbing a change of clothes and going into the bathroom to shower.

I was going to talk to her.

After she had a chance to clean up and relax.

There were too many men around to overhear anyway.

She had the early morning shift the next morning.

I would be there.
It wasn't like I slept anyway.

# THIRTEEN

*Maze*

"What?" I asked, my mouth falling open slightly as my heart started pounding and a stress-sweat broke out over my skin.

"You heard me, Violet," he said, raising a brow. "I wrote down the number last night when they wouldn't stop calling you. Then I got too shitfaced to do anything with it. And today we were all busy. Until I got back a little earlier than you and Repo. So I did some looking around. You know what I found?"

"That K.C.E Boxing Emporium called me?" I asked, sarcasm dripping into my words to cover the fear that was coursing through my system. "Wow, Sherlock, I'm so impressed by your investigative skills. It was almost like they were listed somewhere. Oh, wait, they're a business... so they are."

To that, Renny's lips twitched slightly before they settled back into a straight line, and I saw for the first time that he wasn't the person I had originally thought he was. He wore his disguise really well: the lighthearted, funny, sweet, goofball with a good heart. He never slipped, save for the fight with Duke and, well, they were men and sometimes men just fought because it was in their instincts to settle things with fists, not words. Otherwise, he was one-hundred percent that Renny-disguise all the time.

But the man in front of me was a view of the man who was underneath that.

And he had a little coldness in his eyes, a little hollowness in his voice, a kind of sharpness about him that you'd swear could cut you to pieces if you got too close.

"Let's try this again. What business do you have with a boxing emporium?"

"Why the fuck would it matter? Would you question me if it was any run-of-the-mill gym calling?"

"Would any run-of-the-mill gym call you twenty-some-odd times in one night?"

"If I owed them money, probably," I mused.

"Cute," he said, shaking his head and I saw a struggle there between the two Renny personalities. In the end, the knife-like one won out. "But billing departments wouldn't be calling after hours."

"If they were in, say, California maybe they would."

"Nice try, Violet, but I'm not stupid."

"Why do you care who is calling me?"

"Because it's an anomaly and I don't like those."

"Christ, Renny, I never pegged you as the anal type."

"There's a lot you don't know about me, Maze."

It was that moment that Duke's words came screaming to the forefront of my mind, words he'd said when talking about Renny: *"Not everyone is who they appear to be, Ace."*

Had Duke known back then about Renny? Was whatever darkness that was in Renny the cause of that fight they had had?

Because, quite honestly, with the way he was acting, I kind of felt like going a couple rounds with him myself.

"Interesting. So you're allowed to have your secrets, but I can't have my own?"

"Something like that. At least not from me."

"What makes you so special?"

"K.C.E Boxing, Violet. Why them? Why so many calls? Why did you look so freaked after you called them back. And don't insult me by saying you didn't call them back and that you didn't look freaked because if there is one thing that I am, it's observant."

"Yeah, okay," I said, rolling my eyes. It was childish and it served no real purpose, but confronted with this side of Renny, I was forgetting all the training K had tried to pound into me.

"For instance, you climb trees when you're in a mood. You can cook, but it's not a task you particularly enjoy. So from that, I'm going to conclude that you grew up with someone who did like to cook and he or she, more likely she, was determined to pound that skill into you whether you liked it or not."

Well, he had my grandmother pegged right there.

"Why not a he?" I latched onto, being the only topic that didn't hit too close to home.

"Because girls like you, the take-no-prisoners, I-can-do-everything-a-guy-can, I-don't-need-no-man types... they generally don't come from households with strong male role models. When you have a strong male role model, you learn you can trust men, you can lean on them, you don't have to prove yourself or anything to them. So you, Maze, I very much doubt you had any men in your life. Single mom. Single grandmother. Something like that."

Both of those were true.

God.

*God.*

Was I such an open book or was Renny just a really good reader?

"Do you need more examples? From last Wednesday to three days ago, you had your period. You don't bitch and moan but you get cramps. I know that because you unconsciously rub your stomach. It's not something you do when you're hungry, so one would assume it was because of pain. You and Repo, you have a love-hate thing going on and the sexual tension between you could be sliced with a fucking knife. You..."

"Okay, enough. I get it, you notice things," I snapped, genuinely freaked out that any one person could derive so much factual truths from just... casually watching me.

"And I noticed you call them back and I noticed you fall against the fence like whatever you heard freaked you out."

"So, I got some bad news. Christ, Renny. It's none of your fucking business."

"Everything is my business. Especially when I know that K.C.E isn't just a boxing emporium," he said and I felt myself stiffen and I knew he noticed. "It's a boxing emporium run by the notorious, enigmatic K."

"So?"

"So why is K calling you?"

"Who said it was K calling me? Jesus, for someone so observant, you can be kind-of dense."

"Dense?" he asked, brows drawing together, his face losing some of its coldness, some of its certainty. Maybe that was his Achilles heel. He needed to be right, to be the smartest and most observant guy in the room. If something threatened that, the other Renny could shine through more.

I could work with that.

"Yeah, dense. In case it escaped that keen eye of yours, K.C.E is a business. Meaning it has employees. Plural. More than one. K doesn't single-handedly run the place."

"So you're saying..."

"That my sister works there, asshole," I snapped, eyes widening at him like he was stupid. "She works there and she was having a personal crisis. If you must know, her fiance cheated on her. This is the week of her rehearsal dinner. She was devastated. She needed to talk."

I watched as the rest of his sharpness fell away, leaving someone similar to the Renny I thought I knew, just slightly less easy-going and jovial. "And K?"

"Great guy. He taught my sister to kick ass and then I wanted in and he worked with me a little bit. I wish I had more time with him. He seemed like good people."

"So you seriously don't know what he does?"

"Aside from training boxers and teaching self-defense classes?" I asked, brows drawing together.

"Yeah aside from all that, Violet."

"No. Is it something illegal?" I asked, shaking my head a little. "Because I can't imagine that."

"Yeah, well," he said, his easy smile breaking across his face, "who'da thunk a handsome fuck like me would be a future gun runner?" He moved toward me, throwing an arm across my shoulder. "So this sister of yours... she look like you? If so, I mean... I can heal a broken heart, man," he said as we moved in unison toward the stairs.

I laughed because that was such a Renny-thing to say.

But that being said, there was a swirly feeling in my stomach having him close to me. Not because I had any fear of him. I was still pretty sure that he was some kind of friendly for me. But because something was up with him. Normal, well-adjusted people couldn't flip a switch on their personalities like he could. His unpredictability made him dangerous for my cover. And while I might have gotten him off my case with my lie, there was no guarantee he wouldn't just keep snooping around. I wasn't exactly sure how deep K buried Maisy Mckenzie. I knew he couldn't do anything about my old tax returns, my work history, my college records. He'd deleted me off of every possible website online until if you searched my name, nothing came up except a name on a list of college graduates. But K wasn't a hacker and I had no idea how many traces there were for someone who was.

When we had crafted Maze, choosing the name because it was what my grandmother had called me when she was angry and I would automatically respond to it without any thought or training, we had given her a license, some work history, a few traces of her existence online, but that was it.

If Renny got a wild hair one day and decided to go digging, I wondered how long it would take him to see that I wasn't really who I said I was.

"So what did Repo's test consist of?" he asked, arm still slung around me as he led me toward the bathroom.

"Oh, um, shooting practice."

"Oh, great," Renny groaned, dropping his arm and looking at the ceiling.

"Not a good shot?"

"Haven't had too much practice to be honest."

"Repo is good. Like... he's really good. He's not going to let you come back here until you can hit the target how he wants," I warned.

"You a good shot?"

"I'm... decent. Definitely not good. But decent seemed to be enough to get him off my case. What did you do at Hailstorm?"

"Oh, I got grilled by Lo and some guy named Malcolm. Then Janie insisted on grappling with me."

"Why?" I asked, thinking of the short, waifish woman who had fought so hard to get me in and keep me in, despite the odds.

"I dunno. Looking for the flinch factor maybe?"

"The flinch factor?" I repeated, opening the bathroom door and putting the clothes on the sink vanity.

"Yeah, you know how men who are raised to respect women and not raise their hands to them are forced to put their hands on one. They flinch. It feels wrong and unnatural."

"Did you flinch?" I asked, turning fully to him, watching for any signs of dishonesty.

"Of course I fucking flinched, Violet," he said, looking at me like I was both crazy and insulting him.

"Just asking," I shrugged. "I hear Wolf has some kind of hunting planned for us."

"Thank fuck because just sitting around and staring and grunting at each other would get old pretty quick. Have fun getting all that mud off," he said, running a finger across the side of my neck and showing me the dirt on his finger.

"Yeah they picked a great day to drag us outside," I shrugged, hoping for casual as I closed and locked the door.

That evening before I hauled it off to bed to rest for my early morning shift, we were all gathered in the great room: members and probates alike, just hanging out. I was standing near the bar by myself, my gaze falling on Renny as he seemed to be back to his old self.

"You saw it too, didn't you?" Duke asked, sidling in beside me.

"Saw what?" I asked, turning my head to look at his profile.

He jerked his chin back toward where I had been looking.

"Renny-two-point-oh," he said, his tone a little guarded. But, then again, Duke's tone was always guarded.

"Renny-two-point-oh," I repeated.

"Yeah. Saw that shit on my third day here. It comes and goes. No real rhyme or reason I can find. Something triggers him and he's that fucked up robotic version of himself."

"Has Repo and the rest of them seen it?"

Duke shrugged. "If they have, they have reasons they're not telling us for keeping him around."

"I heard something about his particular skill set."

"Yeah, heard that too. But no one will say what it is. Maybe they like his snake-ish ways."

"Repo hates snakes," I said automatically, feeling a jolt at the casual intimacy of that admission. Duke's gaze went to mine, curious. "His tattoo," I covered quickly. "The one on his back with the snake getting stabbed. 'Snakes and snitches get it where they slither'," I added with a casual shrug.

"Who the fuck knows. All I do know is you keep your cards to your chest around him, okay Ace? There's no telling what someone like him is capable of."

With that, he pushed off the wall and moved away from me to go grab a pool stick, leaving me feeling even more on edge about the whole Renny situation. Because if there was one thing Duke didn't seem like he was, it was an alarmist. So if he told me to worry, to be careful, I needed to heed that advice.

I made a mental note to bring the situation up to K when I spoke to him. He would do some digging, find out what he could about Renny, what his supposed skills might be. And, what's more, he could tell me how to navigate him when he was in one of his moods.

I sighed, making my way back down to the basement and curling up in my bed, back pressed up against the wall and knife tucked under my pillow, my hand resting over it.

--

I woke up later than usual, crawling out of bed with a grumble, my thigh muscles sore from... earlier activities I was actively trying to not think about. Along with the mess with Renny. And, let's not forget, the very dangerous, garrote-wielding Russian traffickers who could very well be looking for me right that moment.

"My life is ridiculous," I grumbled into the silence of the abandoned kitchen, pouring myself a cup of the seemingly always-fresh coffee before making my way outside.

"He's in the back," Repo's voice met me as soon as I stepped out the back door, making me start and splash some of my coffee over my hand.

"Jesus," I hissed, shaking the liquid off my hand and locating Repo where he was sitting on top of one of the picnic tables.

"Didn't mean to scare you," he said.

"It's alright," I shrugged, scanning the dark distance for a sign of Duke. Seeing nothing and knowing it would be another couple of minutes, I took a deep breath and looked over at Repo. His eyes were swollen and red, the purple smudges underneath even more prominent than usual. "Do you ever sleep?" I heard myself blurt out.

Repo gave me a tired smile. "Not often."

"Why not?" I asked, my legs carrying me closer to him despite better sense telling me to keep distance between us.

"Nightmares," he said with a shrug.

"Every night?"

To that I got a wry smile. "I stopped trying to sleep nightly about five years ago, honey."

There was a vulnerability about him in that moment that I felt tug at a similar feeling buried deep within me. It was underneath all the training, under all the determination I built up while lying alone in that panic room every night. It was something I had tried to squish, tried to pretend wasn't a part of me. But it was. And maybe I found it a little comforting that someone as put-together and strong as Repo also had a part of him that was softer, weaker, uncontrollable too.

"Is it..." I started, only to be interrupted by Duke.

"Early again, Ace? You make the rest of us look bad," he said, holding out the flashlight toward me and I took it. "Don't know how the fuck you look so rested so early in the morning. It's unnatural," he said, jerking his chin at Repo, then making his way back toward the compound.

I turned to watch him disappear for a long minute before Repo interrupted the silence. "Is it what?" he prompted.

I turned back, brows drawn together. "What? Oh, um... are the nightmares based on... real things?" I asked, never being the type to suffer from chronic nightmares. Since running from the Kozlovs, I had the occasional one that would wake me up freaked out, but I usually forgot all the details of the dream within minutes of waking.

"Yeah, real things," he told me, watching my face closely. "I haven't always been a good man, Maze."

"I find that hard to believe," I said because it was true. "Besides, everyone has done some shit in their lives that could keep us up at night if we harp on it."

"What have you done?" he asked. The question would have seemed invasive if he hadn't asked in a quiet, smooth voice.

I looked at my feet and let out a breath. "I've been really naive and gullible," I admitted.

"Come here," he said, leaning forward and snagging me at my hips, pulling me closer to the table and between his legs. He waited a minute for my gaze to rise to his. "Maybe you were those things once, but that isn't who you are."

The certainty in his tone made a bit of a weight lift from my shoulders. It hadn't occurred to me that I had been harboring a worry that it was something that was written all over me, like I wore my flaws as a badge for all to see despite how hard I had tried to make sure no one could ever call me those things again.

"Same goes for you, Repo," I said, my hands landing on his thighs.

"I've killed people, Maze."

"Was that supposed to shock me?" I asked, shrugging a shoulder. Quite frankly, I had walked into the compound expecting to find that every member of the gang was, at some time or another, a cold-blooded killer. K had sort-of told me as much. He said he wasn't sure about some of the small-time guys, but he knew for a fact that Reign, Cash, and Wolf had left piles of bodies in their wakes. Reign, mostly as preventative measures, eliminating snitches, taking down rival organizations. Cash, when ordered to in extreme situations. And Wolf, well, Wolf kind-of went bonkers every once in a while and committed some ridiculously violent murders. But he mostly seemed to kill assholes who deserved it.

So Repo admitting he'd killed people? It wasn't a surprise.

"It would shock normal people," he said, his fingers sinking into my hips in an almost possessive way that made my sex clench.

"Who ever claimed I was normal?"

"They killed my uncle," he admitted, still watching for my reaction.

"The people you killed?"

"Yeah. They wanted to overthrow my uncle's *business* so they killed him and whooped my ass."

"That's how you got this," I concluded, hand moving from his thigh, my fingertips tracing down the scar on his cheek.

"Yeah."

"Snakes and snitches," I guessed.

"Yeah, honey," he said, hands closing the rest of the distance between us, making my pelvis push against his.

"If they deserved it, I don't see why you have nightmares."

"Because they didn't deserve the way they died."

"Maybe, maybe not."

"Maze... not."

My head tilted at the firmness of his tone. "I never had you pegged for the self-condemnation type."

"Don't usually do things I regret," he said, his hand moving up to stroke over my cheek.

I swallowed hard, trying to talk myself into stepping away from him. We were right in the middle of the yard. Anyone could see us if they happened outside for a smoke or some fresh air.

"I need to do my rounds." To that, Repo smirked a little evilly. "What?" I asked, brows drawing together.

"Yeah, when one of us takes the guard shift, we just plant

our asses on the roof with a gun. You can see every inch of the fence from up there."

My mouth fell open in mock shock. "You bastards," I laughed, shaking my head.

"We gotta get our kicks somehow," he chuckled. "But you're right. Rounds need to be done," he said, but I didn't trust the look in his eye as he pushed me back a few steps and hopped off the table, taking the Maglite out of my hand and flicking it on before taking off toward the fence.

I paused for a moment before rushing to fall into step beside him, watching his profile as we walked. "Are you... doing the rounds with me?"

"Yeah," he said, nodding slightly.

"Um. Okay. But... why?"

"We need to talk."

Shit.

Shitshitshit.

We most definitely did *not* need to *talk*. What we needed was to move on and pretend that what happened never happened. It was better for both of us that way.

"I think we're all good on that front," I said, pointedly keeping my gaze ahead of us.

We walked that way for a long couple of minutes, each second that passed making me feel more and more like I was going to crawl out of my own skin. But then, nestled far from the compound in the back corner of the yard, Repo's hand closed around my bicep and turned me, pushing me up against the fence.

"We're not all good on that front," he countered my point from several minutes before.

"Repo..."

"No," he cut me off, putting two fingers against my lips to silence me. "Shush for a second, alright? We need to get some shit straight and if you keep trying to interrupt me, this is gonna take all night. Now, I think we both get that my job is to not allow you into the MC. By whatever means necessary. It sucks. It's not fair. But that's the way it is. I get that you're going to resent me for that. And I know it means it's going to be hard to trust..."

"Okay. Hold up," I said, brushing his hand away.

"No, listen."

"No, you listen..."

"Maze, I want to give this a shot," he said over my objection, effectively shutting me up.

"Give what a shot?"

"Whatever this is," he said, waving a hand between us.

"This is nothing. We had sex. That's not a big deal. We can be adults about it and move on."

"That's what you want? You want to move on?"

"Yes, that's..."

Then his lips were on mine, his hand going into the hair at the nape of my neck, curling in and pulling, as his teeth bit into my lip hard enough to bruise. On a groan, I reached out toward his sides, dragging him against me as he pressed me into the fence, tongue teasing mine until I let out a whimper. At the sound, he pulled back suddenly, his breath warm on my face as my eyes fluttered open.

"Sure about that?" he asked, lips quirked up on one side.

"That was low."

"But it proved my point, didn't it?"

"I believe the fact that we're obviously attracted to each other was *my* point, not yours," I countered with a small smile, my lips still tingly from the kiss.

"It's part mine too. We're attracted to each other. We did a pretty ace job on the fucking front. And on top of that, I like what you have to offer, Maze. I'd like to have a chance at receiving all that. When all this is done."

I was with him until the last part, when I felt myself straightening. "When all this is done... meaning when you send me packing," I observed as I used my hands that were still at the sides of his abs and pushed him back a foot.

"Maze..."

"Do you really think it's a good idea to try to build some kind of... relationship on your killing a dream of mine?"

"It's not personal, honey."

"I hate that phrase. It's personal to me."

I closed my eyes, taking a deep breath and letting it out slowly. It was a ridiculous conversation to have. Because if Repo succeeded in kicking me out, which he seemed determined to do, there was no chance of us getting together in any capacity. Because if I lost the protection of The Henchmen MC, I was going to be relocated. Probably clear across the country. I wouldn't be able to keep in contact, not that even if I could it would make any difference. Long distance relationships were for college and temporary work assignments, not girls on the run from freaking Russian traffickers.

"Maze..."

I opened my eyes slowly. "You're telling me there's not a single chance of getting patched in here?"

Repo paused, raking a hand down the side of his face. "Yeah, that's what I'm telling you."

I tried to ignore the swirling, free fall sensation in my belly and reached for the front of his tee, pulling him forward. "In that case..." I said, pulling his lips down to mine.

I would ride it out, continue doing my grunt work, deal with whatever they wanted to throw at me, learn things if anything was offered that would be useful for my future, and I would enjoy every last stolen moment I could with Repo. Because, in the end, what did it matter if I was going to be out on my ass anyway? Soon, and there was no telling how soon, but soon, I would be relocating. So what was the use in denying myself something I wanted?

"Maze, we weren't done..." he started against my hungry, insistent lips.

"Yeah we were," I countered, my lips going to his neck as my hand drifted down his stomach and flattened over the crotch of his jeans where his cock was already hard and straining. My hands moved up the soft, worn material of his pants to his fly, quickly undoing it and reaching inside to stroke him, sliding my thumb over the head at each pass, until Repo made a low, growling sound in his throat and snagged me at the wrist, pulling my hand away.

Giving him a mischievous smile, I lowered myself down in front of him, using my free hand to free him and stroking down his cock to the hilt before leaning forward, head tilted up, eyes on him, I slowly took him into my mouth, using my tongue to tease the head before I took him deep. His deep blue eyes were intense on mine, the lids heavy. A muscle was ticking in his jaw as his hand released my wrist and moved to stroke the hair out of my face.

Encouraged, I ducked my head and worked him with my mouth, a little tentative at first, then faster, deeper, one hand stroking his cock as I sucked and the other stroking over his balls as his hand went to the crown of my head and coaxed me deeper and faster for a long couple of minutes. His quiet groans stirred the desire between my legs until I was wet and aching for fulfillment as well.

"Honey... alright... okay," he said, chuckling slightly as I fought him pulling me backward. I wanted to taste his release; I wanted to own his pleasure. He held me back from him by my hair. "I got one rule with sex, Maze."

"Rule?" I asked, brows raising. That was a new one for

me. I'd never run across a man with sexual rules.

"You always come first," he said, using my hair to drag me back to my feet.

"Well, I think I can get behind a rule like that."

"Right now, I'm getting behind you," he said, smile a little boyish as he released my hair, my scalp stinging slightly. "Hands on the fence, Maze," he commanded, reaching into his back pocket for his wallet and pulling out a condom.

Feeling anticipation flutter in my belly, I turned to face the fence, spreading my arms wide and grabbing the fence as per orders. I stood that way a long minute, long enough for me to almost look over my shoulder to make sure he was still there, before I felt his hands grab the waistband of my jeans and, without bothering to unfasten them, yanking them roughly down my legs. I felt his body move in behind me, his feet settling inside of mine, his cock pressing against my ass. One of his hands slid up my back, sinking into my hair, wrapping it around his hand and yanking roughly, making me arch back. "Hands stay on the fence," he reminded me as I automatically moved to get closer to him and ease the smarting of my scalp. His other hand moved out and squeezed my ass cheek hard once before guiding him between my thighs. I couldn't even build up any anticipation before he slammed hard and deep.

I cried out his name as I clenched around him, my hands pulling at the fence as I stuck my ass out further.

"Fucking perfect view," he said withdrawing slightly, his voice tense as his hand went to one of my hips, digging in and using it to pull me backward as he thrust deep again. There was no reservation after that. He fucked me fast, rough, his fist pulling my hair harder with each stroke of his cock, his hand occasionally slapping my ass cheek as he kept up our frantic pace, me shoving back into him, greedy, needing release. My moans came out loud and uncontrolled, so wrapped up I was completely unconcerned with being overheard.

I didn't get the slow build-up, the expected suspended sensation that always proceeded an orgasm. No, it slammed through my system completely unexpected, my legs going weak and Repo's hand had to go around my waist to hold me upward as he kept thrusting through the rapid waves of pulsations deep inside.

I came down to reality hard, sucking in a breath I hadn't been aware of holding. Repo held me against his chest, his stubble grazing my neck as he teased my earlobe with his tongue and teeth.

"Now," he said, voice still rough and it shivered through my satisfied system, "let's see if we can convince you that nothing ever has or ever will feel as good as my cock in your ass, huh?"

And, well, was there really any way to deny him anything?

Especially with a promise like that and the fact that he seemed wholly capable of delivering on it.

"Okay," I said, turning my head toward the side on his shoulder and he leaned down and kissed the tip of my nose.

"Okay," he agreed, hand going between us and stroking his cock up my slick cleft. "Nervous?"

"No." First because, as much as I trusted anyone outside of K and his team of badasses, I trusted Repo. Second because, I'd dated Thato for a long time then a couple other guys over the years living in the City. And, well, let's face it, every guy made a move to try anal at some point. I couldn't exactly claim those had been altogether pleasant experiences, certainly not orgasm-inducing, but it was a different kind of intimacy and it was fulfilling a desire of someone you cared for.

I felt his cock slide up toward my ass, pressing there hard for a second but not sliding in. "You need me to slow down, tell me," he instructed, one hand pushing against my lower stomach as he slowly penetrated. I closed my eyes, breathing deep as he filled me. "You alright?" he asked as I felt him push fully inside.

"Mmhmm," I murmured, meaning it. Like I expected, it didn't feel like the most amazing thing in the world, but it was nice.

"About to be a whole lot better," he promised, nipping into my earlobe as the hand on my belly slid lower and moved between my thighs, his thumb pressing against my clit and a finger thrusting inside my pussy.

It was right then that I realized Repo was nothing if not an honest man. Because with the way my sex clenched and a rush of wetness coated his palm, I knew he was somehow going to make good on his claim.

His thrusts started slow, tentative, as if waiting for any resistance or objection. But with his thumb working my clit and his finger working my G-spot, all I felt was the strong, almost overwhelming anticipation of an orgasm that threatened to rip a hole through the sky and let me see into heaven for a moment.

"So, how's this going for ya?" he asked through my increasing moans, his tone a little teasing.

"Shut up," I laughed, reaching up behind me and wrapping my arms around his neck as his thrusts got faster, his fingers more insistent.

I felt my sex tightening, hinting at completion. The thrusts got even faster as his finger raked across my G-spot and his thumb pressed in hard and I just... shattered.

There was no other way to describe it.

The orgasm coursed through my system, starting at my clit and G-spot and exploding outward until it overwhelmed my entire body.

"That's it, honey," Repo growled against my ear as his thrusts got harder for a moment as I came back down before he planted deep and jerked once upward as he let out a curse as he came.

We stayed that way for a long time, him still inside me, my arms around his neck, one of his arms low on my hips, the other just under my breasts, our breathing ragged, our heartbeats frantic.

"Fuck yeah," he said after a long silence, his tone sounded sated but also pleased.

"I second that," I smiled out at the fence.

"Alright, gotta deal with this condom," he said, carefully slipping out of me, pulling his boxer briefs and pants back into place then walking across the field to his cars where there was a garbage. I reached down, pulling my panties up then unbuttoning and unzipping my jeans so I could pull them back up. By the time I was finished, Repo was back, grabbing my hand and pulling me along with him.

I looked around a little frantically, worried about being seen, as I was led around the side of the compound to the fire escape. Only then was my hand released and only because we needed both of our hands to climb the narrow stairs.

"What are we doing?" I asked as I followed him to stand on the roof.

"Your job. Without all the unnecessary walking," he said casually, moving to the center of the roof where there were actually milk crates set up to sit on.

"Did you guys sit around and laugh while watching us walk the grounds during the disgustingly hot or rainy days?" I asked, lowering my eyes at him and he looked sheepish.

"Maybe a little."

"Oh, you fucks," I laughed, shaking my head as I moved to sit down on the crate across from him. As soon as my ass hit it, however, he reached across, grabbed the crate, and slid it directly in front of him. His legs went out wide at my sides, his hands landing on my knees. His eyes were intense as he watched my face, so penetrating that I had to resist the urge to squirm. "What?" I asked when I couldn't take it anymore.

"We haven't finished our talk."

"Oh, come on, Repo. We don't..."

"Jesus fuck, since when is it the dude who has to try to force the chick to have 'the talk'?" he asked, rolling his eyes a little and giving me that boyish smile I was really beginning to like seeing. "Look, I'll keep this simple. I know you're going to hate me for a while and resent me or whatever. But regardless of all that, I plan on convincing your stubborn ass that it was just work, nothing personal. Because personally, I'd like to have you here within arms-reach at all times so I can fuck you any time the mood strikes."

"That... wow... that was *so* romantic," I teased though inside, my belly was doing the flip-flop thing again.

"Figured flowers and candy and poems weren't your thing. Thought you'd prefer some honest-to-God truth instead."

He was right. After so much deceit and uncertainty in my life, I really appreciated someone just laying it on the line for me, even if it wasn't particularly pretty.

And with that, I felt the flip-flop sensation get replaced with a big, hard, ugly pit of guilt in my stomach. He was being brutally honest and I was being anything but.

"Tell you what," I started, choosing my words carefully. "I can't make you any promises, Repo. And I will probably resent and be pissed at you a lot, but for the time being, anytime you want to sneak off and find a field somewhere," I smiled, "let me know."

"We're never gonna fuck on a bed, are we?" he asked, his eyes dancing.

"Where's the fun in that?" I countered and he laughed.

"You've got a point."

"So, ah, are you going back in or what?" I asked a minute later when we both just sat there, looking around at the fence line.

"Embarrassed at being seen with me, huh?" he asked, smirking.

"More like I'm not looking for any reason for Reign to kick me out any sooner than necessary."

"Can I ask you something?"

There was a seriousness in his tone that made me stiffen a little. "You can ask."

"Why stick it out? If you know it's not going anywhere, why not just cut your losses and head out? You can't possibly enjoy the grunt work."

"No, but I'm not a quitter. I'll stay until I'm not welcome anymore."

"Hate to break it to you, honey, but you're not exactly welcome now," he said, snagging my milk crate again, this time spinning it so my back was to him. His arm moved around my center, pulling me back against him. Feeling me stiffen, he pulled me tighter. "Don't worry, I'll get out of here before anyone can see us. Just relax."

Relax.

Easy for him to say.

He wasn't going to be kicked out of the organization that could keep him safe from some crazy Russian brothers.

And he wasn't weighted by the knowledge that, by getting kicked out, we would be losing what we had come to find with each other.

But that was my burden to shoulder.

So I leaned back against Repo's strong chest and we did our jobs and I pretended to ignore the growing sadness settling down deep inside me.

# FOURTEEN

*Maze*

The next three days did two things.

One, I was constantly sex-sore because when Repo said 'fuck you whenever the mood strikes', he meant it. And that mood struck at least twice a day. Once, I was pulled back toward his cars under the pretense of handing him tools and waxing the car (both things he totally forced me to do, by the way. Being *with* Repo didn't get me any special treatment) and then he fucked me against the hood like he had fantasized about. There was another time in his back seat, me on top riding him hard and fast, our bodies slick with sweat in the summer heat. And my shifts tended to be at night or in the morning so no one would see us when he would grab me and fuck me hard and rough or slow and sweet. Repo had no standard for how he liked to fuck. He wasn't one of those guys who only had one move, one speed, one preference. He followed the mood and that meant I got not only spoiled by orgasms that threatened to make me dumb, but experience with types of sex other men had never afforded me before.

We still hadn't had sex in a bed.

Two, I sort-of maybe got a little too wrapped up with my little affair to remember why I was at The Henchmen compound in the first place. I still texted and called K. But as the days passed and he heard nothing and I saw nothing, I felt a sense of ease start to settle over me again.

I blamed all the sex.

It got me all hopped up on the endorphins and dopamine.

It gave me a false sense of security.

Yes, false.

On the fourth day after we sort-of unofficially got together, I got called into the kitchen by Reign who had his head stuck in the fridge.

"What do you need, Reign?"

"Food," he said, slamming the door. "Repo usually keeps us stocked. Don't know what the fuck he's been up to." Aside from fucking me nonstop, that was. "Take this," he said, reaching into his pocket for a wad of cash that, judging by the hundred it was wrapped in, made a huge sum of money. "And this," he added, going into a cabinet to grab keys then hand them to me. "That's to the Explorer. You need the trunk room for the bags. And no girly shit. Get the shit you usually find in the fridge."

"Okay. On it."

I didn't even hesitate.

I should have hesitated.

Because K had been very specific about not leaving the compound, especially not alone.

Things had been fine.

I went to the super market. I loaded up on the basic veggies Repo always seemed to like handy as well as: eggs, yogurt, dips, chips, and an obscene amount of meat for dinners. I paid with Reign's money that was all hundreds in that wad. Apparently arms dealing was quite profitable.

I was halfway back to the compound, stuck behind a fender bender for long enough for me to cut the engine to wait it out.

It was then that everything went to hell.

Because out front of Chaz's bar was something I never could have thought to imagine, no matter how much my brain tended to run toward paranoid.

There, baking in the summer heat, was Moose.

I didn't imagine he just hightailed it out of Navesink Bank after his shameful booting, and being insulated at the compound, I had very little cause to ever come across him.

But it wasn't Moose that had me feeling very much like I might ruin the really nice leather interior of Reign's SUV with vomit. It was who he was with.

He was with Viktor.

Viktor who, despite it being close to a hundred degrees outside, was in one of his expensive suits and looked completely unaffected by the heat.

I slipped low into my seat, reaching up to quickly tie up my distinctive purple hair, hoping if they happened to look over that it would be less noticeable if it was pulled back. My heart was slamming hard in my chest, my stomach churning painfully as I fumbled for my burner.

"K.C.E Boxing Emporium," the chipper receptionist said into the phone by the second ring.

"Vermont. Bugging out," I declared, hanging up and wiping my sweaty palms on my pants. She knew what that meant. She would relay it to K.

Bugging out meant getting out. It meant shit hit the fan and I needed to run.

It meant K would have to get on top of figuring out the next move for me.

I felt sick as the cops finally started to wave the line of traffic forward. I turned my head to the side, looking away despite everything in me screaming to keep an eye on them, to see if they noticed me, to see if they were going to follow me. I turned off the main drag that would lead to the compound, hitting the side street that would take me to the train station.

See, that was part of my training too. I learned the streets of Navesink Bank. I studied the maps. I learned where I could escape into to disappear if I was being chased. I found out where the ferry, bus, and train stations were. I memorized the numbers for two cab companies. When I first arrived in Navesink Bank, I was forced to walk, then run the streets with K on the phone, quizzing me on what the next street was, what the cross streets were, until he was convinced I could navigate them even in a life-or-death situation.

So I drove to the train station on mental auto-pilot, parking in the lot, paying the fee, then going over to the automatic ticket machine and getting the first train out that would take me to the station that would, from there, take me to Philly where my bag would be situated. I reached into my pocket, grabbing the burner phone, wiping it clean of prints, smashing it under my boot, then throwing it away.

The burners were dangerous for multiple reasons. One because, despite common misconception, they totally could be zeroed in on if someone found out the number. And two, because of the call log that led back to K.

So for the next two legs of my journey, I would be doing it totally alone.

I had nothing. Literally nothing but the money Reign had given me. I stole a bottle of water out of the trunk and a couple power bars, then locked the car with the keys inside. They would find it. When they came looking for me. I figured I had maybe two hours until that happened.

The twisting in my gut was enough to make me bend forward for a second, sucking in a breath. Repo would worry. He would wonder what it all meant. He would help look for me. What would he think of the SUV parked in the lot at the train station with all the groceries still inside, along with the keys, with the parking fee paid so it wouldn't be towed?

Would he think I had just... willingly walked away?

Would he know better?

I exhaled hard as the train pulled up beside me, willing myself to push those thoughts away, to bury them deep to be dealt with later. It wouldn't help to harp on that. So I boarded the train and I sat down beside a window, watching with a sick rolling sensation inside as I left Navesink Bank behind.

I got off that train two hours later, sitting in an outside train station in an unfamiliar and seedy area because there was some sort of delay with the train that would take me to Philly where I had a bag stashed with money, clothes, new IDs, and a phone to call K.

It was almost nightfall when the train finally chugged into the station, delayed by some sort of problem with the tracks which didn't really inspire confidence as I got aboard, but having very little choice, I did, climbing into a seat beside a woman with two small children as to avoid the group of young men with 'trouble' written all over them.

"I like your hair," the older child, a girl of maybe four with huge brown eyes and endearingly kinky, out-of-control hair, declared.

"Thank you," I said, smiling as she reached up to touch it and wound up yanking it hard. I had started to really like it too. But, just like I had to strip Maisy to become Maze, I figured I'd have to strip Maze to become... whoever else I needed to become at my next stop.

"Hey ladies," one of the guys from the group called and I felt myself jerk upright, shaking off the melancholy that was steadily building.

"Don't look," the woman warned in a firm tone, jiggling her restless son on her knee. "Better off ignoring them. They'll give up and go onto another target."

"Guys can be *such* assholes," the little girl informed me with as much seriousness a four-year old could muster.

"Shayna!" her mother snapped, but only half-heartedly.

"You know what?" I said to Shayna, leaning down.

"What?"

"That's true for a lot of them, but some can be really nice."

"The ones that don't pull your hair," she concluded, nodding with authority before barreling back across to her mother to steal her phone and demand she put on the 'coloring book'.

Her mother looked up at me with a sly smile and shrugged. "Sometimes even the ones who pull your hair can be good too," she added with a wink and I felt myself smile despite the feeling of sinking inside.

I got to the station in Philly another hour and a half later, walking with Sheila, Shayna, and Ray until we were sure the group of creeps were long gone. She gave me a smile. Shayna gave me a wave. Ray gave me nothing because he was finally asleep on his mother's shoulder.

I reached inside my boot, moving the liner aside and reached in for the hidden key as I moved in front of my locker. With a somewhat defeated sigh, I opened the locker and pulled out my bag, taking the whole of it back toward the main station where I could find an outlet to sit and charge my phone for a while so I could call K.

Looking through the contents of my bag, I pulled out a

sweatshirt and slipped it on, pulling the hood up over my hair. There wasn't much inside, not really. And certainly nothing personal. Hell, I didn't even pick any of the clothes out. That was all K, or whoever K farmed those kinds of jobs out to. I ate a power bar and carefully tucked Reign's money into a shoe at the bottom of the bag. I planned to send that back to him when I settled somewhere. K had emptied my bank account when I went to him and the money was moved into another secure account that I could access wherever and whenever I needed to.

I didn't need Reign's money. And, what's more, I really didn't want any of them thinking that I had stolen from them and skipped town. Why, I wasn't sure, seeing as I would never see any of them again. But it mattered. I guess because I had, over my time with them, learned to respect and even like them all individually.

Reign was tough to like at times, coming across cold and detached. But I attributed that to his needing to keep a certain level of distance from his men for them to not see him as an equal, but a leader. Cash was, well, impossible not to like. He was sweet, often funny, and ridiculously in love with his woman just like his brother was with his wife. And Wolf was the one I spent the least amount of time with. And when I did, well, I did most of the conversing. But he was a steady, solid kind of person that you couldn't help but think that you could lean on anytime you needed to and he would never shrug you away.

And Repo...

"Fuck," I hissed at myself, looking down at my feet.

I had a feeling that wound was going to hurt for a while.

But I would move on.

I would be okay.

I hoped.

I called K's office five times, getting the machine. I was under strict instructions not to leave messages. On a sigh, I unplugged the phone and made my way out onto the street: dark, unfamiliar, and therefore scary. I hailed a cab and asked them to take me to a hotel. I got a room under a temporary alias of Daisy because, yet again, it was close to my actual name so my response wouldn't require practice.

The Cranford Inn was a step up from the sleep-and-fuck I had stayed in when first exploring Navesink Bank, but not by much. The tan wallpaper and drapes did match the hideous black and brown comforter, but said wallpaper was peeling in places and the drapes had moth holes, and the comforter looked like it hadn't seen a real thorough cleaning in far too long. Stripping it off the bed, I inspected the sheets that looked and, what's more, *smelled* like they had been in a washing machine in the recent past. The bath and toilet were inside a separate small room with worn tile and bad lighting, but the actual sink and vanity was situated in the main room just inside the door to the hall.

It wasn't anything special, but it was relatively clean and I didn't find any bugs during my inspection.

I reached for the phone and dialed K's cell, but it didn't ring. It went right to the machine, the sound of the robotic voice sending a chill through me. K always answered, always. He had to have gotten my message from his secretary earlier. Unless she hadn't been able to get in touch with him either. What if Viktor or Ruslan had found him? Had found out about him hiding me? It was absolutely a possibility. And while I texted him every day as per our agreement, I didn't get responses back. I didn't expect them. I only talked to him verbally every other day. I had spoken to him the night before. Anything could have happened in that span of time. If Viktor and Ruslan got to him and...

"You need to calm down," I told myself, sitting down on the foot of the bed and thinking about what K had told me once. "If I can't get in touch with K for twenty-four hours, I need to call

Xander Rhodes and ask to speak to his woman, Ellie. If something is wrong, she will help point me in a new direction. I'm not alone." The repeating of the plan always helped, always soothed over the frayed edges.

I kicked out of my boots and curled up in bed, taking a deep breath and watching the city lights through the cracked window dressings.

I tried, and failed, to not think about Repo.

Earlier that morning, I had gotten up to do my shift, walking out into the great room to be snagged around the waist from behind, a hand clamping over my mouth as I was lifted off my feet. I was dragged into the bathroom where Repo turned me and crushed me up against the wall, his lips sealing in the scream I had prepared. And the fear mingled with the desire I always felt around Repo, created a combination that was downright narcotic.

And then I got high off Repo.

There was no other way to explain it.

When we were done and I reached for my clothes, Repo slapped my hands away, taking over the task of dressing me, his fingers lingering over my already overly-sensitive skin in a gentle, but somehow possessive way that made me fight the irrational urge to throw myself into his arms when he was finally done.

"Some day," he said, chucking me under the chin gently with his fist to lighten the suddenly heavy mood between us, "I will be able to take you out and show you off."

There was no denying the little squeezing in my heart at that statement. "Show me off?" I asked with a head shake like he was being ridiculous.

"Hot as shit and you don't even know it," he said, shaking his head right back at me like *I* was the crazy one when anyone with eyes could see he was the real prize between us. But still, it was nice that he thought it was the other way around. Even if that made him mildly delusional. "Get your ass to work, probie," he'd ordered, but his voice was smooth and sexy and he gentled the demand with a long, wet, toe-tingling kiss before pulling the door open and shooing me out.

The night before when I pulled the overnight instead of Duke or Renny, a rare honor that I felt a little proud of landing even though the rational part of me knew I only got it because Repo wanted time alone with me, meaning he would be there to keep an eye as well, he surprised me by bringing me up onto the roof again where he had a small feast set up for us.

When I turned back at him with big eyes, his hands were tucked into his front pockets, his shoulders slumped forward, looking both sheepish and maybe a little insecure. "You're always stuck doing the cooking. Figured it'd be nice for you to be able to eat something you didn't have to make for a change," he'd told me and I'd felt the heart-squeezing thing then too.

Then we sat there and ate the spaghetti and meatballs he made that were infinitely better than the ones I made and I attributed that to the fact that I loathed cooking so all that negativity seeped into my food. Repo seemed to, if not genuinely enjoy it, not mind the task. It showed in the end product. He gave me beers until I felt a shade more than tipsy then he'd taken me on the roof, starting soft and sweet and ending up fucking me just short of violent, under the black sky and bright moon.

Hell, even that very afternoon, before being sent off on some top-secret errand, he had caught me alone in the basement, coming up behind me and rubbing my shoulders while he whispered in my ear all the filthy things he had planned to do with me that next morning while I was 'working'.

I closed my eyes tight, deep-breathing through the sting in my chest at the realization that I would never get to experience those things with him, that I would never know his casual touch, or his dirty words, or his sweet ones, or see his dancing eyes or his boyish smile again.

I listened to the sounds around me for a long while: the horns on the street, the doors in the hall opening and closing, the muffled sound of a game show in the room to my left and a porn in the room to my right, the clock ticking above my own TV set, informing me it was barely nine at night. But every ounce of my tired body and achy heart told me that sometimes, all there was to do was sleep.

--

I woke up disoriented the next day, my heart slamming so hard in my chest that I felt it up my throat. I shot up in the unfamiliar bed in the unfamiliar room, my sleep-foggy brain taking an embarrassingly long time to remember where I was.

In Philly.

In a cheap hotel.

Because Viktor was meeting with Moose.

Moose who knew exactly where I was and the best ways to get into the compound.

Right then, I felt panic seize my system.

*Moose knew the best ways to get into the compound.*

I should have... warned them somehow.

There was no real good reason not to.

It didn't matter if I blew my cover; I was long gone.

If something happened to any of them, especially Repo or Duke or, hell, even Renny, I'd never forgive myself.

I took a deep, steadying breath, reminding myself they were grown men. Not only were they grown men but they were highly trained and criminals. They knew how to look out for trouble and they knew how to handle it when it popped up too. Besides, Viktor against the whole of The Henchmen MC? Yeah, the odds were definitely in their favor.

Hell, Repo could probably get a literal bullseye shot on him from a hundred yards off before he even penetrated the perimeter.

At his name, the stinging sensation shot through my chest again, sharp and shocking enough for me to raise my palm to the left side and rub across my heart.

"K would kill me himself if he saw me right now," I grumbled to myself.

Then I shot off the bed, heart slamming for a whole other reason at the thought of K and how he hadn't responded the night before.

My eyes flew to the clock on the wall and I got another wave of panic. It wasn't morning. I was expecting it was eight or nine in the morning. But it wasn't. Oh, no. All the weeks of near-sleeplessness at the compound must have finally caught up with me because I went to sleep before nine and slept clear through to one in the afternoon.

*One in the afternoon.*

When I was supposed to text K before noon each day.

Shit.

Shitshitshit.

I scrambled across the room to the small, seemingly mandatory mini-desk all hotel rooms possess and grabbed for the burner.

K.
I needed to get in touch with K.

# FIFTEEN

*Repo*

"You guys seen Maze?" Reign asked, walking in from the kitchen.

I looked around at Duke and Renny, wondering the same thing myself. I had expected to see her when I got back, but she was nowhere around.

"Nah," Renny said, shaking his head.

"I sent her out for food hours ago," Reign said, brows drawn together.

"How many hours..." I started when Cash walked in through the front door.

"Bro, what's the Explorer doing at the train station?" he asked, moving over toward the bar to get a beer out of the fridge.

Reign froze and I felt myself doing the same. "The Explorer is at the train station?" he repeated, making Cash straighten, putting his beer down on the bar.

"So... it shouldn't be there?" he asked, sounding suddenly

more serious.

"Sure as fuck shouldn't," Reign said and I was already on my way toward the door.

Reign was quickly on my heels, calling over his shoulder to the probies, "Call if Maze shows up." We both got on our bikes and Reign turned toward me. "You're with them the most. How much do you trust Maze?"

"More than Renny, about the same as Duke," I said honestly as I tried to talk myself out of the uncharacteristic panic that was gripping my system.

With that, he tore off down the road and I followed behind, a lump the size of fucking Texas in my throat. The train station was a short five minute drive. We made it in three. The lot was packed and it took us a few to locate Reign's SUV. When we did, the ticket on the window said it was paid up for another couple of hours. Reign fished the spare key out of his bike, unlocking the door where we were assaulted by the smell of all the food left inside the trunk to bake in the heat for God-knew how long.

"The keys were locked inside here," Reign said, coming out of the front seat with said keys. "The fuck is going on?"

"She bought groceries then... paid for parking and left?" I asked, and even I could hear the slightest trace of worry in my tone.

"What do we know about Maze, Repo?" he asked, watching me move away from the truck to stand by my bike.

"Not much. A small work history. That was kind-of all we got."

"No record?"

"Nothing."

"No connections to any organization?"

"Fucking nothing, Reign," I snapped, immediately closing my eyes at my tone. I needed to get it together. I couldn't lose it. I couldn't talk to him like that.

"Alright, Repo," he said, his tone oddly calm. "I figured you weren't just making googly eyes at her," he said, shaking his head a little. "You guys got something going on?"

"Reign I know you said..."

"Fuck it," he said with a casual shrug. "Doesn't matter. What matters is you know her better than the rest of us. She said anything about old connections?"

"No, Reign. She's... quiet about her past."

"Shit," he said, slamming the door to the Explorer. "Now we gotta figure out if she ran because she was in trouble or ran because something is about to come down on us."

"I told her she wasn't gonna get a patch, Reign. I don't think she'd stick it out if this was some covert shit when I told her there was no chance to actually get in the ranks."

"So you think she ran because of trouble?"

"I don't know what the fuck to think," I admitted, raking a hand down my face. "She didn't act like someone in trouble."

"Yeah, but you told me yourself that she had some kind of training. And she was living behind a gate with a group of men who run guns. If there was anywhere she probably felt safe, it was in the compound."

"Yeah."

"Nothing else really makes sense at this point. This was the first time since she showed up that she went outside the compound alone. Maybe she ran into someone or saw someone, got spooked and ran. Otherwise, she'd take the fucking car, not park it in a lot, pay for parking, and take a train."

He had a good point. "Did she seem freaked when you asked her to get food?"

"No. She didn't even hesitate. I told her to get the shit you usually get, gave her cash, gave her keys, and she headed out." He was quiet as he got back on his bike. "Was she close with the other probies? Would they know more than you?"

"I dunno. They were competition, y'know? She hated Moose and Fox but seemed to get along with Duke and was friendly with Renny."

"But if they knew something they thought we should know about her past, they probably would have told us."

"Exactly. Especially Duke." Renny might too, but not until he got every single goddamn detail he could. He was anal as fuck about things like that. But I guess when you had the fucked up childhood like he did, that shit made sense.

"Alright, let's get back to the compound and make sure. Doubt either would lie right to our faces to protect her when she's already gone. And gotta get one of the guys over here to deal with that mess," he said, waving a hand toward the SUV.

With that, we headed back to the compound.

Reign was as calmly in control as ever while I freaked out.

What if he was right? What if she ran? What if she had been running all along? What did that mean that she kept that kind of shit from me? Not to be a chick about it, but that was kind of screwed up that she hadn't trusted me with that. But, if I were being honest with myself, she shared very little with me. There had been little things here and there, usually after sex when we were just sitting with our own thoughts. She'd been facing away from me, watching the tree line, her back to my chest, when she admitted that her mom was locked up for some social security shit. It didn't sound much like a wound, but I hadn't been able to suss out if that was because she was trying to convince herself it didn't hurt or if it genuinely didn't.

Then when handing me tools one afternoon and I had commented on how much she knew about them, she'd laughed humorlessly and shook her head. "I dated a guy once who I thought was a mechanic."

"Thought?" I asked, turning my head from under the hood of the car to look at her.

"Yeah... he actually ran a chop shop. It was a bit of an ugly surprise when the cops informed me of that. But, before then, I had spent some time around the so-called mechanics and they taught me some stuff. They said it was important for people to know at least a little bit about how to take care of a car. They'd actually been pretty nice guys. Who'da thunk they'd be big criminals?"

"Honey..." I said, giving her a smile.

"What?"

"I'm a fucking one-percenter here..."

"Oh, ha," she'd said, shaking her head at herself like she had genuinely forgotten how The Henchmen made their money. "Yeah, I guess. I must just... have a thing for the bad boys then."

"So he never told you he wasn't working above-board?" I'd asked. "He got you wrapped up in his shit without you knowing what you were getting wrapped up in?" She'd shrugged, nodding. "Dick."

"Well, I mean. I can't be considered faultless there. I was naive."

"You liked the guy. You trusted him to be honest."

"Yeah, therein lied my mistake."

There was a kind of sadness in her tone that I didn't like, like she had convinced herself that trust was some kind of fault instead of a virtue. Only a real asshole made a woman feel that way. "Hey," I'd said, dropping the wrench I was holding and turning to look at her fully. "You can't just assume that everyone you meet is trying to fuck you over. You trusted, you had that shit thrown in your face. But that's on him, not you. You didn't do anything wrong."

"I don't think everyone is trying to fuck me over," she'd objected, but only half-heartedly. "It's just... it's easier to make people prove they are trustworthy than just... automatically trust them without question."

"That's a pretty cynical way to live, Maze."

"Do you just... trust people?"

"I trust my brothers here. That's all I got."

"Even after the people who you and your uncle saw as brothers screwed you guys over?" she'd asked bluntly, surprising me. It was a topic I expected her to pussyfoot around like everyone else did. I appreciated that she didn't.

"They were disloyal. The men here, they've proved time and time again that brotherhood and the old ladies and the kids, they're more important than anything else."

"But did you trust them immediately when you came here?" At my sigh, she'd smiled. "So this is a 'do as I say, not as I do' kinda thing?"

"Maybe it's a 'because I fucking said so' thing."

"Oh, you think you can boss me around, huh?" she'd asked, head tilted, eyes challenging.

"Think I've done a pretty good job of that so far, don't you? Now why don't you be a good girl and hand me that ultra short gear wrench?" I'd asked, ducking under the hood again.

It didn't surprise me in the least when the goddamn thing went sailing past my head, landing with a loud clank against the engine.

Nor did it surprise me that as I reached for it, I was smiling.

But that was the most she had ever really given me all at once. She hinted at other things, she gave me bits and pieces. She hated cologne. She liked watching documentaries. She once broke her leg in three places falling out of those trees she liked to hide in. And, apparently, she maneuvered crutches the way a newborn foal maneuvered their legs, meaning not well at all and with a lot of falling.

We parked the bikes outside the fence and Reign threw the keys at two of the guys standing around. "You two go to the train station. The Explorer is there. Clean it out and get it back here," he instructed, moving across the yard toward the door to a waiting Cash. "She paid for parking with a car full of groceries," he said, shaking his head.

"Well shit," Cash said, sighing.

"Renny, Duke, get your asses out here," Reign called into the door and all of ten seconds later, both men moved outside. "We need to know what you know about Maze that we might not."

"Is Ace alright?" was Duke's immediate question and I was reminded again why I was happy to have him on the team. He didn't immediately condemn Maze. And his knee-jerk reaction was to ask after her well-being.

"Fuck if we know. She's gone," Reign said, his tone a little dismissive, but his shoulders were tense.

"Gone?" Duke repeated, brows drawn together. "No fucking way. She wanted this more than the whole lot of us. And I can't speak for Renny or the recently excommunicated Moose and Fox, but I want this a whole fuckuva lot."

"That's why we're here. We need to know what you guys know. You live with her. You sleep near her. If anyone aside... aside from Repo," he said, giving me a brow raise and a smirk that any idiot could decipher, "it's you guys. What do you got?"

"She's got a sister," Renny supplied, making me start.

"What?" I barked before I could stop myself. She'd never said shit about a sister.

"Yeah," Renny shrugged. "She called her a fuckton of times the night of the BBQ. Apparently there was some issue with the sister's fiance cheating or some shit. She lives in the City."

Reign turned to me with a shrug. "Maybe her sister

needed her?"

"So she just left groceries to rot in your truck at a train station?" I shot back, dubiously.

"I dunno. Bitches can be weird like that when the other needs her. Remember Lo when Summer went into labor?"

I felt my lips quirk up despite the pit in my stomach. I remembered that shit alright. Me and Cash had been in the waiting room of the hospital, Reign giving us a short update when Lo walked in with two rifles crossed over her back, completely oblivious to the fact that they were even there despite the worried looks all the nurses were giving her, until Cash walked over and removed them for her. Hell, Janie had showed up half an hour after that with Alex in toe, Janie bleeding profusely from her nose and Alex's lip swollen from, presumably, grappling practice.

He was right, women seemed to quite literally drop everything when another was in trouble.

"Alright. So this sister..." Reign started, "is there any way for us to get in contact with..."

The rest of his sentence drifted off when all of our attention went to the open gates where a behemoth black SUV with black-out windows came barreling to a stop, the engine barely getting a chance to cut off before the door was thrown open and a man jumped out.

"Who the fuck..." Reign started, reaching for the gun in the waistband in his jeans, me and Cash doing the same. Renny's hands curled into fists and Duke went for his knife.

The man was tall and black with a distinct boxer's build that he had dressed in slate gray slacks with a thin black plaid pattern and a black dress shirt, tucked in, black loafers and an expensive silver watch. It was a fucking ridiculous outfit given the heat, but he didn't even seem to be sweating.

It was Renny who spoke next as the man stopped

advancing, jerking his chin up at our raised guns like they didn't intimidate him.

"She fucking lied to me!" he declared, sounding genuinely offended.

"The fuck you talking about?" Reign asked, not taking his eyes off the stranger.

"Maze. She lied to me about her sister. That number that was calling her? It was K.C.E Boxing Emporium."

"Start making some fucking sense or shut the fuck up," Reign demanded.

"She said her sister worked there when I grilled her about it. She lied."

"How the fuck do you know that, kid?" Cash asked.

"Because the guy who runs K.C.E Boxing Emporium is standing..."

"Right here," the man said in a deep, smooth voice. "Now lower the fucking guns and tell me where the fuck Maisy is."

Maisy?

*Maisy?*

# SIXTEEN

*Repo*

I was the first to drop my gun. Mainly out of surprise.

"Who the fuck are you?"

"K."

Reign and Cash lowered their guns in unison. "K?" Cash asked. "As in *the* K and his *disappearing women?*"

"That'd be me."

K and his disappearing women.

His fucking disappearing women.

Jesus Christ.

"Hey, he was ready to send his woman to you a coupla years back," Cash supplied, nodding his head toward his brother.

"That's great. Where the fuck is Maisy?" he asked, looking directly at me for some reason.

"She's gone," I said, shaking my head. "And that's all you're gonna fucking get until you explain yourself to us."

"Repo," he said, nodding at me. "I fucking knew she had

something going on with you."

"You sent her here, didn't you?" Reign asked.

"Did you assholes have to give her such a hard time?" K shot back, shaking his head at us.

"Alright, let's move this inside. It's hot as balls out here," Cash announced, holding the door open.

With that, everyone turned and headed into the clubhouse.

"Explain," Reign demanded, crossing his arms over his chest and leaning against the wall inside the door.

"Got a call from Maisy about four hours ago. She checked in with my receptionist and said she was bugging out. That's a serious call. It means the shit hit the fan in a big way and she had to run. She's instructed to toss the phone and board a train to Philly where she was to call me immediately after getting her bug-out bag. That should have happened almost two hours ago."

The shit hit the fan.

And it was serious.

"Who is she running from?" Reign was calm enough to ask while my fucking brain felt like it was swirling.

"The Kozlov brothers."

"Who the fuck are the Kozlov brothers?" I asked, the name meaning absolutely nothing to me.

"They arrange Green Card sort-of marriages, but a bit more murky than that. Maisy worked as their book keeper for years without knowing who they were or what they were up to."

Jesus Christ.

She couldn't get a break.

The mom with the social security fraud.

The ex with the chop shop.

Then the bosses with the trafficking?

No fucking wonder she had trust issues.

"Until..."

"Until she realized they were laundering money through their legit businesses. She took the info to the cops who couldn't and wouldn't do shit. They pushed her in my direction."

"How long did you have her?" Reign asked.

"Six months." He gave us an almost wistful smile. "The Maze you know was nothing like the soft little blonde that literally came crashing into my life six months ago."

So she was a blonde. That was also news.

Obviously I knew she wasn't fucking naturally purple-haired, but she had dark brows and, well, no carpeting so there was no other way for me to tell.

I couldn't picture her blonde. It didn't seem to suit her.

But then again, I guess I didn't fucking know her at all.

"Why us?" Reign asked, shaking his head.

"You're safe. You're a very insulated group. You hate the fucking Russians and wouldn't be too receptive to a couple of them sniffing around at all, let alone after one of your members. If you patched her in, you'd protect her."

"So you were just going to plant her here?" Reign asked, brows together. "Indefinitely? Just play-acting at being someone she wasn't for, what, the rest of her fucking life?"

"Better pretending to like riding that bike she used to curse seven ways to fucking Sunday than end up garroted in some alley somewhere, don't you think?"

"They're that dangerous?" Reign asked. "'Cause I gotta be honest, I ain't ever heard shit about them."

"Yeah, well from what I hear you're pretty happy with your arms dealing. You're not looking into selling poor Russian girls to the highest bidders. There's no reason you would know about them. They're a city problem anyway. They don't cross the border."

I was still rather caught up on the image that got conjured at the phrase *garroted in some alley somewhere* to pay them much attention.

"Why do they want her so bad? She didn't fuck them over with the cops."

"She had a copy of the files she gave to the cops."

"I'm assuming you have those copies."

"Yeah. But only until I find some cops I trust to hand it all off to to bring them down. The Russians are always a brutal lot though. They'll kill someone just for stepping on their shoes. So her trying to stab them in the back? They aren't going to let that go. And then a coupla days ago, they closed shop. Their offices are gone. Their legit businesses are still operating but they aren't present. So I don't know what the fuck is going on at this point. And I don't like that one fucking bit."

"Alright," Reign said, uncrossing his arms. "I sent Maze to go food shopping a couple of hours ago. When I noticed she still wasn't back, I started to ask around. Then Cash said he saw my truck at the train station. We went. The trunk was full of festering groceries. She paid for fucking parking for hours and she locked the keys inside. That's all we got."

K nodded then looked to me, brow raised. "You're sleeping with her. You got anything to add?"

I could feel everyone's eyes fall on me. Reign was just looking. Cash was grinning. Renny didn't look surprised. Duke had his brows drawn together, but I had fuck-all any idea why. "I got nothing, man. You trained her well. She didn't let any of that shit slip. All I really know about her is the ex with the chop shop thing and the mom thing and that she has trust issues. Guess now I know why."

"She told you about Thato and her mom?" K asked, looking surprised.

"Thato?" I repeated, almost laughing. Fucking bitch-ass name for a bitch-ass man. "If that's the ex's name, yeah. Why?"

"Because she knew better. She wasn't supposed to tell

anyone anything about her past."

"Yeah well, she's human. She screwed up," I growled, shoving away from the rest of them and making my way toward the door. Where I found my arm snagged in a strong grip. I turned, looking over at K. "Get your fucking hand off me, man."

"Where are you going?"

"We aren't doing any good standing around here bullshitting. I'm heading to Philly."

"Repo..." Reign said in a warning voice that I knew him well enough to read into. He was telling me I didn't have permission to go. And yeah, well, fuck him.

"Be smart," K cut in before I could really fuck myself by tearing into Reign. "We can't go to Philly until we're sure she's not still around here. What the fuck were you gonna do? Walk every street? Talk to every person? Focus."

He was right.

"Janie and Alex," I said, turning back to the group. "Get them on the cameras at the train station."

"Repo..." Reign said in that voice again.

"Don't you fucking dare try to tell me this is any goddamn different than what you did with Summer and Cash with Lo and Wolf with Janie. You all broke rules when your women were in trouble and I don't want to hear a fucking word about this," I said, I think momentarily shocking them all silent before Reign nodded slightly.

"She's yours?" he asked.

"Hell fucking yeah, she's mine." It didn't matter that she'd kept so much from me. It didn't matter that there was so much to her that I was in the dark about. What mattered was the connection we had despite all the secrecy. She melted against me when I reached for her. She sparked when I touched her. She smiled and laughed and bitched and joked with me. She couldn't fake those things. That was real. What we had, however little it was, was real.

"Alright, Cash see if you can get in touch with Breaker and get Alex on this. I'll call Wolf and see if Janie is at the cabin or Hailstorm. Duke, Renny..." he trailed off for a minute. "I dunno. Make yourselves useful. Go ask around in town or something."

"What? Am I supposed to sit on my fucking hands?" I asked, my hands clenching up into fists at my sides.

"You and K can have a talk until we have a direction we can point you in."

With that, the room cleared out, leaving just me and K and the weight of worry between us. It wasn't lost on me that the two people who genuinely gave a shit about Maze were the ones left twiddling their damn thumbs.

"Don't know much about you," K said, breaking the tense silence, "but I doubt you deserve her."

"Why? Because I'm a biker?"

"Because after what she's had to deal with, I don't think anyone does."

"I respect what you've done to get and keep her safe, but fuck off. Just because some asshole lied to her and her mom was a deadbeat and her bosses were dickheads doesn't mean everyone she crosses paths with plans to screw her over. I've had nothing but good intentions with regard to Maze."

"Except to make her life hell to get her out of the MC."

"You think I'd have done that if I knew fuck-all about her situation?"

"You think she'd have gotten in if she was upfront from the jump?"

"No, but maybe..."

"Hey, man. Don't go on an ego trip. Just 'cause you made her come a couple of times doesn't mean shit. Your dick ain't some magic remedy for her trust issues."

"You didn't exactly help those issues by..."

"Listen, she can trust *me.* I was the one who was there for her when no one else was. I kept her safe. I trained her. I got her strong. If, by doing that, I helped enforce her distrust of everyone, well, it was fucking necessary. But it didn't matter because she knew she always had me."

"That's a little short-sighted, don't you think? Maze is young. She's fucking beautiful. She's a combination of sweet and sour that anyone with a cock would want to get a taste of. Did you really think she was going to be a fucking nun? Especially here?" I paused, shaking my head. "Maybe you should have taught her how to spot a decent man instead."

To that, K's lips quirked up on the side slightly. "Didn't I though?"

"What?"

K shrugged. "All these men here... a couple of other probates she was around all the time, was on the same level with, could have more easily connected with without risking her position here. But she chose you. And, judging by your reaction to all this, I'd say she did spot a decent man."

"Janie is pulling up the cameras now," Reign declared as he walked back in. "She's on her way in. Alex is working on seeing if she can find any records for the Kozlov brothers in Navesink Bank or Jersey in general."

"Alright," I said, taking a deep breath. I turned to K again. "How long you been doing this?"

"Ten years. Give or take."

"How many women have you worked with?"

"Dozens. At least fifty."

"How many have you lost?"

"You mean while permanently on my watch, not going rogue?"

"Would Maze go rogue?"

"No."

"Then yeah."

"One," he said, his tone an odd mix of sad and almost... determined. There was a long pause as we listened to a car door slam. "I'm not losing Maze," he added with the same determination.

"Alright," Janie said, bursting through the door with an open laptop on her hand, Wolf walking in behind her. "I got her pulling into the train station. Well, fucking barreling in is probably more accurate. She pulled in, sat there for a couple of seconds then walked up to the machine and paid for parking. She locked the keys in the car. She went and bought a ticket to somewhere..."

"Philly," K supplied.

"If you say so."

"No train out of here goes straight to Philly," Reign supplied. "She'd have had to switch trains somewhere."

"Regardless," Janie rushed on, "that's what she did. She went to the platform and waited. She actually kinda doubled over for a second at one point," she supplied, hitting a button then turning the screen toward us to show the moment she was talking about. The angle was from the front and a little grainy but I swore I could see genuine anguish there. "Then that's it here obviously. I'm working on finding where that train led. We can get footage from there. I doubt anything happened to her from here to there... seeing as she would have been on the train. No way could someone pull her off of that without a major scene."

I nodded, silently agreeing, but finding no comfort in the words.

For the next ten minutes, there was nothing. Janie worked, metal blaring from her speakers and she barked out an order for coffee which I fetched just to have something to do. When I came back with it and sat down beside Janie, one of her hands landed on my knee and squeezed. "Haven't heard from you after midnight in weeks, Repo," she said, the words cryptic to anyone else in the room except maybe Wolf. But it meant a lot to us. When she was in a good spell sleep-wise, sweet-dreams-wise, I didn't hear from her after midnight. I knew that had something to do with Wolf. So when I didn't call her for weeks on end, she knew it had something to do with Maze. While, I generally hadn't been actually sleeping any better than usual, I had other things to focus on so I didn't have to call Janie.

I had Maze.

Janie knew how much that helped.

She felt the same way about Wolf.

I was choosing not to analyze what that might possibly mean.

There would be time for that when I knew Maze was safe.

The door flew open and Renny stormed in, his face closed down, his fists clenched. I had already stood and so had K, sensing something off. And then in walked Duke, his hand wrapped around the back of Moose's neck.

"Guess who made friends with a couple of fucking Russians?" Duke asked, tossing Moose a couple of feet into the room where he crashed into the new coffee table we replaced after Duke and Renny had ruined the first one with their fight the night before the BBQ.

Moose went to push himself up, but found his palm pinned to the table by one of Janie's massive combat boots. "Oh, I don't think so mother fucker," she said, smiling as Wolf reached out and hauled him up.

"Get the fuck off me. It's none of your business who the fuck I talk to. I don't belong to you."

"Forget one thing," Reign said, moving across the room. "Maze does still belong to this MC. At least until I decide otherwise. So you fuck with her and her safety and you fuck with us and our safety. So it's in your best goddamn interest to spill what you know or I'll let those two," he said, waving a hand toward me and K, "take your ass downstairs where no one will hear you scream and rip you to fucking shreds. We clear?"

"Oh, you can talk all big and bad. I was here for six fucking months. You ain't did shit that was the least bit fucking intimidating."

Oh, fuck.

That was the wrong damn thing to say to Reign.

See, Reign didn't need to use his fists often. He wasn't his father. He didn't need to command respect with violence, he did it with fear. Because those of us who had ever seen him in action, with a gun, with a knife, with his bare hands, yeah, we knew he was not someone you tested. And Moose was testing him.

Reign was going to pass.

And Moose would be lucky to be eating through a straw.

I wasn't gonna lie. I was itching to see that mother fucker bleed.

He'd sold out Maze.

He was why she had to run away.

He was why she was currently fucking missing.

"But this isn't my fight," Reign surprised me by saying, waving a hand toward me. "You remember Repo, right? See what you fucks don't know about Repo is he kind of gets a little... psychotic when something threatens his ideas on loyalty. You and your brother, you made an agreement when you prospected that club business was club business and you were never to speak of it. See, now you've spoken of it. To the fucking *Russians* no less. I think that might make Repo a little angry. But, see, what's got him over there with that muscle ticking in his jaw and his hands clenched down by his sides... yeah, that's the fact that Maze is his woman. And you might have just gotten her killed."

If I hadn't been so livid and so bone-deep terrified that something had, indeed, happened to Maze, I might have found the look on his face comical. His eyes went a little wide; his lips parted; his hands went up in front of him in a defensive gesture.

"I didn't know she was yours," he objected immediately.

"Well it's too fucking bad for you that I don't give a fuck about what you knew."

And with that, a darkness I hadn't known in the better part of ten years overtook me, bubbled up inside until it was a bigger part of me than my common sense, my need for self-preservation, my desire to not have any more nightmares to keep me awake at night.

Wolf released Moose.

I released whatever it was inside that kept me sane.

And Moose got to see just how intimi-fucking-dating members of The Henchmen MC could really be.

"We need him capable of speech," K's voice boomed behind me, grabbing me at both my arms and dragging me away from a beaten, bloody, awful version of Moose.

I let myself be pulled backward, looking down at my hands, knuckles broken open from Moose's teeth. I sighed, flexing my fingers to make sure none were broken.

"Get him up," Reign demanded to Duke who had moved to block the door. He reached down, hauling a hissing, spitting Moose off the ground. "Now you're going to tell us exactly what fucking happened with the Russians or you'll be another in Repo's body count."

"They had a fucking picture," Moose almost yelled, wiping blood from his upper lip. "She was blonde, but there was no mistaking her. They'd asked if anyone had seen someone around like her. Said they knew she had been staying at the motel nearby."

"And?" K asked as if sensing he was holding back.

"And then I told him she was here but he got a call."

"Saying?"

"He didn't say much, okay?" Moose exploded, shrinking away from K who had advanced threateningly. "Something about Trenton."

Reign's head nod caught my attention. "Trains don't go to Philly from here," he said, reiterating what he'd said earlier. "She'd have had a transfer. Likely in Trenton."

"On it," Janie said, already sounding distracted as she grabbed her laptop. "Hey, Al," she said to her computer, presumably some kind of video chat with Alex. "Trenton."

"On it," Alex repeated.

"Was it Viktor or Ruslan you talked to?"

"Fuck... I don't know, man..."

"Suit or casual?" K asked.

"Suit."

K nodded and looked at me. "Viktor."

"Is that a good or bad thing?" I asked.

"They're both killers," K said, not comforting me in the least. "But Viktor is a cold son of a bitch. Ruslan is a bit more laid back. And they aren't going to suspect she's as trained as she is. They'll expect her to be the meek office mouse she was before who had a little crush on Ruslan. It might work to her advantage if he's the one who is closer to finding her, if that is the case."

"So we're heading to Philly after all," I concluded, annoyed that we had wasted time.

"Alex found her in Trenton. She got off the train from here and then was stranded there forever. There was some kind of fucking track issue. She's on the camera here, looking a little paranoid, but not super freaked. She got on the train to, I presume, Philly from there."

"She must not have thought she was followed," K

concluded. "Maybe she saw Viktor when she was driving back from the food store and put the plan into motion like she knew she was supposed to. She didn't check in because she was trapped and didn't have her burner. Did you girls pick her up in Philly yet?"

"Working on it, but don't get your hopes up. Thirtieth Street Station gets crazy busy. She could easily get lost in the crowd."

"Did you have a plan for where she was supposed to go when she got there?"

"Yeah, she's supposed to go to her locker to get her bag to call me. Then I was supposed to point her in a direction. I wasn't going to keep her in Philly for more than a night and only a night if she was too tired to hop another train."

"The fuck you guys still here for?" Reign asked suddenly, making me start. "Go get your woman, make sure she's safe. We'll talk when you figure shit out. Here," he said, going behind the bar and grabbing a couple of guns.

K hesitated, shaking his head. "I prefer..."

"Take the fucking guns," Reign demanded and K reached for one. I reached for the other two. Then we took off toward the door.

"I'll keep you updated," Janie called. "Keep your phone charged."

We jumped into K's giant SUV and hit the road, K checking his phone as soon as he turned the car around and blinked to turn out onto the main drag. "What the fuck..."

"What?" I asked, stiffening. We really couldn't afford any more bad news.

"My fucking phone is fried..."

"Fried?" I repeated, reaching for it as he tried to fuck around with it and drive at the same time.

"Left it on the fucking charger in the fucking car in this

fucking heat," he growled, slamming his palm down on the wheel.

Fuck.

"She can still contact your office though," I said, reaching for my cell. "Call them and tell them to give her this number."

Then, plan in motion, we drove to Philly.

It wasn't a long drive. It took us somewhere around two hours, having to abide traffic laws lest we be pulled over with a bunch of illegal guns on us.

"Where the fuck do we even start?" I asked, looking around as we climbed out of the SUV on the street by the station.

"First, I'm making sure she got her bag. Then... fuck if I know. I know what her alias is here, but hotels won't give out information on guests. She's not familiar with this area so it's not like she'd have known where to go from experience."

Turns out, she had gotten her bag.

And when Janie called with an update later that night, she'd caught sight of Maze leaving the station and getting in a cab. She got the plates then sent us toward the cab company headquarters which was locked for the night. Of fucking course. Without anything else to do, we got food and coffee and waited until fucking nine A.M when they'd reopened. Then we had to wait another hour for the boss to show up, leaving us with a skittish secretary who looked at us like we were constantly on the verge of jumping her. When he eventually arrived we'd tried to bribe the information out of the owner, who refused. Then, well, I got to witness K's considerable boxing skills for the next half hour before we finally got the name of the driver. Then we'd had to wait a-fucking-gain for the driver to be called in from his job. He was much more forthcoming with information, likely due to the punching bag that was his boss' face.

He'd dropped her off, safe and sound, and a little sad-looking (his words) at The Cranford Inn the night before.

A little more hopeful, we made our way there. Bribing worked immediately to the man at the front desk of the inn and, a little after one-thirty the afternoon after she went missing, we made our way down the long hallway to the room she had booked.

K knocked and called her.

I knocked and called her.

Then, stomach churning painfully, I reached for the key the guy at the desk had been all-too happy to hand over. The door beeped and opened and we stepped in.

To an empty fucking room.

But it wasn't just an empty fucking room.

Her shit was still there.

And there had been some kind of fight judging by the mess and broken items thrown around.

"Fuck," I shouted, slamming my fist into the wall beside the bed, feeling all hope drain away.

I looked to K, hoping to see something there, some hope or plan or something.

But all I saw there was devastation and a hint of determination.

# SEVENTEEN

*Maze*

When I still hadn't been able to get in touch with K, I felt sick to my stomach. I didn't want to have to make the call to Xander. I didn't want to focus on the realization that something really awful must have happened to him if he was leaving me completely on my own.

I went over to the sink and rinsed my face with cold water, trying to focus, trying to calm myself down. That stinging in my chest hadn't gotten better with sleep. If anything, it felt amplified, like it was trying to overtake my entire chest cavity.

Stomach growling, I grabbed my knife and slipped into my boots and went to the door to see about grabbing lunch. There was a bagel shop next to the hotel. I could sneak in and out and no one would pay me any mind. Then when I got back, I promised myself that I would call Xander and get in touch with Ellie.

When I pulled the handle for the door, I hadn't expected

it to be pushed violently forward, catching me off-guard and sending me flying backward, tripping over my bag and sending the contents scattering around the room and sending me flying onto the bed.

"Kotyonok," Ruslan's deep, rough, sexy voice greeted me, sounding almost amused. "I had no idea you wanted me that bad."

And all I could think right then was: no, nope, hell to the fucking no.

I'd been through enough.

There was no way I was going to get assaulted by my former employer on top of it all.

I rolled off the bed onto my feet, reaching for my knife as Ruslan moved inward and closed the door with a quiet click.

He looked as good as ever. Still handsome. I don't know. I guess I had figured that knowing what he did for a living and knowing he was a garrote-wielding killer would somehow take away his good looks to my more keen eyes. But that wasn't the case. He was still tall and broad with his great bone structure, deep eyes, easy smile, and strong body wrapped in his usual jeans that he had paired with a simple v-neck white tee.

"No need for the knife, Maisy," he said, holding out his hands wide as if he meant me no harm.

Unfortunately for him, I was through blindly trusting anyone.

"Sure there's not," I said, trying to find an escape. He was approaching me in the only walking space. My only choice was to climb across the bed. Making my decision, I flew at it again before he could get any closer to me.

I got, say, in the center before his hands snagged my ankles and pulled my feet out from under me. I flew backward, my stomach dropping out as my back slammed against the mattress. I had barely landed before Ruslan was on me, straddling me at the waist, his hands slamming down on my wrists and pinning them to the bed.

"Relax, kotyonok. I'm not going to hurt you."

"Is that a garrote in your pocket or are you planning to rape me?" I spat, feeling his unmistakable hard-on, trying to plant my feet and buck upward like K had taught me. But the mattress was too soft and I couldn't get the footing I needed.

"Maisy," he said, shaking his head. "You think I'd do that?"

"I didn't think you'd *sell women,* Ruslan. I was wrong about that so I don't know what to believe anymore."

He sighed, making some kind of ticking sound with his tongue as he released my wrist so he could wrestle my knife away. He took it, throwing it toward the wall where it hit and landed with a clatter that filled me with hopelessness.

"I sell no one," he said, his voice harsh.

"Oh, bullshit. I'm not stupid and I..."

"Viktor."

"Don't insult me," I shot back. "You're not innocent, Rus."

"Innocent, no. But I don't lie to poor women in the homeland and promise them handsome, rich men who will treat them like gold. That is Viktor. You know him. You've seen him with women. He's cold. He's... he's..." Ruslan's face scrunched up slightly, struggling for the right phrase. "He's soulless."

"And yet you went along with it."

"Past. That's the past, kotyonok."

"I'm not your *kitten,*" I snapped.

"No, but you wanted to be. Don't try to deny it."

"I'm not denying it. I'm claiming temporary insanity."

To that, he sat back on my pelvis, releasing my wrists and letting out a deep chuckle. "Was this spirit always under there?" he asked, shaking his head, but he was smiling like he enjoyed it.

"Are you planning on killing me or what?"

"My job was not to kill you. I am to retrieve you so Viktor can find where the files are. He says you're too smart to have only made one copy. He had a lot of respect for you until you betrayed him."

Huh.

That was news.

I always felt like an ant under his shoe.

He'd certainly never made it sound like he was pleased by me, let alone respected me in any way.

"So we're still here, why?"

"Because I know what Vik will do when he gets the information he wants."

"He'll kill me."

"That," he said with a casual nod, then looked away for a moment. When he looked back, he seemed sad. "Maybe. But Vik is nothing if not an opportunist."

"Opportunist?" I croaked, already knowing to dread the meaning there.

"You're young, Maisy. You're beautiful. Vik makes a fortune on young beautiful women."

"I'd never do that willingly," I objected, shaking my head.

Rus leaned forward slightly, tucking a strand of hair behind my ear. "There are men who will pay more for women who *aren't* willing."

I closed my eyes, taking a deep breath, trying to keep it together. Losing my shit wouldn't help.

"Maisy," he said, his voice as soft as such a deep, rough tone could be.

"What?"

"I'm not letting that happen."

"You've been too chicken shit to do anything about it before. Why the fuck should I believe you now?"

"I've had enough, *kitten*," he said, the word sounding

unnatural off his tongue and he gave me an almost sheepish smile as if sensing it.

"Enough of what? Watching women get hauled off to live out a nightmare?"

"That, yes. And Viktor. And having to follow orders like a *fucking* dog. But you, malysh, that was the... final straw."

"Why?"

"Because I can't watch him toss you to those wolves like a gutted pig. They'll tear you apart."

"And you care because..."

"Because, Maisy, we both know something was developing here," he said, gesturing to the air between us.

And, well, he wasn't wrong. I'd certainly had a crush. He had, at least, shown interest in taking me to bed. I hadn't possessed the vanity to believe it was more than that. But maybe it was. Maybe that was why he was always hanging around the office, not to be a slacker, but to be around me. It was certainly within the realm of possibilities. It was also something I could work with.

"But I betrayed you," I tried, making my tone a little softer, making it more how it used to be before K got a hold of me and taught me how important it was to speak with conviction no matter what I was saying. It spoke of confidence, of power, of someone who you shouldn't fuck with.

"You gave me a chance to get away from that life," he countered. "It was the push I needed. By this time tomorrow, he will know that some of his coffers are a bit more empty than they were the last time he went in to admire them."

"You stole from Viktor?"

"More than enough to get us out of this godforsaken place."

"You want to... leave the country?" I asked, stiffening a little.

Still sitting on me, he felt it. "What is left for you here, kotyonok? Come with me. We will get somewhere and live like kings, fuck like teenagers, and grow old together like generations past did."

"Rus, that's all nice and all... but I can't get out of this country. I have no passport. Not in my real name or my alias."

"That is easy enough to fix. We will leave here. Vik will be here soon. We need to go, find somewhere safe to disappear until we can get documents for you. Shouldn't take more than a couple of weeks. Then we can go anywhere. Where do you want to go? Islands? Europe? Anywhere."

"Rus, I..." I said, shaking my head. Honestly, I wasn't sure I could offer a good lie right then with my head spinning.

"Okay," he said, holding up his hands. "Okay. Too much. All you need to know is that we need to go. Now. Can I let you up?" he asked, genuinely waiting for an answer.

It hurt to nod my head. Literally, it made it feel like my neck was fighting the motion. But I needed to not piss him off. I needed him to think that I was going to go along with him, that I wasn't a captive but a willing partner in crime.

If I kept my head and managed to be convincing, I could make him trust me. If he trusted me, I could get a chance to get away or get alone long enough to contact K or Xander.

When Ruslan's weight lifted off me, I took a slow, deep breath, trying to ease the fluttering of my pulse and the dread in my belly.

"Come," Rus said, holding out a hand as he stood off the side of the bed.

"Can I get changed first?" I asked as I took his hand and let him pull me to stand in front of him. "I, ah, crashed last night without changing after all that traveling yesterday."

"That depends," he said, giving me a smirk as he ducked his head a little to look me in the face.

"On?"

"On if you're looking for another weapon to stab me with."

"Want to frisk me?" I challenged, cringing a little at my snippy tone.

But apparently Russians, like badass bikers, liked their women with a little spunk and he laughed. "Much as I'd enjoy that, Maisy, I don't want it like this."

"What like what?"

"Malysh," he said, taking a step closer and reaching out to tilt my chin up. "You, I wanted to see all of you the second I walked through the office door that first time. But I don't want it out of pride, fear, or some misguided power play. I trust you."

With that, he dropped his hand and moved toward the door, turning away from me and giving me what little privacy I could have in such a small space. I quickly dashed around to grab clothes, falling twice and knocking over the freaking lamp when my leg got caught in the cord.

"I guess I had no worries," he said, sounding amused.

"About what?" I asked, watching him closely as I grabbed the cell and quickly tucked it into the pile of clothes.

"You being some kind of danger to me. You're more of a danger to yourself."

I small-eyed him because he couldn't see me, but did feel my lips quirk up a little. It just reminded me so much of the teasing he used to do when coming into the office.

"Can I change in the bathroom?" I asked.

He turned slowly. "Whatever you want," he said, but I was pretty sure I saw a little disappointment there, like he was upset that I didn't trust him to not look.

"Thanks," I said, ducking my head a little as I dashed into the bathroom and closed the door. I chose not to lock it, trying to inspire him to not get suspicious of me as I stripped out of the clothes from the day before and into the black skinny jeans and white wifebeater I had grabbed along with fresh undies and my boots.

I checked the phone with still no contact from K, the pit in my stomach growing. I made sure the sound was off, then powered it down, knowing that whatever battery life I had on it was going to need to last until I got somewhere I knew we would be staying long enough to warrant some kind of rescue or whatever. I tucked it into my boot and tied them up tight so it couldn't be spotted, fixed my crazy hair into a tight top-knot, and opened the door.

Rus was standing against the sink vanity inside the door holding my stash of cash and fake IDs. "These are yours," he said, handing them to me. "You need anything else?" he asked, waving toward the disaster of a room.

"Um, I'm just gonna grab a sweater," I said as I took and stashed the IDs in my pocket and the cash into the boot that didn't have my cell. At that, I grabbed a sweater and turned back to him with a small shrug.

His head tilted to the side as he reached to open the door, looking at me for a long second. "I kind of like the hair."

With that, I followed Rus into the hall then down to the streets to a pickup that wasn't familiar to me. It was either rented or maybe bought outright with whatever obnoxious sum of money he took from his and his brother's stash. It was a late model black truck with a cab and short bed. He walked up to the passenger side door, opening it for me and actually helping me inside.

Then I tried to force myself to calm down as I watched us drive out of Philly to God-knew where. And, well, with nothing to do but think, I did a whole helluva lot of that.

First, I was present enough to try to assess the situation with Ruslan. And, well, the only real conclusion I could come to was that he was genuine. If I had been paying closer attention to the details back when I worked for them, I would have seen how deeply unhappy Rus was anytime Vik sent him off to do some job. I would have seen the way Viktor talked down to him and the way Ruslan's jaw would clench like he was struggling to hold back his words. For someone as laid back and even-tempered as Rus, that really said something. He'd wanted out. Maybe it was just the money that kept him there for as long as he did. Granted, he didn't seem to spend it as lavishly as his brother, but Rus had some nice things. He had a nice apartment. He took lavish vacations. He ate at nice restaurants to impress the women he fucked. So maybe that had been enough to hold him there.

I wasn't delusional or naive enough to think that Viktor was the only violent one between them. I was sure there was blood on Ruslan's hands as well. But maybe whomever he had been told to beat or eliminate had been men who had, in some way shape or form, deserved it: people who tried to steal their business, people who tried to take them down, people who threatened what they had worked for.

While a part of me still cringed away from the idea of torture and murder, having grown up in a relatively non-violent cushion of the world, the older, more worldly part of me understood it. Fact of the matter was, some of the men I had come to love and respect were men with blood on their hands. First, K. He never expressly admitted to killing anyone, but it was alluded to. Still, he was the most selfless, giving, skilled, amazing man I had ever met. Then there was Reign who the reports proposed he had done his fair share of murder and mayhem. Hell, Wolf was a wild animal when he felt the occasion called for it. Cash had killed and he was sweet, good-natured. Christ, even Shooter. He was a fucking contract killer but the most easy-going, charming, sweet person I'd ever met.

Then of course, there was Repo.

At the thought of his name, the stinging sensation in my chest amplified until I had to rub my hand over my heart again to try to ease it.

Repo had admitted to killing men in awful, violent ways.

But Repo was a *good* man.

There was no question in my mind about that fact. It was in every thing he did. It was in him cooking for me. It was in the way he took care of his brothers. It was in the way he made sure I understood where I stood with him. It was in the fact that he shared all his ugly details with me, without even hesitating. He didn't hide himself. He didn't lie. He was upfront. He was loyal.

And, well, let's not forget that whole 'I don't come until you come' rule with sex.

So it wasn't hard for me to accept that while Rus might have hurt or killed people, it didn't necessary make him a bad person.

The selling the women thing though? That was never going to sit right with me.

I didn't care what they tried to convince themselves that the women willingly signed up and it was a mutually beneficial situation, that it was a new type of arranged marriages. I called bullshit. They knew better.

It was human trafficking plain and simple.

It was no better than stealing a woman off the street and selling her.

But, yeah, I was pretty sure I was okay with Rus. At least for the short-term. He could have easily beat or raped me back in that hotel. Granted, I'd have put up a hell of a fight, but chances were... he would have overpowered me.

He didn't.

Not only didn't he even attempt to, but he had seemed insulted about the whole frisking thing.

He would only want me willingly.

And, well, there would be no willingness from me.

But that was just another hand I had to play.

I trained for it.

I trained to make and keep a cover.

The fact that I let those rules slide a bit with Repo was beside the point.

It would not be a problem with Rus.

I just had to sit tight and wait for my chance at getting away.

"How does Miami sound?"

It sounded like a seventeen fucking hour drive was what it sounded like.

"I could use to even out my tan," I said instead, giving him a smile that was at once flirtatious and shy.

Judging by the way his eyes got bright, he bought it.

I took a deep breath, and silently repeated a mantra in my head.

And maybe, just maybe, that mantra had something about Repo in it.

But I was just going to let that slide.

# EIGHTEEN

*Repo*

To say we didn't handle the empty and trashed room well would be a bit of an understatement. K managed to punch a hole in the wall and I had frantically looked through the mess to try to find something that might have some kind of clue as to what had happened, who had been there, where they had gone, if she was hurt.

While I was glad I found no blood, I also didn't find a goddamn thing else either.

After ten minutes, we made our way back downstairs, K twirling Maze's knife absentmindedly around in his hand, completely unconcerned about the people who watched him like he was a lunatic. We rounded the front desk where we had talked to the spineless shit earlier, the guy who had been easy to bribe for us and, well, likely for whomever had Maze as well. He grabbed the kid by the throat and pushed him through the office door behind the desk, almost slamming the door in my face in the process.

Apparently when K got angry, he got *angry.*

"Now you're going to tell me every fucking thing you know about the comings and goings in room 28B or I am going to take this knife," he said, angling it so the point was digging into the man's Adam's apple, "and I am going to start slicing off parts you've become attached to. And I won't be starting with fingers..." he warned.

"There was another man," the guy immediately rushed to say through clenched teeth, careful to not let his throat move too much as he spoke lest the knife dug in.

"Details," K demanded, slamming him back against the wall hard enough for his head to make a sick cracking sound.

"Tall, wide. Dark hair. Jeans, t-shirt. Nothing too distinctive except..."

"Except?" I prompted.

"He had an accent."

"Russian?" I asked.

"I don't know. I suck at accents. Maybe?"

"Ruslan," K concluded, letting his hand with the knife drop down by his side. "Maisy said Viktor only ever wore suits. Rus was the jeans and tee guy."

"Did you see them leave?" I asked the guy who was watching K like a grenade without a pin, like he might explode at any second. I had to say, I barely knew the guy, but that seemed exactly what K was when he was worked up.

He held up his hands when K turned his attention back to him when he paused to swallow. "Willingly! Willingly. I might be an opportunist, but I'm not a monster. I'd have called the cops if I'd seen a woman getting dragged out of here. He went up there for I dunno... maybe half an hour. When he came back down, she was right behind him out of the elevator. She... she didn't even look freaked, I swear. When he opened the front door for her, he put his hand on her lower back. Like they were friendly."

I felt myself stiffening a little at his words, my guts twisted in a way that made me both want to puke and haul off and hit something despite my crusted-up bloody knuckles. K said Maze had a crush on Rus. Maybe if he slipped her the right words she'd have followed him blindly, willingly.

I didn't like that one fucking bit.

"Car?"

"Pick-up," Mr. Accommodating supplied immediately. "I saw it because he illegally parked it right outside the doors. Black. Had one of those mini backseat things."

"We're going to need a plate number," K said in a way that brooked no argument.

"Um, we have cameras up front..."

"And you're still standing there like a fucking idiot because..."

The guy rushed toward a computer, hitting keys frantically and having to retry three times before he could get his shaking fingers to cooperate. "Okay here," he said, turning the monitor.

I pulled my phone out of my pocket and punched in Janie's number, rattling off the number before she could even finish saying 'what's up'. "They're paper plates. The truck is new. Find out where it's from. Try to get it on cameras heading out of the city."

"On it," she said, hanging up.

"You got anything else to tell us?"

"That's all I know, man. I swear. I have noth..."

"Shut it," K said, turning to me. "How long until they find something?"

"Ten, fifteen depending on where he bought the truck."

"Alright. Coffee then we'll get out to the highway until

we get a direction."

Ten minutes later, inside his truck with coffees in the holders, my phone started screaming. "Tell me you got some good news, Janie."

"He bought the truck outright in New York. The plates will do nothing as they're temps. But, get this, the truck came with six months of On-Star."

"That's supposed to comfort me because..."

"Because On-Star has tracking," she declared like I was an idiot. I drove bikes and vintage cars. I was clueless to all the bells and whistles of late-models. "They have major security, but with me and Alex on this... we should be able to pinpoint a location."

"How long?"

"An hour? Can't say for sure. But Alex said they headed south out of Philly so it won't hurt to get on the road and head in that direction so they don't get too much of a lead."

Janie's voice drifted off and I heard Reign pick up. "Repo, got Duke, Renny, Cash, and Wolf out looking for Viktor. Called in Hailstorm, Breaker and his crew, and the Mallicks. Even put a call out to the Grassis to let me know if they see him. They're no fonder of the Russians than we are. Someone will find him and bring him to us. From there, well, I guess that's up to K and Maze to decide what to do about him."

"Right. Thanks, Reign. I really..."

"Fuck off. This is what we do," he brushed off my gratitude and hung up.

And, I realized, not for the first time, that he was right. In our little, albeit ever-widening circle, there didn't need to be questions and explanations. All one needed was a phone call and the others were on board. It never occurred to me before how thankful I should be for the whole fucking lot of them. When all was said and done, I owed everyone a couple rounds at Chaz's.

Hitting the lowest corner of Pennsylvania, the last sign

we'd seen was for some bumfuck town called Stars Landing, we pulled off the highway and waited for a call from Janie before we got too far out of town.

Half an hour after parking, both of us knowing we should get some rest but neither of us willing to do so, the phone screamed in the quiet space, making both of us jump.

"Janie..."

"Yep, all us bitches are interchangeable," came a voice that was distinctly not Janie.

"Hey Alex, you got something for me?"

"Aside from very possible carpel tunnel?" she asked and actually laughed at the growling noise I made in response. "Touchy. Anyway, yes. That's why I'm calling." I switched the phone to speaker at K's impatient snap. "Janie is tracking them now. They're in Maryland." With that, the SUV turned over and peeled out of the lot we were parked in. "They're not slowing down so we can't really pinpoint anything helpful. Besides, you're behind them by a while. Best bet is for us to keep guiding you in general directions until they pull off and call it a day. But it's early and they haven't been on the road that long yet so I wouldn't count on them stopping until nightfall."

With that, we made our way to Maryland.

The phone rang again half an hour later, a number I didn't know, so I put it on speaker immediately. "Repo," I said as K's hands gripped the wheel.

"K, it's Shelly. Vermont called."

I looked over at K whose eyes were completely off the road, confirming what I had suspected. Vermont was Maze. "What did she say?"

"She said..." Shelly trailed off for a second, shuffling paper and then reading back what she had obviously written so she wouldn't forget anything. I didn't blame her. K seemed meticulous as fuck about details. "'This is Vermont. I haven't been able to get in touch with K since I bugged out. I don't know if he's okay or if I should be calling Xander. But I don't have a lot of time. Ruslan Kozlov has me. We're in a black pick-up heading toward Miami. We're almost in Virginia now. I can't leave my phone on because I have no charger. I'll check for a message when I can or call back if I can get free or have an address where someone can come find me. Um... okay. I'm safe. He won't hurt me but, ah, he fucked over his brother so Vik is an issue. I gotta go.' She rushed that last part, her voice dropping and I heard someone calling her name."

"Thanks, Shelly. Keep us updated."

"Triple overtime since I have to sleep on the couch in the office," Shelly said and didn't even wait for an answer from her boss before hanging up.

"She thinks something happened to me," K said hollowly. "I'm such a fucking idiot."

"You were worried. You weren't thinking str..."

"It's my fucking job to think straight. Otherwise what the fuck good am I to these women?" he countered and, well, I really had no other words of comfort.

We all fucked up.

We all looked over shit we shouldn't have.

But I understood him being so hard on himself. Maze was one of his girls.

I felt the same kind of regret and anger at myself even though there was nothing I really could have done any differently.

The issue was, she was mine. She was mine and she was scared and alone and I hadn't protected her from that. That shit didn't sit right with me.

The phone rang again sometime around ten that night. "They stopped," Janie said, her voice with an unmistakable over-caffeinated edge to it. "Greenville, North Carolina. 334 East

Road. At the Hampton. I'll see what I can do about trying to get the guest room registry so you guys can get a key when you get there."

"Thanks, Janie," I said, the words heavy and I knew she picked up on it.

Both of us visibly relaxed for the rest of the drive, finding ourselves about two hours behind them so either they were speeding or we'd needed to stop for fuel more or who knew what the fuck. All I knew was it was midnight before we pulled into the lot of the Hampton. K parked right beside the Russian's truck and we made out way in to the lobby, guns in our waistbands, not entirely sure what our plan was aside from going in and getting her out.

As promised, Janie or Alex or both of them came through. We had a key and a room number. I owed them fucking huge some day down the road.

We walked out of the elevator and down the hall in unison, nothing around us but the occasional low grumble of a television set behind closed doors.

K was fishing the key out of his pocket as we moved to stop outside the door.

When suddenly it pulled open and Maze came to a halt with a yelp, head jerking upward to look at us.

All of us were stunned silent for a long second before Maze's lips turned up in a strange little smile. "This is kind-of anti-climactic, don't you think?" she asked, dragging a strangled chuckle out of me as K reached out, grabbing her, and hauling her against his chest.

I stood there for a second, itching to get my hands on her as well, but it was only right that he got his real proof of life first. He had invested so much in her, got so much time with her, had even longer to fall for her. Of course, with him, in a strictly platonic sense.

"Where is he?" I heard K ask quietly, near her ear as he still crushed her to his chest.

"On the bed," she answered back as he released her finally and stormed inside, reaching for the gun. She turned to me a little hesitantly, like she wasn't sure where she stood with me.

"Maisy, huh?" I asked, head tilting to the side. "From Vermont?"

"Once upon a time, yeah," she agreed with an unsure little nod.

"I think Maze suits you better," I said but her shoulders didn't relax in the least. "You gonna give me a hug, honey, or what?" I asked, opening my arms. Her shoulders went down then she flew at me, knocking me back a foot as my arms went around her. "Hey, you're alright," I said when she made some sort of whimpering sound into my chest, her arms holding on like her life depended on it.

"I..." she started, but was cut off by K's smooth, rolling laugh.

"Do I want to know?" I asked, smiling into her hair.

Maze snorted, pulling back from me, her hand sliding down my arm until it found mine, curling around it. She squeezed once then turned to pull me into the room to where K was standing at the foot of the bed and Ruslan...

Yeah Ruslan was tied to the fucking thing with what looked like a belt on one wrist and an assortment of shoe strings and bedsheets on the other.

"Fucking seriously?" I laughed as the very-conscious Ruslan glared at me.

"He sleeps like the dead," she informed us and, if I wasn't mistaken, sent Ruslan an apologetic smile.

"I wasn't going to hurt you. I was going to save you, kotyonok," he said, his voice soft and with a conviction that even

I didn't question and, well, the fucker stole my woman.

"I know that," she said and I knew I wasn't mistaken, she felt bad for tying the bastard up. Hell, I felt bad for him. That shit looked humiliating. "But I didn't want to be on the run from Vik for the rest of my life, Rus. I didn't want to leave the country. I didn't want to leave..." she stopped suddenly, looking over at me a little self-consciously.

"Go ahead and finish that sentence," I said, brow lifted.

"You. Okay? I didn't want to leave you. Is your ego stroked enough now?"

"As much as I'd like you two to get your touchy-feelies out," K broke in waving a hand toward the bed, "but what the fuck are we supposed to do about this?"

"You didn't have to sneak off when I was sleeping, Maisy," Ruslan broke in, shrugging his shoulders as much as the awkward position would allow. "If you had told me you didn't want me, that you didn't need my help, I would have let you go."

"Well... I didn't know that!" she said, rolling her eyes at him. "It didn't exactly feel like I had much of a choice."

"Because you needed someone to protect you, kotyonok. I didn't know you already had people doing that for you."

"I guess we should untie him," Maze said, looking between us.

"You sure that's smart?"

"I'm in the room," Ruslan interrupted. "It's fine to untie me. I won't try to take you on."

"Don't all move at once," Maze grumbled, going to the side of the bed and working on the complicated assortment of ties holding his right wrist to the headboard. K moved to his other wrist and I stood there, not sure what the fuck to do. "What are you planning to do now, Rus? Obviously you can't stay around here with Vik looking for you."

"I wouldn't count on Vik being a problem for long," I said and Ruslan's eyes snapped to mine. "Half of Navesink Bank is looking for him. My money is on them finding him. Then it's up to K and Maze what to do with him."

Ruslan nodded, looking over at a suddenly horrified-looking Maze. "He's too powerful," he said.

"You're saying he needs to be neutralized," K said, freeing his arm and moving back.

"If you want to keep Maisy safe, yes. Otherwise, he'll never stop."

"He's your brother," Maze objected, shaking her head and staying on the bed despite finishing her task.

"Kotyonok, he'd kill me soon as he'd wish me a good morning," Ruslan said, sitting up, his hand landing on Maze's thigh and squeezing.

And, well, that was about enough. I reached out, grabbing Maze at the waist and pulling her to stand and put back against my chest, one of my arms going around her waist. "Repo, what are..."

Ruslan's face twisted up in a smirk as he gave me a chin raise. "Loud and clear."

Maze looked over at K who gave her a shrug. "Ever see a dog piss on what belongs to him?" he asked with a white-toothed smile.

I couldn't see her face, but I'm pretty fucking certain she rolled her eyes.

"All seriousness though," K said, "Maze isn't in on whatever does end up being done. She doesn't need that on her back."

"K, I'm a big girl. I can handle..."

"Not a word," I agreed immediately. She'd had enough to deal with, she didn't need to think there was blood on her hands.

"This might help," Ruslan said, moving off the bed,

jerking his chin up at K who took a long second to move out of the man's way. He went over to the desk, grabbing a piece of paper and a pen. "Vik fucked up five years ago or so. He convinced an unhappy girl to come and marry in the States when he was visiting home. Turns out she wasn't just a poor girl with no prospects, she was the younger sister to one of Russia's biggest importers." It didn't take a genius to know he meant drugs. "The brother, he's looked for her. But Vik hid her well when he figured out what happened. This," he said, pointing something out to K on the paper, "is how to contact him. This," he pointed lower on the paper, "is where to find her. You all," he said, looking up at me, but focusing more on Maze, "you will have nothing on your conscience. This is righting an old wrong."

"And what about you, Rus?" Maze asked.

"Me? I'll be fine. I will hide out living large on this money until I get word that Viktor is no longer a... obstacle for me. Then I can go back to New York." Maze must have looked upset because his face softened as did his voice. "Kotyonok, no. Never. I will go back and run the real businesses the way they should have always been run."

"If I find out that is not the case, that you're selling girls again, I will personally drag my ass up there, tie you to another bed, cut off your cock, and shove it down your lying throat."

Damn if my girl didn't mean every word of that.

"I believe you," he said, moving toward us, running a hand down her nose, then heading toward the door. "On that paper is a way to contact me. Please do so if you have news for me. I will be in Miami as planned... *evening out my tan*," he said in a way that suggested it was some secret between them.

With that, he grabbed keys off the table and left.

"Seriously though," Maze said a tense minute or so later, pulling from my hold so she could look at both of us, "how much did that kill the 'save the girl' thing you guys were going for?"

she asked, smiling.

"We were just happy to find that you were okay," K said, shaking his head at her.

"Oh, bullshit. I call bullshit. You totally wanted to burst in and start knocking heads. What happened to Repo's fists? And yours for that matter?" she asked, nodding toward K's hands.

"Me, that was Moose. K, that was the hotel room wall back in Philly annnd... the owner of a cab company's face in Philly too. And almost the face of a clerk at the hotel in Philly. But he pissed himself before there could be any real fun. He's been busy."

"And this wasn't some macho thing?" she asked dubiously.

"It was a 'our girl is missing' thing, Maze." That effectively shut her up, her lips parting slightly.

I know I told her that after her whole probate thing was over that I planned to pursue something with her, but I hadn't exactly explained what I meant by that. I meant she was mine. I meant I was hers. I meant that I was going to do everything in my power to never be another reason she couldn't trust a man again.

And judging by the look on her face, she sussed out the deeper meaning in those words.

"Alright," K said, clapping loudly. "You two can get into that later. We need to get the fuck out of here. Not that I don't trust Rus, love," he told Maze, shaking the piece of paper he had folded, "but we can't stay here. At the very least, we need to get out of North Carolina. Let's cross over into Virginia and get another couple of rooms before we head back tomorrow. Sound good?"

With very little option, we both agreed and shuffled down toward the car where K promptly jumped into the driver and Maze in the passenger, like it was an old habit. With a shrug,

I got into the back and listened as K filled Maze in on everything that had happened over the course of the last two days, covering everything from the phone frying to the boring hours we spent waiting for more intel to work with.

K finally parked in a hotel lot at almost three A.M. Maze had fallen asleep in the front a half an hour before, K flipping on the radio to a classical station to drown out the sounds of the road. He hopped out, telling me he would get rooms and left me to wake up Maze. I climbed up front and opened her door, watching her for a long second. The only time I'd ever seen her sleep was when she was sick. Her lips were parted slightly, her eyelashes soft against her cheek. Up close, I could see her blonde roots hinting through the purple.

"Honey," I said, touching her cheek, smiling when she grumbled and swatted at my hand. "Come on, honey. Let's get you inside," I said and her eyes fluttered open, looking at me then behind me as she rubbed at her eyes.

"You just want to get me into bed," she said, her voice still sleep-foggy.

"Well, I can't deny that, but right now I think you need sleep more than sex so let's go get you comfortable."

"Ugh," she growled, swinging her legs out of the car. "Walking..." she added, curling her lip up at me as she jumped down.

"It's ten feet to the door. I'm pretty sure you can make it."

"Yeah yeah yeah," she grumbled, waving a hand at me as she walked.

"I thought you were supposed to be a morning person," I said, trying not to laugh at her as she flung the front door open.

"Three A.M is *not* morning. Especially after the day I just had."

"Here you go," K said, handing Maze a key. "4B. I am in 9D."

"9D?" Maze repeated.

"They had a room next to yours. And we're close, love, but I don't need to hear you two fucking."

"Sleeping," she corrected, moving past him toward the elevators.

"Is she always this moody when she wakes up?" I asked as we followed, both of us smiling at her back.

"Only when she's *woken* up."

With that, we rode the elevator up to the second floor where Maze and I got off, agreeing to meet K for breakfast at ten, then going toward our room.

Maze paused once inside, staring at the bed.

"What's up?"

She turned back to me, head tilted. "We've only slept in the same bed once," she informed me unnecessarily, "when I was sick."

"Mmhmm," I said, rocking back on my heels. "You had a bad dream and asked me to not let them get you. I told you I wouldn't. Guess I failed there, huh?"

For the second time that night, she threw herself against me, squeezing me tight enough to almost cut off my air. "You came for me," she told my chest, her voice muffled by my shirt.

"Of course I came for you."

"You claimed me to Reign."

"You got a problem being mine?"

There was a short pause, making my heart lodge itself in my throat, thinking she was looking for a way to tell me it wasn't something she wanted. But then she tilted her head up, her chin resting on my chest. "None come to mind," she said, smiling.

"Good."

"So... this sleeping thing," she said, her smile turning a little mischievous.

"The sleeping thing?"

"Yeah, do you have your heart set on it?"

"I might be able to be persuaded out of it."

"Well, I guess it's good that I can be rather... persuasive," she said, her hands sliding up my stomach and chest then back down, her hand sliding over the crotch of my jeans.

"You think? I don't know, honey. I'm pretty beat."

"Really, because this particular part of you seems... rather awake," she said, her palm stroking over my cock. She slowly lowered herself down on her knees before me, reaching up and making short work of getting my cock out and into the warm velvety wetness of her mouth. I reached down, dragging her hair out of her knot and watching it flow down her back and shoulders. She sucked me deep, twirling her lips around me in a circular motion as she moved back upward, her tongue sliding over the tip and licking off the pre-cum beading there.

I twisted my hand in her hair and pulled her back onto her feet, crushing my mouth to hers, kissing her hard and demanding until her entire frame wavered against me. Then I took her hips and turned us, me sitting down on the edge of the bed and pulling her to stand between my legs. "Take your clothes off, honey."

"Take my clothes off?" she repeated, showing me a hint of uncertainty I hadn't seen there before.

"Yes."

"Repo, I..."

"Rye," I corrected.

"Excuse me?"

"Rye. When we're alone, it's Rye. You want me to call you Maisy?"

"No," she said immediately, shaking her head. "I'm not Maisy anymore, not really. I want you to call me Maze."

"Okay. Take your clothes off, Maze," I demanded again.

Her hands balled up for a second before she unfolded

them and reached for the hem of her wifebeater and quickly dragged it off. Her hands slid down to her jeans, unfastening them and bending at the waist to drag the tight material down. She stumbled forward toward me in trying to free one of her ankles, her hand slamming down on my thigh to steady herself, giving me a shy smile that was very likely the cutest fucking thing I'd ever seen in my life.

She righted herself, reaching behind her back for her bra clasp and letting the material fall to the floor, her nipples hardening immediately likely due to both desire and the marked coolness of the air conditioning in the room. She hooked her fingers into her panties next, pushing them down and shimmying out of them.

I watched her for a minute, eyes raking over every inch of her: her round breasts, her slim waist, the flare to her hips that made her perfect ass possible, her thick thighs.

"Rep... Rye..." she said, shuffling her feet and drawing my attention back to her ridiculously perfect face.

"Like how it sounds when you say my name, honey," I said, patting the bed next to me and she moved to sit. "Lie back," I said, lowering myself onto my knees and moving toward her knees, pressing them apart and before she could even fully flatten her body to the mattress, my mouth was on her sweet pussy, licking up her slick slit and finding her clit, already swollen with desire, and moved my tongue around it in soft, barely-there circles. Until she was so wet that my face was slick, until her inner thighs were shaking, until her moans got loud enough to warrant loud rapping from one of the rooms on the side of ours. Then and only then, I flattened my tongue on her clit as I thrust two fingers inside her, raking over her G-spot and feeling her pussy milk my fingers hard for a long minute until the waves subsided.

"Rye, please," she pleaded, her hands reaching down to

grab my head and drag me upward.

"Please what?" I asked, kneeling between her thighs and reaching up to drag my shirt off.

"Please get inside me," she begged, hands going to my hips and dragging my jeans and boxer briefs downward as she sat up, planting kisses across my stomach as I fumbled for my wallet, pulling out a condom and pushing her back on the bed so I could slip it on. I kicked out of my boots and the legs of my pants then moved over her, planting my hands by her sides and running my tongue up her stomach from the navel upward, tilting my head to take her nipple in my mouth, sucking hard until she arched up into me before I went to her other breast to continue the torment.

"Rye..." she groaned into my ear as I bit into her neck, her fingers digging into my back hard as her legs wrapped around my lower back.

And, well, there was only so much restraint a man could demonstrate.

I shifted my hips and slammed forward, hitting as deep as her body would allow and rocking my pelvis against hers to rub over her clit again.

Then there was no teasing, no softness. I slammed into her: hard, deep, fast, driving her back upward and sending her crashing over before she could realize she was close. Her pussy clenched hard around my cock and I buried deep and came, cursing out her name as I rested my head in the crook of her neck.

"Rye," she said a minute later, her voice sounding almost a little amused.

I pushed up enough to look down at her. "What?"

She smiled then, open, carefree, a smile I hadn't seen from her before, not really. "We totally just had sex in a bed."

I felt my own lips tip upward, a surprised chuckle rolling

in my chest. "Yeah we did."

"It was pretty damn good, but I don't think we should give up open fields in thunderstorms or the yard at the compound just yet."

"Or the roof," I added, leaning down and dropping a quick kiss on her lips. "Or the bathroom. Or my cars."

"Exactly," she said, unconsciously running her hands up and down my back. "But the bed does have an advantage."

"What's that?"

"I can sleep here," she said, bringing a hand to cover her mouth as she yawned.

I laughed, planting a kiss to her forehead and pulling away to go deal with the condom. When I walked back out, she had already moved up the bed and climbed under the covers, the light off on her bedside table.

"You weren't fucking around about being tired, huh?"

"Hey some of us require sleep to keep functioning," she said, curling up on her side toward me as I got under the covers, reaching over to turn off the light, leaving just the one over by the door to the hall on to be able to see each other by. "Besides, it's not my fault. You stole the last of my energy."

"Get used to that," I said, pulling her up and onto my chest, feeling her soft body meld perfectly to my harder one. My arms went around her back and hips to anchor her to me, not wanting her to roll away in sleep. It was a new feeling for me.

But then again, it was all new to me.

I never stuck around long enough to have a woman fall asleep with me.

"Okay," she said, her voice already a little far away like she was falling asleep.

"Okay," I said back, squeezing her a little and feeling her relax against me as she passed out.

To my complete and utter shock, less than an hour later, I

did as well.

# NINETEEN

*Maze*

For no damn good reason, I was twisted in knots as we drove into the compound the next afternoon. Repo, as if sensing the tension in me over breakfast, had tried to smooth things over, telling me how on-board Reign had been with helping, calling in the other friendleys in the area, claiming I was part of their club even though I was only a probate.

But regardless of that and the absolutely mind-numbingly hard, borderline brutal sex we'd had in the shower right before leaving, so rough that I'd had three orgasms and some soreness between my legs the whole ride back to Navesink bank, I was still freaking out a little bit.

First, because I'd lied.

I didn't know Reign as well as Repo did, but he really didn't seem like the kind of man who was going to be forgiving about being lied to, repeatedly.

Second, because I didn't want any of them to think that

my situation in any way made me weak. They, being bikers, outlaws, testosterone-driven men, tended to settle problems with bull-headed confrontation. There was no running away. That was what pussies did. It was not what a one-percenter did. Ever.

So yeah, when I followed Repo into the front door, K taking my six, I was pretty fucking close to throwing up all over my boots.

I had half-expected to walk into some sort of damn tribunal, all the patched members standing in a line, arms crossed over their chests, ready to throw me out on my ass. But when I walked in and found everything pretty much business-as-usual in the clubhouse. Men were playing pool or bullshitting, watching TV. At the bar were the men who held my future in their hands: Reign, Cash, and Wolf. Janie was nearby with a woman I had learned to know as Alex. I looked around, expecting to see her man, Breaker, but not seeing him anywhere.

Duke and Renny were standing on opposite sides of the room, Renny by the door to the hall, Duke leaning against the wall by the couch. I know from what Repo and K told me that the two of them had teamed up to track down leads and bring in Moose, but things still seemed a little tense between them.

"Hey babe," Reign greeted me, noticing us first. He'd half-turned from the bar, giving me a chin jerk. "You're on the gates overnight."

I felt myself falter, crashing back into K whose hands settled on my shoulders as I watched Reign turn back away from me, falling back into conversation. "Um..." I said, looking at Repo who gave me a small smile and a shrug as he moved over toward the bar to talk to his brothers.

"Don't look a gift horse in the mouth, love," K said, squeezing my shoulders then stepping away from me. "I can't stay long. I need to get back to work, get a new phone situation squared away, and see a Russian about another Russian."

I felt myself nod tightly. I knew that was going to happen. I wasn't K's only case. He had a lot of girls he needed to keep tabs on and while Shelly could hold down the fort for a limited amount of time in an emergency, she had a life and K's girls needed to hear from him to feel safe. That was the way I felt too. I needed to know he was still on the job to feel like I could breathe, to keep the faith.

And, well, my case was closed.

Or all but.

Ruslan wasn't an issue.

Viktor was on his way to being no one's issue anymore but some Russian dude back in the motherland.

My life was mine again.

I was pretty sure that was what was absolutely freaking terrifying me.

It was easy to be Maisy, the girl with the con mom, the amazing, but dead grandmother, the ex-boyfriend who almost got her locked up for his crimes, the employee who had been way too trusting of her bosses. She was easy. Clueless, naive, effortless to take advantage of, but easy.

And Maze, the girl with no past who was a hardass and cold and distant and secretive and wholly incapable of trusting anyone, who questioned every minute little goddamn thing. Yeah, she was easy too.

But this person left in the wake of it all?

I had no idea who the hell she even was, but I was pretty sure there was nothing easy about her.

If the night and morning in the hotel room with Repo/ Rye was anything to go by, it wasn't going to be easy to reconcile both sides of me. Because that was the case now. I wasn't Maisy and I wasn't Maze; I was a hybrid of both those women. I was someone who could be soft and sweet and emotional like I had been in my life before. But I was also someone who knew she could make a full grown man unconscious in seconds if she needed to. I had thicker skin and sharper edges.

My immediate instinct when I threw my arms around K and then Repo when I first saw them was to cry. Legit, that was the knee-jerk reaction. I wanted to let all the stress and worry and fear burst out of me in one big, ugly show of emotion. That was the soft side of me. But I had pulled it together and tried to joke around, pulling out my thick skin and keeping it together.

Then after being lulled to sleep with some seriously amazing sex that was deeply akin to actual lovemaking and waking up in Repo's arms to find that he too had fallen asleep, well, the thick skin thinned out and Repo woke up suddenly to the loud hitch in my breath as the tears streamed down hot and relentless.

"Honey, hey, what's the matter?" he'd asked, reaching out and wiping the wet from my cheeks as his eyes slowly cleared of sleep.

But I just face planted into his chest and let it all out.

Then, later in the shower, wishy-washy emotions all exorcised, Repo and I had went at each other like animals, like a battle, like survival of the fittest. There was nothing even remotely like lovemaking about the way we fucked, hair-pulling, skin-biting, ass-slapping, airway-constricting.

The Maisy I used to be would have been horrified by the violence of it.

But Maze thrived on it.

So, yeah, to say the least... my little personal identity crisis was an issue.

Especially because I had decided to keep trying to get my patch. I knew it was a long shot if it was even possible at all. But I wasn't a quitter. I wanted to prove it to them that I could take whatever they threw at me and handle it.

I also wanted needed to prove that to myself as well.

But was the new hybrid me going to be badass enough to pull it off? And was it going to change things that Repo and I were now openly... um... dating? Fucking? I wasn't entirely sure what we were. He'd claimed me. So I guess that meant more than fucking. Repo didn't exactly suffer from communication issues, so the fact that things were slightly hazy were either because I was over-thinking them or because he was waiting to clarify them when he saw how I was going to handle the whole situation.

That made sense.

And...

"Maisy," K's voice cut in, brow raised like he noticed I had totally spaced-out. "You alright?"

"My head is spinning," I admitted.

"Okay, here's the plan," he said, tone serious and no-nonsense. I immediately felt some of my anxiety slipping away. "You are going to buck up and you're going to fight for your patch. You've put in the work. Don't you dare give in now. They won't give you one, give them a giant 'fuck you' and move on. You and me, we aren't done just because your trouble is all but a memory. If you're my girl, you're my girl for life. So if this blows up in your face, I'm there. You need to come back to the City and be Maisy, but slightly improved, I'm there. You need to be Maze and start over again somewhere else, I'm there to help you navigate that. You end up falling head-over for that blue-eyed biker of yours and you need someone to walk you down the aisle or be a godfather for your first child, *I'm fucking there.* Got it?"

I felt my lips curve up as tears stung my eyes. "K..."

"Blink those tears away, love. It's not the time or place. Now, I gotta get going. Stay safe and kick ass, Maisy."

With that, he chucked me under the chin, slapped Repo on the back while whispering something near his ear, shook

Reign's hand, and was out the door.

Despite knowing he would always be there for me, I felt a little stabbing in my belly at watching him leave.

Repo walked back toward me then, face a little guarded. "What?" I demanded before he was even within five feet of me. He reached up, scratching his cheek, and gave me a smirk. "So yeah, the men are complaining that all their sheets need cleaning."

"You're serious?" I asked, feeling my mouth hanging open slightly as I looked over at the bar to find a particular group of said men watching me.

"Afraid so, probie."

I felt myself snort, shaking my head, then declaring to the room as a whole, "Wow, it's a good thing I'm back seeing as Duke and Renny seemed to have had all four of their hands amputated while I was busy being hunted and kidnapped and found themselves suddenly incapable of doing your laundry. Can't have you guys rolling around in dirty sheets like a bunch of *pigs,* now can we?" I asked, giving Reign the saccharine smile he had come to expect whenever I mouthed off. Then jerking my chin up at him when he saluted me with his beer, I made my way toward the hall to go collect the fucking sheets.

And as much as I was annoyed at the current of sexism under the request, it felt good to know that things hadn't changed. I was still just a probate. And I was the first female one to boot. I got ragged on. I got the shitty jobs. I got shit kicked at me then got told to sweep it up because it was stinking up the joint.

There was a certain sort of comfort in that I realized as I shoved the first batch of sheets into the dryer and turned it on before putting another batch in the washer, adding detergent, and flicking that on as well.

"You didn't get the sheets off my bed," Repo's voice said

from behind my shoulder as his hand slid around my belly.

"Whatever I am to you, Rye, I'm not your fucking maid."

"It's only fair," he said, nipping into my earlobe and sending a rush of wet between my thighs.

"How is it fair?"

"We're both going to be participating in dirtying them up."

"Gee, I dunno what you think, Mr. Boss Man Biker. But I'm just a lowly probate. I sleep in a bunk bed in a cold basement like a hated third cousin showing up for Christmas uninvited."

"Like fuck. You'll do what you need to do when someone needs you to do it, but when you're sleeping, you're doing that shit in my bed next to me," he declared, his hand moving under the waistband of my jeans and stroking me over the material of my panties, finding my clit easily and pulsing his fingertip against it. "Got it?" he asked, his finger sliding under my panties and plunging inside me.

I held back a groan, my head falling onto his shoulder as I took a deep breath. "Fine, bring down your sheets."

"But first this," he said, finger raking over my G-spot.

Then we added the laundry room to our long list of places we had amazing, wild, inventive, amazing, perfect sex.

# EPILOGUE

*Maze- 3 Months*

"This is complete and utter *bullshit*," I shrieked to the whole group of them at large as I watched Duke and Renny stand with them, patches in hands.

Three months. Three extra fucking months of waiting on them hand and foot, cooking for them, cleaning their sheets, fetching drinks, washing bikes... all for nothing.

Nothing.

Because they had stuck to their guns.

I wasn't getting a patch.

I wasn't being allowed into The Henchmen MC.

I swear they picked this particular day to let me in on that fact because Janie was still off on her Honeymoon with Wolf, Lo was out of town on a job, Summer was down with morning sickness until well into the evening, and the rest of the girls club only happened over to the compound if they were called to. So there was no Alex or Amelia around either to pitch a fit with me.

I was, quite literally, completely and utterly alone.

Repo stood with his brothers.

I hadn't exactly thought it would be any other way when it came down to it. It wasn't that he was standing against me, he was just standing with the decision his boss had made. I understood it. But that didn't mean there wasn't a tiny little pit of resentment in my stomach over it, no matter how sad his eyes looked when my gaze slid to him.

He knew what it meant to me. He knew every little bit of torture I went through, how above and beyond I worked and trained to make myself an important member of the MC.

"Babe..."

"Don't," I snapped, loudly and without restraint. I wasn't a member and I wasn't a probate anymore. So talking back to Reign wasn't disloyal. It might have been a bit risky and stupid, but it wasn't against some code of conduct. "Don't you dare fucking 'babe' me," I yelled, crossing over toward him, watching Vin and Cash shrink away from his sides because, I imagined, they knew women well enough to know that when we got on a tear, we didn't give a good flying fuck in space about collateral damage.

"Maze this is for the..."

"Best?" I cut him off. "You know what... fuck that. And fuck you and your sexist bullshit. One day, Reign, Ferryn is going to be all grown up. And on that day, I'll be around and I won't hesitate to tell her what a chauvinistic pig her fucking father..." I started to punctuate each word with a shove to his massive chest, barely managing to make his body move at all.

"Maze..." he broke in, tone calm, not even mildly phased by my outburst. Possibly due to the fact that he was pretty much only ever surrounded by women who were in no way shy about sharing their thoughts and feelings.

"Take your half-assed explanations and go to hell," I spat,

turning on my heel and moving across the field toward the front yard.

"Hey Maze, maybe you should shut the fuck up for a second and listen," Reign called. If I hadn't been seeing, hearing, and feeling red... I might have heard the humor in his tone. As it was, all I heard was 'shut the fuck up and listen' and, well, I had just about enough of him. I moved to spin around, almost crashing into Reign himself, not realizing he had followed me. "Stop," he said when I opened my mouth to spit more fire. "Listen," he said, ducking his head a little to look me in the eye. "Things are changing around here a little."

"Really? And how long before you come out of the seventeenth century gender-role wise?"

He ignored that completely. "Most prominently, Maze, the law is changing around here a little. There's a lot of new blood. There's no telling who might want to cut their teeth by trying to gnaw away at Henchmen business."

"And this matters to me, why? Remember? I'm not part of The Henchmen."

"It's a strategic move, babe. You are but you aren't, okay?"

My brows drew together and I sighed, feeling some of the anger fall away under a sea of questions. "Alright, explain."

"We have to start going part legit. Repo is going to open a garage, stop fucking around in the field when he feels like it and do some real business. Cash, Janie, and Lo are going to be opening a gym that focuses on martial arts and kickboxing..."

"Why are you telling me this?"

"Well, see, Maze... you have a particular set of skills the men and I decided might come in handy."

I felt myself straighten, knowing where he was going and not sure how I felt about it. "Go on."

"Well, see, babe. Took you years to sort out what was going on with the Kozlov books it was so well hidden. I was thinking maybe you could... point us in the right direction with that kind of thing."

"You want me to help launder your money?" I asked, feeling my smile spread a little. Oh, what would Detective Conroy Asher think if he saw me now?

"No. Of course not," he said, grinning a little devilishly. "I want to hire you as an accountant to handle the books for the mechanic shop and the studio. If Repo just so happens to find out how exactly to hide money so well that not even the finest IRS agent could find it, well, that would just be a crazy coincidence."

I paused, biting into my cheek, wanting to choose my words carefully. "This wasn't always the plan, Reign. I'm not stupid."

"No, you're not. And, no, it wasn't. But it was the plan by the time you walked back in after that shit with the Russians. This has been something heavy on all our minds since they started fucking with the NBPD a couple years back. Everyone is sweating it. The Mallicks, they have a shitton of businesses to protect them. The Grassis have their restaurant. Breaker and Shooter are big time, but are still small fish. These guys will be itching to take down an organization, not individuals. We need to branch out. You couldn't be a member, babe. Not because you're a woman. You've proved to pretty much all of us that you have what it takes. But we need you on something else and to be on something else, you can't be associated to the illegal side of business. Make sense?"

It did.

Damn them.

I really wanted to be angry about not getting patched-in.

Hell, I had started to take on a 'doing this for all women' attitude about the whole thing.

But if they were trying to go legit, then things had

definitely gone bad with the law. The Henchmen had been around for a long, long while without ever sweating any kind of heat. And, well, I was a lot less offended that they weren't choosing me if they were trusting me to take care of their money. And, in doing so, I would help ensure their safety.

It wasn't such a bad deal.

No patch, sure.

But a helluva lot of responsibility and respect.

I could live with that.

I took a deep breath and nodded.

"Alright."

"Alright?" he asked, brows drawn together.

"Did you expect a fight?"

"From you?" he asked, smiling. "Fucking always, babe."

"Well, for once, you won't be getting one. I'll take the job."

"I have a feeling there's a catch here somewhere," he said, brow lifting.

"I'm sure there is. I just haven't thought of it yet," I said with a smile.

"I'll be eagerly awaiting that battle," he said, shaking his head. "Welcome aboard, Maze."

"In my non-official capacity," I emphasized.

"You're a member in all the ways that matter, babe. Don't nitpick."

With that, he turned. I did too, smiling huge because no one could see me.

*Repo- 1 Year*

The ring felt weighted in my pocket.

There was no other way to put it. It was a simple square-cut diamond on a platinum band. It was big, but understated. The box was black and tucked into my back pocket.

It weighed little in a literal way.

But figuratively, it was heavy as fuck.

It carried with it all my future good times, all the bad days, all my sleepless nights, all my plans, all my hopes.

It was such a little nothing.

But it was also everything.

Maze had seemingly effortlessly made the transition from probate to unofficial club member. The first couple of months, with nothing really to do, she hung around and pitched in still in little ways, doing a little cleaning or cooking, but only when she wanted to, not when someone tried to tell her to. I say 'tried' because she had, on more than one occasion, knocked fellow members onto their asses. And maybe they would have tried to retaliate if she was just any other member, but she wasn't. She also belonged to me.

She moved out of the basement, where Duke and Renny still lived until Reign put in the plans for an expansion of the club rooms, and into my room with me. I liked having her there, but it made me realize real quick that I needed to get a place of my/our own. I was pretty fucking laid back about a lot of things, but the first night I walked out into the clubhouse and got hoots from the guys about overhearing me and Maze fucking, yeah, I flipped shit.

Sure, we fucked like porn stars half the time.

But that was mine and Maze's business, not everyone else's.

The ring was the first surprise.

The house was the second.

With all the money I had socked away rebuilding and selling vintage cars over the years and having next to no living expenses save for the cut I gave The Henchmen, I had a nice chunk to sock away on a small cape-style fixer-upper right off the closest side street to the compound. It was within walking distance for the nights when we had one too many to drive home. It was seconds a ride away if the shit ever hit the fan and I needed to get my ass there.

It felt almost wrong to be deciding to move out after being the only real live-in member at the compound. But, that being said, Duke and Renny stepped into the place I vacated. They were there. They kept an eye on things along with some of the older men who had nothing else to do with their time but hang around.

The garage was supposed to open in another two months. It was nothing special. Reign bought one of the old, abandoned ones in town, just a simple shop with two lifts, a bathroom, and an office. He'd gotten a bunch of the men in and had them clean it up, fix any issues with the the Sheetrock, plumbing, and electrical. Then he'd had Summer, the only one of the girls club who seemed to have any interest in interior design, and had her fix up the office. The promotional fliers were going out in a few weeks and then we would be in business.

Lo, Janie, and Cash's gym was about another six months out due to both all the strong personalities involved and expected head-butting and some issues they ran into with construction and certifications.

And Maze, well, she'd somehow talked Reign into paying

for an office for her in town to do her official business. The money for which, at first, was completely off the books. She'd been surprisingly undemanding though. When I say it was a small office, I mean that I was pretty sure you could touch both walls if you spread your arms out. But she loved it and spent a lot of time getting it just how she wanted it, insisting she not only cover the books for us, but as many of the local businesses and individuals as she could. Within a few weeks of opening her doors, she had us, a few legit small businesses, and several individuals she called clients.

"Maze," I called as I walked into the compound.

"How'd you miss her up on the roof?" Renny asked, shaking his head at me like I was an idiot. Renny was Renny. Some things never changed.

I went back outside and went around the building to climb the ladder to the roof where I found Maze sitting with a gun propped up on a milk crate and an open folder full of papers on her lap. Her hand was tapping a pen against her lip as she tried to concentrate. She was wrapped up in tight blue jeans and a big, bulky white sweater against the only mildly cool Fall weather. Her hair, which she had kept purple, was in a thick braid down one of her shoulders.

I knew it was supposed to fade, to grow old, but I never got over the punch-to-the-gut sensation I got whenever I saw her and realized she was mine.

She turned, hearing or sensing me, her head tilting, her smile tugging her lips up slightly. "Hey Rye," she said, looking a little more tired than I was used to seeing her. But she had taken to working on her accounting business with the same single-minded determination that she took to prospecting for The Henchmen MC. I walked over toward her, tucking the papers back into the folder and slipping it under the milk crate. "Everything alright?" she asked, brows drawing together.

"Yep. I got you something," I said as I crouched down in front of her. All the crates being used, it didn't seem unusual.

"Is it the grease-less hands? Because that is quite the treat," she teased, her hazel eyes bright.

I reached into my pocket, grabbing the box and flipping it open before she could fully register what I was doing.

"Rye..." she said, her eyes going huge as her gaze went from my hands to my face.

"I didn't even know your real name when I knew you were it for me. I didn't know where you grew up or your favorite flower or what song makes your soul hurt. But I didn't need to know those things to know you, Maze, to know you're determined and strong and stubborn as all fuck, but that you're also giving and sweet and snarky and sexy as all hell..." I added when her eyes started to water up, trying to lighten the mood. "There's only one thing in this world that means more to me than my brotherhood, than The Henchmen, and that's you honey. So I figured it was time to..."

"Mark your territory?" she asked, swatting at her cheek, giving me a wobbly little smile as I took her hand and started sliding the ring on.

"Something like that," I said, pushing it fully on then curling my fingers between hers. "So, yes?"

"One condition," she said, eyes getting a little mischievous.

"Anything."

"The wedding night..."

"Yeah..." I smiled, liking where this was heading.

"Come up with somewhere really fun for us to, ah, seal the deal."

"Done," I agreed, reaching for the back of her neck and hauling her toward me, lips hard and hungry and full of the neediness I hadn't been aware I had been practically exploding with until she accepted me.

*Maze- 1.5 Years*

"Really, the shop is small guys," I objected, but only half of my heart was in it. One, because I knew it was absolutely useless to try to fight the girls club when they got united on an issue. Two, because I actually genuinely wanted them there.

See, getting Repo meant I got The Henchmen. Getting The Henchmen meant I got The Henchmen women. Getting The Henchmen women meant I got their friends, namely Alex and Amelia who were Breaker's and Shooter's girls respectively. It meant I had Lo there to make sure I never got taken advantage of, that I was always at my best. I also got Janie who always had my back should I need it, even though she was a new mother with little (but not quite so little given that Wolf was his father) Malcolm on her hip. He was named after one of Janie and Lo's colleagues over at Hailstorm. Little Malcolm was the spitting image of his father with dark hair and almost unnatural honey-colored eyes.

He was on her hip as the whole lot of the girls club stood in my minuscule office. Lo was at Janie's side, holding her baby backpack. Summer was beside them, Ferryn at her feet desperately trying to pull her hand out of her mother's so she could grab the elephant paperweight off my desk. Summer also had her other new addition in a sling; little Fallon was sound asleep which was an absolute rarity for him. Behind Summer stood Amelia. And then, barreling through the door was Alex, shaking her head like an apology, a tall, leggy, Barbie-perfect blonde at her heels. Elsie was a relatively new addition to the girls club too. She had come aboard around the same time I had apparently, but because her man, Paine, was less associated with The Henchmen than Shooter and Breaker, we didn't see him or her all that much at first.

At least that was until the girls club got their claws into her.

Then she was having her ass dragged up to Hailstorm for grappling practice just like the rest of us.

"Okay, we're here," Alex declared abruptly. "Let's make this easy for you before we even get to the dress store. Amelia, Elsie, and Summer are going to want to wear dresses. Lo and I can go either way, but don't you dare stick us in heels. And Janie, well, just fucking agree to let her wear her black skinny jeans and a tank top or I swear to Christ you are going to want to pull your hair out before this day is over."

"Umm... we're picking out *my* dress today," I informed her.

"Oh, thank God," Alex said, letting out a breath she had apparently been holding.

Then we went and picked out my dress. Amongst the quiet opinions of Elsie, Summer, and Amelia and the yelled objections or encouragement from Lo, Janie, and Alex as well as the crying of babies and the herding of a very mobile, very attracted to the 'pretty princess dresses' Ferryn, I did actually manage to find a dress. It was, well, a full-on ball gown with a ton of filmy layers to the skirt.

As the sales lady told me, 'pear-shaped' gals like me were the only ones who could pull off the coveted style. So, with a silent 'fuck you' behind her back for actually calling me 'pear-shaped' to my freaking face, I picked out the dress and tried it on.

And, well, let's just say that if you put on something that actually made Alex and Janie swipe at their eyes, that was the dress you wanted to marry the love of your life in.

*Maze- 2 Years*

To say I had very little input on the wedding decorations would be putting it mildly. Apparently Summer, Amelia, and Elsie had it all covered. Then, financially, Reign had it covered. Yeah, badass leader of the fucking Henchmen MC paid for my wedding.

Though I do think that was due less to some warm and gushy underneath all the dark and dangerous and a lot more to do with the fact that I was the best fucking accountant slash money launderer on the East coast. Though I only extended that particular service to a very select handful of people.

Fact of the matter was, going partially legit was bringing in an almost obnoxious stream of cash to the MC on top of the already obscene amount of money they already made from the gun trade.

He could afford my little wedding.

And it was little.

On Repo's side, he had The Henchmen and their associates: Breaker, Shooter, Paine, and the Mallick family.

On my side, I had my people from New York. It was a group that was, admittedly, quite a bit smaller than Repo's. I had K and Shelly. I had Xander and his wife Ellie. I had Gabe. I had Faith and her man who, apparently, caused quite a stir with his presence back in Navesink Bank. Back, because he had been there before and, let's just say... his actions caused a helluva headache.

But that was a story for another day.

I kicked the girls club out of my room for the five minutes before the ceremony, trying to de-frazzle myself and fix my hair. I still had it purple because, well, fuck the people who thought it would look tacky to have purple hair on your wedding day. I looked like a freaking fairy with it all straight and around my shoulders, the white, understated floral crown on top to tie it into my dress.

My makeup was barely-there and I had been convinced to go commando underneath.

No bra.

No panties.

No boundaries.

I had pestered Repo about where our consummation was to take place, but he was keeping real tight-lipped about it. I figured having easy access would make things simpler in case the place he picked ran the chance of being happened upon if we stayed too long.

There was a knock on the door and, figuring it was K to come and fetch me, I told him to come in.

I saw my mouth fall open in the mirror as I watch someone else's reflection approach me.

"Kotyonok," Ruslan said, giving me a sweet smile, his hand going to his heart.

"Rus?" I asked, standing suddenly and spinning to face him. "What are you doing here?"

"You think you'd get married and I'd miss it?"

"I haven't seen you in over a year," I said, shaking my head at seeing him in an actual suit. It was deep gray and cut perfectly over his wide, strong frame.

It was true.

The last time we had seen Ruslan was when he came to visit the compound the year before to inform us he was officially done with Miami and on his way back to the city. K had located the Russian importer and gotten in touch within a week of getting back to the city after saving me. Let's just say that Viktor met a fitting end. It was what anyone would expect from a Russian mobster: violent, brutally so.

Then he and said Russian had teamed up to get Illeana out of her arranged marriage.

Last I heard, she had refused to go back home with her brother and decided to finally live her own life in the city. K kept tabs on her. And, well, let's just say... she was the kind of personality that could give Janie, Alex, and Lo a run for their money.

But since then, Rus had been next to nothing to us. He was an occasional text on holidays. That was about it.

To see him in my suite on my wedding day, despite the invitation, was a complete shock.

"Yes, well, I had a lot of work to catch up on, Maisy. But I'd never miss this. I was there when the man thought he was coming to rescue you from me. I thought I should be here to watch your happily ever after play out. You deserve it, kotyonok, after all you have been through," he said, crossing the room and going on his knees in front of me. Reaching out, he took my hands, running his thumb over my engagement ring. "I might always regret never acting sooner, but I'm happy to see you happy."

"Stop it," I demanded, looking up at the ceiling and blinking furiously. I was not, was *not* going to be all sappy because it was my wedding day.

"You look like a fairy," he informed me and I felt the smile stretch wide, causing one stray tear to trail down my cheek. He released my hands to carefully brush it away. "You have someone to give you away?"

Oh, lord.

I blinked harder.

The men around me all knew I was fatherless.

And so far, not only K and Rus had offered to walk me, but so had Cash, Shooter, Renny, and, no lie, *freaking* Duke.

It was just... all too much.

"K," I croaked out, my voice thick with the unshed tears.

"Perfect," he said, giving me a warm smile as he took his feet. "I will see you out there, kotyonok. Best wishes."

I turned back to my mirror and touched up my cheeks and eyes then stood just as K let himself in the door to take me to the ceremony. One look at him and the tears struck again.

He fought back a smile and got all serious on me. "You're

going to suck it up and blink back those tears. Then you're going to take my arm and I am going to walk you down the stairs so you don't break your neck in that skirt. Then I am going to walk you down an aisle surrounded by people who love and respect you and I am going to give you to a man who has proved time and again that he is worthy of you."

Immediately, I felt my shoulders relax. I felt my tears ease away.

Good old K.

He always knew just what to do.

"Okay. Let's get me married," I agreed, taking his arm and letting him follow through with the plan.

The inside of the hall was, with Reign's money and Summer, Amelia, and Elsie's vision, well, a freaking dream come to life. It was all soft cremes and whites, understated twinkle lights, and flawless flowers.

Quite frankly, it looked like the kind of room Cinderella would get married in.

Yeah, it was that good.

I owed Reign, Summer, Amelia, and Elsie huge.

"Deep breath," K said as I searched the room for a second, taking in everyone's smiles. Then the music started and my gaze found Repo's and everything else fell away.

*Repo-*

"Shot?" Duke asked in the room before the ceremony, brow raised, message clear: he was having too much fun being young and free to even consider the fact that there was nothing nerve-racking whatsoever about my wedding day to me.

"He's not nervous," Renny corrected, shrugging a shoulder. "He's anxious."

"Stop fucking analyzing my men, Renny," Reign said, shaking his head. Renny's best asset was also a real pain in the fucking ass to live with day-to-day. He drove half the men up the wall. It wasn't exactly uncommon to find out he was in another fight much like the one he had been in with Duke back when they were probies. It was just how he was. He was a testament to the life-lasting effects fucked-up parenting caused.

"They're ready for you," Cash said, leaning in the door.

I nodded, standing, the suit feeling foreign on my skin. Can't say I could remember a single instance outside my uncle's funeral that I had the occasion to wear one. But, well, Summer wouldn't hear of me wearing anything else. She got Reign, Cash, and Wolf in suits as well.

When the music started and everyone turned to look at Maze, I felt my stomach clench hard as I turned to do the same. It wasn't fear. It was something else I didn't fully recognize, like excitement and nerves mingled together.

And, fuck.

I was pretty sure nothing in the world would ever compare to seeing her walking down the aisle in that white gown, a wobbly smile on her face, her purple hair down her shoulders, her arm wrapped with K's, wearing one of my rings and making her way toward me to get another, the one that promised everything I had to offer... for the rest of our lives.

K shook my hand, pulling me close, and saying low and threateningly in my ear, "You fuck her over, I fuck you up." He clapped me on the back and gave me a huge smile as he handed me my woman, the significance there almost overwhelming. He was *giving her* to me. He expected me to step up, to do whatever was necessary to keep her safe and happy, like he would do. And that smile he gave me didn't mean dick. His words were not an empty threat. If I screwed up, I knew I could count on K showing up on my doorstep.

"I know you're safe now," K said to Maze, giving her a smile that was warm and open, "so just keep kicking ass, love."

Then he kissed her cheek and we turned to the preacher.

Judging by the way she kissed me back after we were pronounced, I was pretty sure she was excited about my conjugal surprise for later.

*Maze*

"Thank God you listened to me," Alex said as the girls club sat around a table at the reception which was in no way any less lavish than the ceremony itself. It was as if it was a continuation of the same room. The flowers, lights, table cloths and settings, it all matched perfectly.

Alex was referring to the clothes the girls club were wearing.

I say clothes, not dresses, because I had, indeed, listened to Alex. I had learned that if you wanted straight honesty and practicality with absolutely no girly embellishments, you went to Alex. So when she showed up at my office the afternoon after I picked out my dress, sat down and informed me about the fights that had erupted over bridesmaid dresses for Lo's wedding, I listened.

Lo, Amelia, Summer, and Elsie were in dresses of varying styles dependent upon their body shapes but in the same unusual rosy-creme color that I hadn't been aware existed until Elsie showed it to me. Alex and Janie were in cream slacks and silky blouses that matched the dresses. Amelia, Summer, and Elsie were in heels. Lo, Janie, and Alex were not.

I hadn't had one single complaint.

It was a beautiful thing.

Thank God I listened to Alex indeed.

"I still can't believe Ferryn decided half way down the aisle that she didn't want to be a flower girl anymore, abandoned her basket, and went to sit on Vin's lap instead," Lo said, smiling like she approved.

"He told me that she told him that she thought flowers are boring," Summer laughed, rolling her eyes.

"They *are* boring," Janie shrugged. "Give me a nice new shiny gun any day of the week."

"Yes, well, we are trying to keep a gun out of her hands until she's at least twelve," Summer laughed.

"Excuse me, girls, can I borrow my wife for a second?" Repo asked, snaking a hand around my belly and kissing under my ear. I'm not gonna lie, my belly did a little flip-flop at the word 'wife'. It still felt weird, but in a way that was too delicious to ever want to have it stop being weird.

Lo, Janie, Alex, and Amelia shared a look that was both devilish and knowing, leaving Elsie's brows to draw together until Alex leaned over and explained it to her, making her choke on the wine she had been trying to drink.

So, yeah, Lo and Cash on their wedding day consummated their marriage in a closet because they couldn't wait to get to their room to get their hands on each other.

They figured that was what we were doing as well.

Which was totally right.

Except we weren't grabbing a closet.

Oh, no.

"What are you doing?" I whisper-yelled at Repo, looking down the empty hall as he grabbed a lock pick out of his pocket and was working on a door.

"Shh," he said, kneeling down to undo the lock in an impressive ten seconds, the handle releasing and the door pushing open. "It's your surprise," he told me, pulling me into the darkened room, closing, and locking the door before reaching for the switch and flicking the light on.

I felt the smile spread slowly across my face until my cheeks hurt as I looked around.

"Right there," Repo said, pointing.

To the altar.

Where we had just been married.

I turned to him, big smile in place. "Perfect."

With that, my hand was snagged and I was hauled against his chest. His lips were slow, explorative, teasing. But it wasn't long before the nerves and excitement and the weight of our actions that day made us needy, frantic, uncontrolled. His hands roamed my body as best they could with the endless yards of material covering it.

"Jesus Christ, how much material is there?" he asked, ripping his mouth from mine after having tried to gather up my skirt... and failing. "Fuck it," he said, pulling me to the altar and pushing me down onto it, getting down on his knees and pushing my skirt up so that it gathered around my waist... and chest... and shoulders. What can I say? It was a *ball gown*... the mass of the skirt pooled everywhere.

But I had, say, two seconds to muse on that before I felt Repo press my knees open and his mouth was on me, his tongue sliding up my cleft and circling my clit before his lips closed around it and sucked hard. I held the back of his head to me, my legs closing around the sides of his head as my hips rose to meet his mouth. His hand slid from my thigh and moved between us, shoving inside and raking over my G-spot until I felt myself tightening around him, threatening oblivion.

But then he yanked against my hold, sitting back on his ankles so his hands could work his fly. Imprisoned by my impractical dress, I couldn't do much but lay there and wait for him to come to me. Which he took his sweet time doing, sitting there, looking down at me for what felt like forever, one hand stroking his cock, the other sliding almost absentmindedly down my inner thigh.

"Mine," he said finally, planting his hands on either side of me, his cock pressing into my thigh.

"Mmhmm," I agreed because, well, I was.

I hadn't even stopped agreeing when he slammed inside me to the hilt, claiming me completely.

*Maze- 6.5 Years*

It was Seth's third birthday party.

He was turning three and he was the spitting image of his daddy who was a spitting image of little Seth's namesake, all dark hair and deep blue eyes. Minus the face scar, but already sporting a ton of others on his arms and legs. He was fearless, taking some kind of pride in scaring me half to death with new and inventive ways of injuring himself.

But, I guess I couldn't expect any different when he grew up around The Henchmen, their friends, and their offspring. All of which were in attendance for the event, the grounds at the compound decked out with blue and red balloons and a Spiderman theme.

Over by the snack table, four year olds Jackson, Paine and Elsie's son and Junior, Breaker and Alex's son, were trying to find a way to sneak cupcakes despite the group of adults standing to their sides. Fallon and Malcolm were off in the back of the field tossing a ball, both six and too big for the little kids. Ferryn, the oldest at nine years old, was in no way bothered by the fact that she had no playmates her own age. She made up for it by bossing the whole lot of them around. As she was doing to newly three year old Seth and his age-mates, Bri and Alexis, Shooter and Amelia's three and four year olds who couldn't seem to grasp the concept of duck duck goose much to the chagrin of the all-knowing Ferryn.

"How's the morning sickness?" Summer asked, moving in beside me, a hand on her belly. It was her third and, she claimed, her last. She was six months along and finally over her whole day need to be near a toilet to puke her guts up.

I was only three months and not quite there yet. "Ugh," I said, curling up my face.

"I feel you," she said as she laughed at Bri sticking her tongue out at Ferryn. "She needs someone to put her in her place," she said, shaking her head at her daughter who was small-eying the four year old.

"Fallon and Jackson are getting bigger. They won't tolerate her bossiness much longer."

"Fingers crossed. It's all Reign's fault," she said, looking over at her husband who seemed to sense the inspection and turned his head to give her a smile. "He's help build up that ego of hers."

"There are worse things in the world for a girl to be than confident," Janie said as she joined us. "I like her spirit."

"Well of course *you* do," Summer laughed.

"Hey, if she's gonna hold her own around all these sure-to-be biker boys as they grow up, she needs to be able to stand her ground.

We all watched as Lo moved across the field toward Ferryn, taking her hand and leading her off toward the pack-and-play where Willa, Paine and Elsie's baby, was situated under a tree. Without the dictatorship, Seth, Bri, and Alexis jumped up from their circle and started running around and laughing.

"Hey, honey," Repo said, coming up with some enormous wrapped box that made me shake my head. I had no idea where the hell we were going to fit all the new toys in a house that was already bursting with them.

"Who is that from?" I groaned as he set it on the table with the rest of them.

"Rus. So I guess we can expect something loud and obnoxious," he said, moving behind me and wrapping his arm under my chest and resting one hand against my belly. "Come up with anything yet?" he asked, meaning name-wise. With Seth it had been easy. The name was obvious once we knew it was a boy.

"Something with a K," Repo suggested, nuzzling into my neck.

K.

He'd been there to walk me down the aisle.

He'd been there to become a godfather to our son.

He'd just... always been there.

But the crazy thing was, I still didn't know his whole first name.

He was K. Case closed.

So I couldn't exactly name a kid after him in the traditional sense.

"Something with a K," I agreed, leaning back into him, cringing as I watched Seth take a head-over-feet tumble then immediately take his feet, laughing the whole thing off, pieces of grass sticking to his clothes randomly and what looked like a smear of blood on his knee.

"What the fuck..." Duke's voice called suddenly, making all the adults tense and turn to where he was looking at something at the gates.

And while the kids weren't aware of it thanks to some very fast and effective distracting from the girls club as a whole, that was when Seth's birthday party became the day when the peace The Henchmen had known for almost a decade came to a screeching halt.

Because what was at the gate was a woman.

And she was barely clinging to life.

And she had a Henchmen "H" carved into her back and the words "you're all next" written in her blood on a note tucked into her pocket.

Duke stooped and cradled the woman to his chest, bringing her inside the compound as Lo made a call to Hailstorm to have one of her medical team come and check the girl over and Repo, Cash, and Wolf called all the rest of the patched members to come to the compound for an emergency church meeting.

All the girls club shared a look, knowing what it meant.

It meant war.

"Here we go," Reign said, shaking his head.

XX

# DON'T FORGET

If you enjoyed this book, go ahead and hop onto Goodreads or Amazon and tell me your favorite parts. You can also spread the word by recommending the book to friends or sending digital copies that can be received via kindle or kindle app on any device.

# ALSO BY JESSICA GADZIALA

**The Henchmen MC**

Reign

Cash

Wolf

Repo

Duke

Renny

Lazarus

**The Savages**

Monster

Killer

Savior

--

DEBT

For A Good Time, Call...

Shane

Ryan

The Sex Surrogate

Dr. Chase Hudson

Dissent

Into The Green

What The Heart Needs

What The Heart Wants

What The Heart Finds

What The Heart Knows

The Stars Landing Deviant

Dark Mysteries

367 Days

Stuffed: A Thanksgiving Romance

Dark Secrets

Unwrapped

Peace, Love, & Macarons

# ABOUT THE AUTHOR

Jessica Gadziala is a full-time writer, parrot enthusiast, and coffee drinker from New Jersey. She enjoys short rides to the book store, sad songs, and cold weather.

She is very active on Goodreads, Facebook, as well as her personal groups on those sites. Join in. She's friendly.

# STALK HER!

Connect with Jessica:

Facebook: https://www.facebook.com/JessicaGadziala/
Facebook Group: https://www.facebook.com/groups/314540025563403/

Goodreads: https://www.goodreads.com/author/show/13800950.Jessica_Gadziala
Goodreads Group: https://www.goodreads.com/group/show/177944-jessica-gadziala-books-and-bullsh

Twitter: @JessicaGadziala

JessicaGadziala.com

<3/ Jessica

<<<<>>>>